Knight of Ash

The Venomous Tempest

By
S.C. van Doorn

Copyright © 2022 by S.C. van Doorn

All rights reserved.
No part of this book may be reproduced in any form or by any electronic or mechanical means, including information storage and retrieval systems, without written permission from the author, except for the use of brief quotations in a book review.

Cover Art: By S.C. van Doorn and Carolina Cruz
Map Art: By S.C. van Doorn

For little autistic me, eight years ago. You've given others what you needed.

Table of Contents

I

Chapter I: The Apprentice	6
Chapter II: A Road Ahead	24
Chapter III: A Stop in Laketon	44
Chapter IV: Learning the Ropes	69
Chapter V: Ashfallow	100
Chapter VI: Titans	112

II

Chapter VII: Patrol	131
Chapter VIII: Words for a King	148
Chapter IX: Too Many People	167
Chapter X: The Cruel Monarch	182
Chapter XI: Dragoncrown Peak	203
Chapter XII: The Visit	222

III

Chapter XIII: Trailing a Titan	247
Chapter XIV: Tyranny	263
Chapter XV: The Black Flame	280
Chapter XVI: Reunion	295
Chapter XVII: Knight of Ash	313
Epilogue	341
Afterword	344

I

Chapter I:
The Apprentice

A pair of armoured men rode through the gates of castle Hyghwing on a clear autumn day. The red faulds on their gambesons provided a contrast with their silvery plate armour. As they entered the grounds, a well-dressed man accompanied by a set of guards met them in the courtyard. He addressed the eldest of the two knights, the one who wore a yellow cloak over his shoulders.

"Greetings Sir Arran, I trust the journey here went well?" the lord asked. Arran turned his head to look at his host. Arran's face was perhaps a little broad. His grey hair lit up gold in the light of the sun. A beard in a slightly darker shade hugged his jaw. He made eye-contact with the aristocrat who had greeted him. He knew this man as the lord of house Hyghwing, though he'd never quite gotten his name.

"Nothing to hold us up for once," Arran replied.

"That is good to hear," Lord Hyghwing said, "I was wondering, who is the boy you've brought with you? I don't believe he was with you the last time you visited?"

Arran turned his head towards the young man on horseback close behind him, and then back at the lord, who'd backed up slightly to allow them to dismount.

"He's my apprentice, Laras."

Laras' grey eyes met Lord Hyghwing's. He greeted him politely, though perhaps a little half-heartedly. Both he and Arran got down from their saddles, handing over the reins to the stable boy who came to lead the horses away.

"You must be tired from the journey here."

"Only a little," said Arran, looking past the lord.

"I trust that you ran into no problems, nothing like those rumours I've heard?"

"No, it was pleasantly calm, actually, definitely nothing to complain about." He shook his head quickly. "I do think we should get on with our business. Could you bring me to the recruits you've had trained?"

Lord Hyghwing turned to his advisor and said something to him in Yilgran before looking back at his guest.

"If you'd follow me," he said to Arran and Laras. He brought them to the castle's training ground, where four recruits were practising on a patch of well-trodden dirt. Their instructor told them to stop and line up before Arran when he saw the three men make their approach. One of the trainees was tall, another short and the two remaining were both somewhere in between. They hadn't lined up in any particular order and simply waited for what was to follow.

"Now if I'm not wrong ... I believe you were the boys picked as possible recruits?"

One of the boys nodded but the others kept looking at the knight in front of them.

"No girls. Surprising," remarked Arran as he looked at the four young men before him. The instructor scratched his head.

"I wasn't aware we were allowed to train those," he said. "Lord Hyghwing specified only boys."

"I figured as much. It's a bit of a shame, too," Arran replied. He quickly turned his focus back to what he came here to do. "You, on the right."

The tallest recruit turned his attention to Arran.

"You're going to show me exactly what you can do," he said. "That dummy over there, focus on that as your target."

The boy quickly did as he was asked. He took a thin sword that was just a bit shorter than his arm. It didn't seem unlikely that he would've taken up a larger weapon, had he looked stronger. He made elegant and overly telegraphed slashes at the target in front of him.

Arran took notice of his flamboyant movement. Not long after, his fist shot up into the air and his voice rang loudly before the trainee could hit the dummy again.

"You're going to be fighting dragons, not dancing at a fancy ball. Try again," he said to the young man. "There's always more to learn."

The boy did make another attempt. Though his swordplay remained just as below average as it had been, he didn't exactly do any better than he did before. Arran tilted his head towards his apprentice and whispered something.

"He looks like he's spent very little time paying attention. If at all."

Laras nodded. He'd been training under Arran for quite some time now and he'd learned quickly how to pick up on the mistakes of others.

"Next!" Arran shouted. The shortest boy stood to attention and instantly knew what to do. He took hold of a broader sword than his predecessor and picked up a shield as well. He'd chosen quite a large barrier for his short frame, and had he held it to his chest it would've covered him from his knees to his shoulders. Arran took note of this and endorsed the boy's decision.

"Good choice; a shield to protect yourself is invaluable when fighting an enemy that could take you out with one hit." Arran spoke with enough volume that the other boys would hear him. The trainee appreciated the comment and carried on. He hit the dummy once and raised his shield, lowered it and hit twice before repeating. After some time spent nodding approvingly, Arran decided to try and get his attention.

"Hey!"

The trainee looked back.

"Don't let yourself get distracted," Arran said as he shook his head.

Laras opened his mouth but shut it again immediately.

"But I thought you wanted me to—" the boy objected, but Arran interrupted him.

"Getting distracted is a fatal error. I would've told you specifically to stop if that had been the case. Next."

The boy walked back, dropped the sword and shield back at where he got them, and returned to stand in line again.

"Don't you think that was kind of uncalled for?" asked Laras, raising an eyebrow. Arran felt inclined to agree with him, and in a moment of reconsideration he decided to at least walk back on his words slightly.

"You did well though. I'm sure you'll make our ranks soon enough," Arran said to the boy as he walked past them.

"You there." Arran pointed at one of the other young recruits. He stood with his shoulders slouched and he was distracted by his surroundings. He pointed at himself when Arran called out to him.

"Yes, you, pick up a weapon and show me how you would fight a dragon."

The boy shrugged. He struggled as he tried to pick up a mace that was far too heavy for him and began to aggressively smack away at his target.

"Stop, stop, stop, stop!" Arran shouted. He stepped forward for a second, perhaps intending to physically restrain the boy himself. "Listen, we don't need someone to stand around with a weapon they can barely use while people are in danger. You're more of a liability than the dragons you would be fighting."

The boy turned and walked away, appearing to care little of what Arran thought.

"Last one!"

The fourth recruit wasn't exceptionally tall or strong. He picked up a sword and slightly smaller shield than the boy who had done so previously. His fighting style was efficient but careless, which was something he should've ironed out with the time he'd spent training. He made several mistakes that would've gotten him injured or killed had he made them out in the field.

"Thank you, that's enough," said Arran, pleased with the results he'd seen that day. Two out of four trainees were capable of joining the Knights of Ash in the near future. He turned away and towards the lord, who was standing on a balcony.

"Was that all of them?"

"Yes, have you come to a decision?"

"Not ye—"

Arran was cut off by the sound of a blade clumsily being taken off a rack. He turned around, where he saw a figure vigorously but tactfully hacking away at the training dummy. They hadn't picked up a shield, but their rapid pace made up for their lack of defence. Whoever they were, they must've quickly gleaned how to do any of the things they were doing. There was no sign of formal training, only messy self-taught techniques and things that might've been observed from a distance.

"Hey!" shouted Arran. However, the figure ignored him. "STOP!" he followed up as he walked towards them. He gripped the blunted blade with his gloved hand to prevent them from continuing. They stopped and let go of the hilt before turning around.

"Who might you be?" he said as he got on eye level with them. Now that he'd gotten closer, Arran could see that "they" were actually "she". She was a short, skinny girl with shoulder length pearl-blonde hair styled in a low-hanging ponytail. Her brown eyes intentionally avoided Arran's own, and his stern expression wavered for just a second. He hesitated slightly.

"It's Yara," she answered as she continued to avoid making eye contact with him. "That's my name."

Arran felt her attempt was rather daring, and frankly he was interested in why she wasn't formally presented to him like the boys had been. "Well, hello Yara. What do you think you're doing?" he asked.

"I was hoping to be picked as a recruit," she said bluntly, clearly sparing no time for nuance or flowery language.

"Oh really?" Arran asked with a grin. "Would you be willing to show me a bit more of what you can do?" He looked back and his grin melted away. Behind him Lord Hyghwing came running down the staircase that ran from the balcony to the courtyard. He'd seen the entire exchange from above and was fuming. Clearly he didn't approve of her actions.

"YOU MOST CERTAINLY ARE NOT!" he huffed, the short yet careful sprint down the stairs having worn him out. Yara was unimpressed by his shouting and even rolled her eyes as he approached. She crossed her arms and looked away.

"Why can't I?" she asked, her tone irritated and indignant.

"Because I won't allow it. You getting foolhardy ideas is exactly why I decided against training girls," he said as he looked at Arran. "You can't seriously think she's a suitable candidate."

Arran stepped in between the girl and Lord Hyghwing. "That is, I'm sorry to say, still up to me." Evidently he was not going to take Lord Hyghwing's side, instead opting to defend the person he'd very clearly chosen the moment he saw her perform. The lord had started to fluster his words.

"She's my only daug—"

"I'm your ward, not your daughter!" Yara yelled out. "Stop calling me that. It's embarrassing."

Lord Hyghwing's temper had already been lost at that point. He was torn between storming off or shouting at either her or Arran, and possibly against his better judgement he decided to go with the latter.

"Sir Arran, you could clearly see that she refused to follow the instructions. You appeared to reject a perfectly good student who only got distracted once. By your doing, might I add! Why should you choose her?"

Arran looked at him and then back at Yara; her eyes turned downwards again. He noticed that she did this a lot, though he didn't fully understand why.

"How long did it take you to learn any of this?" he asked. He noticed that she glanced up at him for only a second.

"I started half a year ago," Yara answered quietly. She looked up again, but her eyes were focused on something behind him, likely intending to feign eye contact. "Only when I found out what they were being trained for."

"You're a quick study," Arran remarked, then turned to his host. "When did the boys start?"

"Two years ago – I would say that would be the minimum for being a recruit," answered Hyghwing with a pompous tone.

"Unfortunately for you, you don't get to decide the rules about that," said Arran. Yara started nodding in agreement, but once her guardian took notice, she stopped.

Almost like a toddler having a temper tantrum, the lord stomped his foot on the ground. "You were put in my care to keep you away from monsters!" he shouted, his tone shrill. "I won't have you run off to join some military group that will only bring you closer to those ... those beasts!"

Arran shook his head. He quickly intervened to interrupt him before he could continue ranting.

"You were going to offer us a drink before; I think I'll take you up on that now."

Lord Hyghwing was in awe at the audacity his guest showed, but Arran gave a cocky nod, like he'd dealt with his sort before. He didn't even let a tiny, snide smile or smirk sneak onto his face, which made him look dead serious.

Their host relented and chose to lead the two knights and his own rebellious ward to the dining hall.

***

The hall they entered was made from the same white granite as the rest of the castle, and the room's oaken floorboards creaked under the heavy footsteps of those who entered. Arran sat down at one of the tables and was soon followed by Laras, who took a seat next to him. Yara took her place at the table as well and to her annoyance Lord Hyghwing then sat down next to her.

"If you'd be so kind, could you get the boy and I something to drink?" Arran said to a servant. They ignored their guest, and in response Laras got up from his seat.

"I'll go and get it," the young man left the room to find out where the taps were. Arran sat patiently at the table while he and his hosts waited for his student to return. He turned his attention to Lord Hyghwing as they waited. In the short time he'd been at the castle, the Lord had already formed a dislike for Arran.

"I will no—"

"Please, at least wait until I've had a sip, my throat is parched."

Arran grinned and quickly glanced at Yara before he looked away. In the small glimpse he got he saw she was trying to contain a grin of her own. Laras re-entered the room not long after he'd left, one mug of beer in each hand.

"Ah, finally!" Arran exclaimed with relief as he let his gaze slide over them. Laras sat down and handed a tankard to Arran, who put the mug to his lips and took a large swig. He then slammed the now mostly empty tankard down onto the table and let out an intentionally obnoxious sigh of relief, before wiping his mouth with his sleeve and the back of his hand.

"Now, about our little ... predicament," Arran chose his words carefully to avoid angering their host any more. There wasn't really any point to trying that. Lord Hyghwing appeared like he was going to pop a blood vessel any minute now.

"Yes, about that."

"I am under the impression there's a total of three possible recruits for the Knights of Ash, is that correct?"

Lord Hyghwing shook his head in disagreement and tried his hardest to contain his temper.

"No. There's only two."

"So you're telling me the second or fourth trainee isn't ready yet? Regardless of my reaction to them I thought they did rather well," Arran replied, chuckling at what he thought was a rather clever joke. It evidently went unappreciated by Lord Hyghwing. Arran knew that this would get a tilted reaction from his host and he got exactly what he bargained for.

"NO, Yara is NOT a candidate. Take the boys but please let her stay."

"Why isn't she? She's capable enough to learn," Arran replied, "she's certainly left that impression, anyhow."

"Learning to fight is too dangerous for her, I mean ... look at her!" He gestured broadly at the girl sitting next to him, "she's like a twig, How am I to be sure she won't injure herself?"

Yara took offence at what he said and crossed her arms in protest. She frowned and looked down.

"Aside from that, she had a leaden tongue until her 6th year. How am I to be sure she is ready for something like hunting fire breathing beasts!?"

"Well, she hasn't injured herself yet, has she?" said Arran in response, "and she seems to be doing fine at speaking right now."

"No but—"

"The boys are skilled, that much is true, but I'd like them to keep practising here. I don't believe they'd learn as quickly as she can."

Yara had to hide the smile that was growing on her face as Arran and her guardian argued.

"That's not ... I've been entrusted with her protection, to defend her from evil like dragons or demons," Hyghwing was running out of things to say and began to repeat what he'd said before.

"And where could she possibly be protected better than with a group of dragon-hunting knights?" Arran said in an attempt to reason with Lord Hyghwing. "If we teach her how to defend herself she won't need protection."

"Do you even have women in your order?"

"M'lord, I was recruited by a woman," replied Arran calmly, his stare focused on the Lord's face. Laras looked on and grinned as he watched his mentor stand his ground and defend his position.

"She's far too young!"

"Laras?"

Laras perked up when he heard his name and looked at Arran.

"Tell the Lord how old you were when you were recruited, please?"

"I was ten at the time, m'lord."

This revelation startled their host, who must've found it astonishing that someone so young would be inducted into an order of dragon hunters.

"How old is she? Sixteen? Seventeen?"

"I'm sixteen!" Yara piped up.

"Sixteen, that's more than old enough."

Lord Hyghwing was dumbfounded, evident from the fact that his reply was a series of stammered words before he finally put together something coherent, "I— I'm not entirely sure yet. I'll need to think about it."

He stood up and the wooden seat he sat on scraped over the oak floor. He then promptly walked away and out of the room.

"When's supper?" Arran yelled after the Lord. He was joking, of course but an answer wouldn't've hurt. Once her guardian was out of earshot Yara jumped up.

"Thank you so much for talking him into it!"

"Calm down now," Arran laughed, "I haven't succeeded yet."

"But thank you for even trying," she said, "I don't think you know how much it means to me."

"I know perfectly well how suffocating living in a castle can be and I wasn't going to leave here without at least making an effort."

The girl's eyes widened.

"Really? Were you a ward too?"

'No," Arran smiled and shook his head, "I've seen plenty of young people in your position," he looked down. Now he was the one avoiding eye contact, "and I don't want you to be another runaway."

Yara looked at the ground. Arran stood up, walked towards her and lifted her head with his finger.

"Chin up now, the dragons are above you, not below," Arran smiled warmly. He put his hand on her head and ruffled her hair. She smiled back.

"I'll be outside with Laras if you need me," Arran said to her while walking away with his apprentice in tow.

***

A few hours had passed and it was already getting late when Lord Hyghwing walked out with Yara behind him. Arran had spent some time in the training grounds practising with Laras as he waited for Lord Hyghwing to reach a conclusion.

"Sir Arran..?" the Lord begged the knight's attention. Arran turned to face the man who addressed him.

"Ah, Lord Hyghwing, we were planning on leaving just now," Arran said, "is there something you need from us?"

"I have spoken with Yara and thought about my decision … "

Arran cocked his head.

"And?" He could see Yara grinning from ear to ear behind the Lord. Arran could already take a guess at the outcome.

"And I— I, as her guardian … " he stammered, "have decided that she is to join you."

Arran was glad to hear him say those words. Yara came running towards and squeezed past him. She essentially used him as a hiding spot.

"You must promise me one thing Sir Arran."

Arran twisted to look behind himself at the young girl.

"You are to be her teacher and she is only to part from your side when a task is too frightful or her training is complete, no sooner," said Hyghwing, "is that understood?"

Yara stepped out from behind her new mentor and guardian to stand next to him. She turned and faced Lord Hyghwing before she looked back at Arran. He calmly put his hand on her shoulder and answered.

"You have my word, I will do whatever I can to keep her safe, as I am sure the others will too."

Lord Hyghwing nodded in apprehensive approval, "I wish you good fortune Sir Arran."

"Likewise, m'lord," Arran replied as he helped Yara onto Laras' horse. He then climbed into his own saddle before the trio rode out of the gate and left the castle. Lord Hyghwing looked on at the riders as they rode down the trail and away from his castle, right up until they were out of his view and disappeared under the cloak of night.

Chapter II:
A Road Ahead

"We should stop here for the night," Arran said to both his students. The group of three rode over a cobble road which led them to a village. Laras dismounted and helped Yara down.

"Why are we stopping now?" Yara asked with a hint of protest in her voice. "Wouldn't we get there sooner if we kept going?"

"Because it's getting late and I'm an old man. I need my rest," said Arran with a snicker.

"But we can sleep later on the journey!" She objected further to try and persuade him, clearly anxious to keep moving.

"I'd rather get some rest in a comfortable bed if I were you," said Arran, "chances are you won't have the opportunity or the luxury to do so nearly as often as you'd like." He then turned away and towards the door of the low-built inn. The building's front door was weak and Arran almost broke it out of its hinges despite his gentle push. Inside stood and sat a few people, likely there for their evening drink after work. Arran walked in, followed by Yara and Laras. He looked towards the bar, where he saw a relatively short man with a plump face and a short neckbeard. Arran assumed he was the owner of the establishment.

"What can I do for you?" asked the innkeep. He appeared only mildly perturbed by the fact that this new arrival had nearly forced the door out of its rotted wooden frame. Arran scratched his beard before responding.

"I need one room with two beds."

Again the innkeeper looked at his new guests. "You're with three." He observed bluntly before he began to clean the mug he held in his hands. Arran nodded.

"Two beds, both for them. I'll sleep on the floor." The knight dug into a coin purse he had taken from his saddlebags earlier and handed over two spiral-shaped and patterned pyrite coins. "That should cover it."

"Need feed for your horses?" asked the innkeeper absently.

"Yes, actually. That'd be appreciated."

The man behind the counter gestured at one of the doors and pointed out that it was theirs. Laras walked towards it, opened the room and entered. Yara tugged on Arran's sleeve.

"Why didn't you take a bed?"

"If I sleep on the ground I'll wake up more quickly."

Yara clearly disliked his logic and didn't agree with it, however she accepted his decision regardless. Arran had retrieved a bedroll from his saddlebags and silently laid down on the soft fabric after he meticulously removed his armour. The stone floor under the bedroll was hard and he could feel the cold pierce through it. Not only was the floor frigid, but the mortared cobbles made the ground slightly uneven. Arran looked under the beds when he opened his eyes and closed them again right after. Carved stone bricks made up the floor the beds stood on. Probably meant to prevent them from wobbling. He grumbled to himself and tried to sleep despite the hard floor he laid on. Nevertheless the bedroll was comfortable enough, and Arran quickly fell sound asleep.

***

The next morning the knight woke up early. He looked at the room's single pane window which he could see from where he was lying. Only recently had the comforting light of dawn graced the skies. It was early morning and outside people were already hard at work, as was expected from a small rural town.

What's the harm in lying down and resting a little longer? Arran thought to himself. He looked at the two young people he was now responsible for before glancing to his sheathed sword. It stood propped up against the back wall of the room.

The weapon helped to remind him of what he was supposed to be doing. The knight groaned as he got up reluctantly. He gently shook Laras awake by his shoulder. Laras shrugged his mentor's hand off.

"Been awake for a while now," he said with a groggy and tired tone. "Waking up is hard." If he had been awake it mustn't've been for long. Arran then turned to Yara. She laid on her side and had curled up into a small bundle with her hands tightly held onto the bedsheets she'd wrapped herself in. Her pearl-blonde hair was spread across the soft surface of the mattress.

"Yara?" Arran whispered as he gently shook her shoulder. She threw off his hand somewhat violently, opened her eyes and let go of her bedsheets before she attempted to sit up.

"What?" She groaned as she wiped the sleep out of her eyes.

"You need to get up. It's morning."

"But it's still so early," she protested. Though she had wanted to stay on the road the previous night it was likely that she hadn't gotten used to waking up early beforehand. She had grown too attached to the soft bed in the short time she'd spent in it.

"The sooner we arrive the faster you can begin your training," argued Arran. He had a point, after all it was Yara who wanted to get to their destination as quickly as possible. Fortunately using her own reasoning against her seemed to work.

"Alright, I'll—"

"Come on, we don't have all day," he added swiftly as he nearly failed at hiding a smirk. Arran left the room along with Laras, who'd gotten up from his bed while Arran had been talking to Yara. Inside the main hall of the inn Arran had asked the innkeeper to prepare them some simple breakfast. The man looked like he himself was still half asleep. Arran and Laras sat down.

"Now that you've got yourself another student, what are you planning on doing with me?" Laras asked with a chuckle. He looked in the direction of the room they'd slept in the night before.

"That's a good question," said Arran. He grinned. "What am I going to do with you now? Now that I've got her to teach I wouldn't want you to get in the way."

They both laughed and began to eat their breakfast after it arrived at their table, while Yara's plate stood unattended to. It'd take her just a little longer to get up and leave their bedroom. She walked across the cold stone floor towards where her companions sat.

"Took you long enough didn't it?" Laras said with a grin. His comment was meant as a joke. It seemed unlikely that Yara picked up on it however.

"I'm sorry …" Yara apologised quickly before she found the food on the table. She took some of the bread to eat and scarfed it down like a starving dog. She wasn't exactly well-mannered, behaving instead as if she'd never even set foot in Lord Hyghwing's hall. She was practically mashing the bread into her mouth.

"Slow down! You're gonna choke," Laras said worriedly. The speed at which she was stuffing her face was concerning to look at. She paused and seemed to rationalise his words before chewing her food more slowly.

"For us there is never really a thing such as "too early'," Arran said as he finished his plate. In truth he was right. It was better for them to be up early. More daylight meant more distance to cover.

"It won't get better at Ashfallow's Hold," Laras said to Yara before putting a piece of bread in his mouth. "I had the luck of being a farmer's boy so I didn't have to get used to getting up early."

The three of them didn't speak much as they ate their food. After sitting in silence for a moment Arran stood up and walked out of the room, probably to gather the horses. Yara was curious about the boy sitting opposite her. He hadn't said anything to her at castle Hyghwing.

"You said you were a farmer, right?"

"Mhm," Laras took a sip of his drink, looked down and hung forward over the table.

"Well, why aren't you anymore?"

He put his mug down and crossed his arms before answering her. "You want me to tell you the entire thing?" he asked. "I should let you know that I get kind of ... carried away when telling stories. We might be here a while," he said with a smile.

Yara nodded. Once something piqued her interest she wouldn't easily let it go. "Sure, go ahead."

Laras obliged, "So I was ten years old. It was early in the morning and I was helping my father with moving the cattle out of the stables and into the field."

"Is he your father?" she asked and pointed at where Arran had sat before. Her words were muffled and hard to understand on account of the food in her mouth.

"No. Can I continue?" Laras shook his head. It wasn't in an impatient manner but he made it obvious that he didn't like being interrupted with questions. "Out of nowhere a green dragon, bigger than the barn I just walked out of, descended onto our farm. First it took my father, then it set our house on fire with my mother inside."

It was obvious that he didn't like talking about the subject but he also wasn't going to leave anyone willing to listen without an apt description. Sometimes Laras' voice seemed to shudder with certain details like he remembered it as if he was still there.

"It then turned to me. I thought of hiding in the barn, but I would only have been covered in its burnt debris as it collapsed. The monster was terrifying. I remember falling to the ground. I was ready to accept my fate when suddenly I heard heavy hooves gallop over the road that led to our farm."

Yara listened closely, appearing near enthralled by Laras' story.

"Then, I heard the sound of boots hitting the ground, followed by seeing a man with a shield projecting some sort of flickering barrier standing over me. He held it in front of both of us," he continued, gesturing with his fork as he spoke. "I couldn't see his face because it was covered by his helmet, all I could hear was him saying 'go'." Laras took a short break to drink something before he continued his story.

"So naturally, I climbed onto my feet and ran — or at least tried to run — away from the farm. Once I was far enough I looked back at the fight. I saw the man hit the creature on the head before jumping aside. Then, he swung at its wing with his black sword and jumped onto its neck. He pulled out a broadsword and buried it in the back of the dragon's head." Laras gestured to imitate what he saw before slamming his hand on the table, making their cutlery rattle. "I still remember how it howled before the man climbed down and ran towards me. I was scared at first. The stranger might've defended me but I didn't know who he was or what he wanted. When he was close enough he kneeled down and removed his helmet. Underneath was the same face you first saw yesterday. I remember that he looked worried at first and asked me if I was alright. Then he asked me if I had any family left. I told him no. In response he offered for me to come with him, and I did."

Yara sat back. As her interest grew she — without noticing it at first — had begun to lean forward over the table. Arran had walked back in while Laras told his story to Yara.

"You done?" he asked, "if so, we're ready to leave."

He then left the building again, but left the door open behind him. Laras stood up and turned away from Yara before he walked out as well. She watched the young man leave as she finished her food. Yara left the warmth of the building behind not long after and stepped out into the chilly, late autumn outside. A gust of wind blew up a few leaves that were scattered across the ground. Yara turned to her left when Arran's distinct voice called her name. He stood next to Laras' horse and was very obviously waiting for her to get there.

"Well, come on then," he said. "I'm not going to stand around and wait all day." He didn't sound impatient. In fact he probably meant to come across as humorous or playful. Yara misunderstood his joking remark however and bolted over to him. She had trouble climbing onto the back of Laras' saddle, but managed to do so just fine after she got a little help. Arran walked towards his own horse and got in the saddle as well. He then rode out a bit farther ahead which left his students a short distance behind him. Together they rode out of the village and returned to the road to resume their journey homeward.

***

The cobblestone road they travelled over lay between golden crop fields. Short wooden fences separated the road from the farm fields. The harvest was going on at the time they passed by. After a fair bit of travel they visited a small village that seemed to consist of nothing more than five houses, a well, an inn, and a couple of barns. Its population most likely consisted of about ten people and their children, and triple that amount for the cattle. Arran had already gone past most of the small hamlet when a plump, short man with little hair on his head and his hat in his hands tried to get his attention.

"M'lord? M'lord? Could I have a moment of your time?" he spoke in a thick country accent and a slight tremble commanded the tone of his voice. Arran stopped his horse in its tracks and turned his attention to the farmer.

"Do you need help with anything?"

"Oh thank you m'lord. I've been asking men the likes of you all morning you see. It doesn't seem the guards give the slightest hoot."

"What did you need me for?" Arran asked. He needed to know more if he was going to help this man. The farmer shook his head and continued with what he wanted to say.

"Last night a giant beast flew overhead, must've been as big as that there barn." He pointed at a small building with a roof made of freshly harvested thatch. "It broke in and took a calf from its mother. I beg ye m'lord, please find it and slay it. I don't want it to kill all my cattle."

Arran looked ahead. He sighed and turned his head back to the man before he asked him a question with a serious tone.

"Do you know where it went?"

"Last I heard it, it sounded like it went northward."

Arran turned around. Laras and Yara were still a short distance behind him. They were talking with each other, though Arran didn't know what about, and he didn't care that he was interrupting them either.

"Laras, it's a cattle thief."

The young man turned his attention to his mentor and frowned.

"Cattle thief?" Yara asked. "don't dragons usually steal cattle?

"Not the big ones, usually just lindworm," explained Laras. "Occasionally though there are young wyverns or dragons that take an animal from its flock or herd." He then ordered his horse to ride up closer to his mentor.

"I need your help with this one. If it can nick a calf from its mother, then it's definitely not small," said Arran after he turned his head to Laras.

Yara was quiet as she listened along. She knew that if she tried to interject and ask to assist in fighting that the answer would most likely be a no. She hadn't yet been given equipment to fight and thus she'd either get in the way or be in danger.

"What do you reckon? The forest?"

"Mhm. If it's trying to hide it's likely to be there," said Arran. "Lindworm can't carry their prey for too great a distance, especially if it's an entire calf. Usually they go for lambs. It's safe to say that this is a bit unusual."

Both Arran and Laras talked about what the best course of action would be. Yara listened to what they said without knowing all that much about what they mentioned. She knew that she wouldn't be allowed to fight along but she was dying of curiosity and excitement. Regardless of that fact, what would she even do in the meantime?

"Can I watch?" she asked apprehensively. It took most of her courage to even try asking.

"Well, yes you can—" Laras was cut off by his mentor before he could continue.

"From a distance, you won't learn anything by just reading about it or only following the same drills," Arran continued, "but don't get too close. I don't want you to get injured."

The answer was satisfying enough for her. She'd get to see it happen. For the first time in her life she would get to see someone slay a dragon.

***

Burnt trees and shrubs marked where the creature had been. Seeing the scorched plant life was strange, however. To Arran's knowledge Lindworm didn't usually have the ability to breathe fire. They weren't like their more powerful cousins. He recalled that there were rare cases of half-wyvern lindworms that could spit a fire-like stream of sparks. That wouldn't explain the damage that'd been done here however. Maybe it was a new kind of beast. Arran didn't particularly care if it was new, as long as he knew how to fight it. It sounded cold when he thought about it like that, but at the same time these things were dangerous. Empathy wouldn't get him very far with a majority of dragons. The trio got down from their horses at the edge of the forest and stayed on guard. Each of them looked around for more signs of the creature.

"Now, like I said — Yara, you have to stay back. Laras, when I call your name I need you to move in immediately."

Both of the apprentices nodded. Arran took his shield off the back of his horse and grasped it firmly with his left hand, to the point where it covered most of his forearm. It couldn't have been bigger than a regular heater shield. Laras carried one of his own, about the same size. Yara didn't quite understand why their barriers were so small. Laras had mentioned something about a projection before. She assumed the shields made use of some kind of magic

The men traversed the charred remains of the woodland area first, followed by the youngest of the group. Yara made sure she stayed a fair distance away. After following the trail for a short period of time it just stopped.

"Shh ... It's behind here," whispered Arran before he gestured at the shrubs he was crouched next to. The knight then beckoned to Yara but also put a finger on his lips, gesturing to her that she had to be quiet. The knight unsheathed his sword and looked at his students. Arran gestured at Laras in a way that Yara didn't understand. He then looked back and forth between them. "Yara."

She looked him in the eyes and nodded quickly.

"Please stay back."

Yara and Arran then nodded to each other. They could all see it through the foliage. It was an animal no larger than a horse. Its body was long and slender like that of a snake and it had two hind limbs and two wings folded up like a bird's. It didn't appear to have arms and its head was hornless. Exactly what Yara had imagined a lindworm to look like.

The lindworm had been gorging itself on the calf's carcass. The poor thing hadn't been dead for all that long, and likely met a gruesome end. Arran stood up slightly and raised his shield to be positioned in front of him. A shimmering barrier appeared before it. He continued to walk slowly and carefully through the bushes, assuming an even slower pace the moment he stepped into close range of the creature. It noticed him and changed its stance into a defensive one. It opened its wings in an attempt to intimidate the approaching man.

The lindworm let out an angry hiss, meant as a warning. It then roared as another warning to try and make sure that Arran would leave it alone. The creature backed away slowly before it lunged towards the man that approached it and used the long and curved talons of its solitary extended wing fingers to slash at Arran. He grunted when the full weight of the creature hit his shield. The lindworm pressed its foe down into a compromising position, or at least attempted to. Arran looked at its head as it opened its mouth. Inside its maw he could see two rows of sharp, barbed teeth on both its upper and lower jaws. What made him doubt his previous assertions about what he was fighting caught most of his attention.

In the back of the lindworm's mouth and just above the tongue there were two round and dark holes. They looked like the organs a dragon would typically use to breathe fire. When he saw those it hit him: this wasn't a lindworm, instead he'd been fighting what he presumed to be a very young wyvern. It pushed Arran down further and in response he raised his sword as much as he could under the wyvern's weight.

"Laras!" Arran shouted. The wyvern then put one of its feet on the shield to apply more weight. Immediately Laras ran in to help. He raised his own barrier right away and held his sword in his right hand.

The beast's throat swelled up as if it were about to release a blast of flame on Arran when it looked up to observe its new assailant. Arran pushed his shield up the moment the creature was distracted to put it off balance.

Yara watched the fight closely as she hid in the bush. She was enamoured by what happened before her and made an effort to pay as much attention as she could. Yara saw what Arran was doing, how he'd walked in with his shield raised first as he let the creature think it would have the upper hand, before tricking and bashing it with his shield. Arran hit it a second time. The sudden impact took it off balance and it hopped backwards and screeched to try and frighten its attackers; once again it was to no avail. The young dragon spread its wings in an attempt to get away, however Laras in a stroke of pure luck, managed to cut through its membrane. Arran got closer again.

The wyvern turned to Laras and tried jumping on him. He managed to dodge the attack just in time. Arran hacked into the creature's tail, which cut the end clean off. The severed tip twitched and spasmed around on the forest floor after being separated from the rest of the animal. Eventually the dragon was cornered and again it focused on Laras.

Arran threw his shield off of his arm and jumped onto the creature. His tackle made him take the wyvern down with him and they both landed on the ground with a thud. Once they'd hit the floor he put his arm around the wyvern's neck in a tight hold and pressed it down to immobilise it. It roared before Arran gave his sword to Laras. Arran used his now free hand to keep the animal's mouth shut.

Yara saw it all happen very quickly. Her eyes followed every move that took place before her. She took notice of the mistakes the creature made and how the two men reacted to it. Yara saw how Laras held Arran's sword tight with the tip pointing down at the creature's head. First she heard a muffled roar, followed by a hiss and soon those sounds gave way to a sad squeal as the black metal was driven through its head.

The first dragon she had ever seen being killed by a human. It was a gruesome sight to be sure. Her heart started to beat faster simply by watching the short fight between Arran, Laras, and the wyvern. Blood pooled in the animal's mouth and seeped out once it reached the edges of its jaws. Arran stood up and wiped a small bit of mud off his face.

"That's done and over with," he said. Laras handed him back his sword, which he then promptly sheathed. The knight looked at Yara through the shrubs. He was pleased to see that she hadn't turned tail and ran or interfered in the fight. "You can help me cut its head off, if you'd like."

***

Now hanging from Laras' saddle, the dragon's head bobbed up and down with every movement the horse made. Occasionally blood dripped from the dead wyvern's mouth. Its jaws hung open in a limp manner and naturally, it smelled horrific as dead things tend to do. Once they'd returned to the village, Arran delivered the head to the farmer that'd asked him to get rid of the small dragon. The darkened and now dried dragon's blood was still on Yara and Arran's gloves.

The job was dirty but it's done. Yara thought to herself as they rode away from the small hamlet. They left behind them the work that they had completed. Arran of course rode out ahead again much like he had done on the previous leg of the journey. Yara wanted to ask him why he kept doing that, but instead she chose not to. She felt that as a new apprentice it wasn't her place to bother him about it. The dragon hunt in its entirety, including the encounter and return to the village, had taken almost the full day. All three agreed to not stop to rest that night but instead to continue onwards.

Chapter III:
A Stop in Laketon

They'd been on the road for just two days since they left the village. Arran had his two apprentices keep close in order for them to feel safer as they kept travelling during the night. His gauntlets still stank of the dragon blood that they'd been soaked in. It was a rank scent that truly started to reek when dried into leather gauntlets and Yara and Laras could smell it from the short distance they were behind their mentor.

Not long after the sun rose they crossed a hill that looked out over a lake with an island between itself and two rivers. On that island stood Laketon. The city had been destroyed by house Delvor not too long after Yara was born. In the end the cathedral was the only building that remained mostly intact. At the time it had been scarred but was still standing among the ruins. People didn't really talk about now that the city had been restored. It looked perhaps like someone had slapped a new coat of paint onto an old wall.

"I've never been all the way out here before," Yara said, "it's kind of strange to actually see it for myself."

"After you've been there once you wouldn't want to anymore," said Arran. He chuckled subtly before commanding his horse to move a little faster. Their mounts were quite tired and Laketon would be the best place to stop and rest.

The green fields and pastures that ran up to the river were fenced off to keep cattle off the road. Yara had often overheard Lord Hyghwing ordering his men or servants to travel to Laketon to retrieve something. Occasionally she'd catch details of the outside world too, but a lot of her time had been spent cooped up in the castle. Sometimes the things Lord Hyghwing wanted sounded strange to her, but they were more likely to be completely ordinary.

Something Yara noticed was that Laketon had no real walls around it, completely different from where she'd grown up. The swift currents of the rivers and the lake to the west served as natural barriers to keep out any attackers. The city wasn't entirely siege proof though. The only fortification she could see clearly was a low bulwark built along the shore of the island, but that was about it. Only that low stone structure which didn't reach higher than the city's streets themselves served as a defence against any assailants. From what she could see as they rode down the hill there were only two large bridges connecting the town to the mainland, each on opposite sides of the city, and both of them appeared to be made of easily collapsible wood in the event of an attack. Each bridge had two guard posts on either side of them. Yara's fixation on observing her surroundings was broken when Laras waved back at a farmer standing in his field, likely more out of politeness than recognition. At the guard post built on the river's south bank they were halted by two men of the city watch.

"State your name, affiliation and intention," one of the guards said with a disinterested tone, "please do follow our requests, it'll make this easier for all of us."

"Sir Arran Stormcleaver of the Knights of Ash, we're here to restock provisions and rest before continuing with our journey northeast."

The guard's face looked as unimpressed as humanly possible and he'd rolled his eyes at the mention of the Knights of Ash.

"And the children?" he nodded at both Yara and Laras. Neither of them were anything close to being children, but it didn't seem like he cared.

"Yara and Laras. They're recruits for the order and here for the same reason that I am," replied Arran in a calm and stately manner to the man in front of him. The guard let out a disgruntled "hmph" before letting him through.

"Why so dissatisfied, friend?"

"Arran we ne—"

Arran interrupted Laras. "You go ahead, I'll have a talk with this man."

Laras nodded to let his mentor know he understood. They continued over the footbridge where he slowed their pace down to let Arran catch up. A pained "ow!" was heard over the bridge followed by the hastened tapping of hooves over oak timber. Arran rejoined his apprentices. A bruise grew more visible on his cheek.

"What happened?" asked Yara.

"He said some things, I said some things, both of us ended with a fist in our face," said Arran. He chuckled. "You should see the state of his nose."

"Why'd you punch him?" She asked with her head tilted.

"He thinks we're a waste of crown resources. I couldn't help but feel like I should return the favour." Arran shrugged. "Probably a bad idea. I don't think it improved his opinion of us, but we hear it more than enough."

They rode through the busy streets of Laketon. People in the crowd around them rarely looked up from their businesses. A man in the background was yelling about his stockpile of fresh fish, and another about his vegetables and how great they were. The open market in the city was a place of fierce competition over sales, stall owners pushed items of possible interest up to the three riders.

The masses were hard to get through, large groups of people often blocked the streets and only stood aside when they noticed the small group of visitors approaching. Eventually they reached the town's square, a large open space of paved stone that laid before the city's cathedral, which loomed over the area and cast a shadow over it throughout the entire day. Arran turned his horse and looked his older apprentice in the eyes.

"I want you to go and look for an inn. I'll be at the lakeside smithy if you need me."

Laras nodded and turned away to look for a place to stay. Yara, still being on the back of Laras' horse, didn't really have a choice other than to go with him. Arran told Laras to stop, however, and he addressed Yara directly.

"I told Lord Hyghwing that I wouldn't lose track of you," he said. "You'll be coming with me."

Yara climbed down from Laras' horse, followed by her mentor getting off his own. She didn't mind having to stay with Arran. In fact she preferred it to being around someone she liked but didn't necessarily know yet. On top of that, she was experiencing so many new things she figured it'd be better to stay near Arran.

The streets were as busy as ever and filled to the brim with people. The crowd thinned as they edged closer towards the lake side of the town. The street on the reinforced bank of the lake had its own smaller crowds of course. Standing in the middle of the road here meant they could see at least a bit ahead of themselves. Not all of the people they passed lived in the city of course. Laketon had been built in a favourable position for trade, right at the heart of southern Anglavar. Most of the people that were present in the city were traders or visitors.

The hooves of Arran's horse audibly clacked on the cobbled pavement as they walked through the streets. Eventually the crowd was thin enough that they could move around more freely. Small fishing boats lay still on the gravel and pebble beaches as their crewmen unloaded their nets. The sound of a hammer hitting metal was clearly audible. It echoed loudly over the streets and the surface of the lake and increased evermore in volume with every step they took in the direction of the smithy. Arran eventually stopped and hitched his horse to one of the support beams that kept the roof of the smithy upright. A man with a tan skin tone that stood at around the same height as Arran if not a little taller was hammering away at an anvil. His gloved left hand was holding a heavy hammer close to its head. He was dressed in a grey shirt and a black, leather apron to protect himself from the heat. The smith was forging nails, probably meant for a customer or a local construction effort. When he cooled the set of nails in a trough positioned next to the anvil. Arran cleared his throat to make his presence known.

"What do you ... Oh, Arran!" His complaints died on his lips as he turned and saw who had entered his shop. Yara assumed from the change in reaction that they were old friends.

"I haven't seen you in two years now, how have you been?"

"The same as always really," answered Arran. "Nothing ever changes with me."

The smith laid his hammer down on top of the anvil and continued. "Well, except for your beard," He laughed. "That and you've brought a new one with you." The smith pointed to Yara with his hammer before he returned to work, "where'd you pick her up?"

"Hyghwing."

"Delvor's old lands? Surprised you even wanted to set foot there." He stopped himself when he saw Arran's frown darken just a little. "Right, sorry, I shouldn't bring it up."

"What's got you working on nails of all things?" Arran changed the topic.

"I've been commissioned for them. The docks are nearly falling apart and every other smith is too busy," he answered. "Any reason you're in this particular neck of the woods?"

"You remember that boy I had with me three years ago?"

The smith nodded. Arran looked at some of the weapons that the blacksmith had hanging around his shop.

"He's becoming a knight soon and I need to make him his own sword."

"You're not gonna give him that one?" The smith asked as he pointed at the weapon which dangled from Arran's waist. He turned back around to face his forge, taking an ingot from a stack and putting it in the fire using his tongs.

"No, Skycleave is for my family only."

"Ah, so you don't have to share." He laughed, perhaps realising too late that his joke was a little too crass. Arran threw him a quick glare. "So you want *me* to make it or ..." he asked Arran as he removed the metal from his forge. "I need to know what you actually want."

Yara wandered around the smithy as they spoke. She looked at the different weapons and armour for sale. The large majority of the shop's stock consisted of weapons such as axes or maces, but hardly any swords. Even compared to that he sold very little armour. She continued to overhear the conversation between Arran and the smith.

"I need something like two metres of black steel."

His friend turned away from the cooling iron, which he'd only just begun to shape, and walked into what Yara could only presume was his storage. He came out with what Arran had asked for.

"I can't imagine having to make that climb that often. must get tiring."

"It's not all bad. The exercise keeps me sharp." Arran laughed and so did the smith. "Though the weather could be better."

The smith's face turned dead serious out of nowhere. His smile was just gone in an instant.

"That'll be fifty pyrite pieces."

"You drive a hard bargain," Arran sighed but handed over a purse that was likely filled with more than enough. "Did it get more expensive?"

"I do what it takes to have my business survive," the smith replied, "that black steel doesn't come cheap, especially not with the King stirring up trouble."

"I haven't kept up much."

"Best if you don't. If you're done, I do have an order to fill." The sudden turn in his mood was unexpected and honestly quite strange to Yara. He'd been so friendly before and she couldn't put her finger on what'd changed. Arran stowed his new purchase on his saddle and helped Yara climb on, then he mounted the horse himself as well.

"Why did he suddenly get so rude?" Asked Yara when they were out of earshot.

"He's strange like that, always has been," answered Arran. "He lets people know when he doesn't want to talk to them anymore. He's a great blacksmith though. I'm inclined to prop that up to his self-isolation."

"I'll take your word for it."

***

On the main street to the town square and subsequently the cathedral — which towered high above all other buildings — they met up with Laras, who had come to find them and tell them where they'd be staying.

"I paid for a bed for you as well, Arran," said Laras sternly. In that one moment he seemed more responsible than his mentor. Arran immediately protested against that decision.

"I don't need a bed," he said.

"You've never told me exactly what you're punishing yourself for," said Laras, "but sleeping on the floor in late autumn isn't going to do you any good."

Yara recognised that Laras was right, but to her it didn't seem like Arran was happy with his decision. On their way to the inn they rode past the church and over the bustling town square again. More people tried offering them goods to trade.

A Yilgran woman caught Yara's attention. The woman held up a pendant to her and she asked Arran to stop his horse for her to take a closer look. The woman offered her a simple leather twine with a tiny crystal vial on the end of it that held a dark crimson liquid.

"What's that inside of it?" asked Yara hesitantly. She wanted to ask Laras or Arran for help but both were distracted by other things. The colour of the liquid inside the vial should've given it away, but she didn't understand what it contained until the woman told her.

"Dragon's heartblood, recovered from a beast slain nearby," the woman then looked at Arran's saddle and took note of the heraldry adorning his barding: a golden Wyvern with a black greatsword stitched onto the yellow fabric. She rapidly changed her attitude once she noticed.

"Normally I'd ask ten pieces of pyrite for it, but you are with the ones that protect us from these creatures. It's the least I could do."

Now Arran took notice. He turned his head to face the woman.

"Give it here please." He made an attempt at being polite, but took the item from the woman's hand, removed the cork and sniffed the liquid inside. He put the cork back on and handed it back with a disapproving look on his face. "I hope you have an actual one. I'm intimately familiar with how dragon's blood stinks, and this isn't it."

The woman scrambled through her stall and found one vial. The vessel was more roughly-cut than the others she had in stock.

"This one mayhaps?" She handed it over and let Arran sample the scent again. He approved this time, put the cork back and handed it back.

"I'll give you fifteen for it. It's the least you deserve for finding something like this," said Arran as he dug into his coin purse. The woman gratefully accepted her payment and she held up a hand when Arran handed over the coins. The knight then gave Yara the pendant. She held it up to the Autumn sunlight. The rough texture of the crystal vial gave it a more natural look and made the blood's harsh opaqueness quite obvious. Immediately after getting a better look at it she put it around her neck. The woman that'd sold it to them returned her attention to the rest of the crowd, eager to swindle more people out of their money. Yara looked at her mentor and thanked him.

As they continued to ride over the busy street she stayed focused on what was quite literally ahead. Mostly to make sure Arran didn't bump into people. Her mentor and fellow apprentice were talking about something. Yara couldn't tell what the subject was because she was too tuned out, though she managed to catch something about a dragon that had threatened a nearby village. Unfortunately exactly what they said was still a mystery. Her straying thoughts were disturbed when Arran called her name multiple times. "Yara?" He asked with a concerned undertone. He'd clearly been trying to get her attention for a while now. She shook her head and turned to look at Arran's face. "Yara we're here."

"Where where?" she asked, confused by what he meant. Laras laughed, it seemed like he didn't expect her to drift off that far.

"The inn, dummy."

"Oh right," she fell silent again. This time she was undistracted by the bustling town around her. She dismounted like her mentor and fellow recruit had done before her. All three entered the building together.

It was warm inside, which was a welcome change from the chilly autumn wind. Poultry was being spitroasted in the fireplace and a barmaid was passing around drinks. Arran nodded at the woman and gestured at her that he wanted a drink before he pointed to his apprentices. Laras told Yara that Arran wanted them to find a place to sit and took her with him to look for one. Arran was relieved that he didn't have to discuss the sleeping arrangements. Asking Laras to do it for him had been one of his better decisions that day. Once seated at the bar he let his eyes wander until he saw kegs, barrels, and bottles stored behind the counter and in clear view of the customer. He looked at his apprentices again. Laras seemed to have told a joke, as he saw Yara chuckle nervously. She'd been so excited before, but now she seemed anxious. It was understandable, of course. Being so far away from where you'd spent most of your life was always both exciting and scary. She was in a place she'd never been to before to become something not many would want to be. Maybe something else played in her head that Arran could only guess at. The knight was given his drink and then asked if his two young companions could get some water.

***

Laras had just finished telling Yara another story like he'd done before. She'd laughed nervously in response as if she didn't feel at ease.

"Something wrong?" he asked with a concerned tone.

"No ... not really," she said. Yara quickly amended her words however. "I usually have trouble with large groups of people ... " she looked at him but quickly turned when a woman approached them. It was the same one that Arran had gestured to earlier. She brought them both something to drink, and when Laras discovered he was given water and not ale he shot Arran an irritated look. His mentor laughed heartily in response.

***

Arran got up early the next morning, or at least earlier than his students. The sun hadn't even come close to touching the horizon. He left his room and quietly walked down the stairs. From the steps he could oversee the inn's tavern section. The dying embers of the previous evening's fire still flickered within the fireplace. Behind the counter stood a short innkeeper. The man's head only barely reached the top of the bar. From what Arran could tell the man was cleaning glasses from the night before. He proceeded to walk towards and sit on one of the stools. The innkeep looked up and raised an eyebrow. "It's a bit early for a drink isn't it?"

Arran chuckled and leaned forward onto the bar. "It's not for now," he said, "could you fill this up?" He handed his flagon to the innkeep.

"What with?"

The knight shrugged and read the names written in elegant calligraphy on each of the small barrels behind the counter. One of them stood out, a vat of northern Yilgran wine.

"That one," Arran said as he pointed at it, "water it down a bit though, it's usually too strong for me."

The barman happily obliged and filled Arran's flask before he added some water. "I noticed you brought two children with you, they yours?"

Arran was lost in thought, but snapped out of his trance when the barman put the flagon down and tapped his hand.

"Sir?"

"Hmm?"

"Sir, are the children yours?"

"No, no they're not."

Arran's answer was clearly not what he'd expected. "Bit strange to travel with kids that aren't yours."

"Right, poorly phrased answer. I'm their guardian, just not their father," said Arran. His answer appeared to be enough for the innkeep, who shrugged and turned around to get back to tidying up his establishment. Arran himself went back upstairs and knocked on the doors of his apprentice's rooms. Laras opened his and let his mentor know he was up. The knight then calmly entered Yara's room. She was half awake and sat up in her bed.

"Hrm ... Time to go again … ?"she asked, her voice slightly groggy. Arran was pleasantly surprised to see her already awake and took it as another sign of her adaptability. He nodded and she got out of bed quickly, if a little reluctantly. Laras had already begun packing his own belongings and halfway through he decided to help Yara. The older knight left the room and walked out of the inn, where he prepared their mounts.

***

All three of them rode out over the same bridge they crossed when entering the city. The early morning air was filled with a frigid, thick fog that allowed them to see barely anything in front of them. At the guardpost outside the town stood the same watchman as the day before. His nose had been bandaged up. Arran saw that despite the bandage a little blood had run down his upper lip. He had to contain a filthy grin when he noticed.

Laketon was soon far behind them. As the sun rose the fog withered and disappeared, which revealed the bare trees and dead leaves on the ground. The day itself was cold and unforgiving, like any day in autumn, or even most of the year for that matter.

Late in the afternoon they stopped. The road had led them to a wide and simple stone bridge crossing a narrow river.

"That," said Arran as he pointed to the stream, "is Green Maw Run. We should rest here and wait for the morning."

"Why? it doesn't look like there's anything there," asked Yara. She'd tilted her head as she looked at the bridge.

"A basilisk sleeps under the bridge this time of day. They're mean beasts," answered Arran. He was right. As Yara looked closer she noticed it. A big reptilian creature covered in scutes and with spines sprouting from its back slept on the stone bridge not too far away from them.

"Don't you think, with that in mind, that camping here would be a mistake?" asked Laras. Though this hadn't been the first night they'd spent outside he wasn't thrilled about sleeping this close to a basilisk.

"Yup," Arran replied with a grunt as he bent down to look for stones for a campfire.

Laras shrugged and helped collect material for the camp. After he picked up a couple of sticks his face turned to a confused and most of all questioning frown.

"Hold on, this early?" he asked as though the thought had just occurred to him.

"Well we don't have anywhere else to go, do we now?"

Yara lost herself in her surroundings while the two men argued about where they'd be staying. There wasn't much to look at this time of year, but it was still unlike what she had seen close to home — forests of oak that lost their leaves and woods of pine that stood green even in the coldest of winters. Eventually Yara snapped out of her observational trance and helped set up the campsite. She took their bedrolls from the saddlebags and laid them down on the ground around where Arran was building a campfire. Yara just now caught onto how cold it actually was. She noticed that she could see her breath in front of her face.

More and more small bits and pieces of wood were added onto the pile until Arran deemed it enough. He began to search through his saddlebags and grew more frantic and frustrated the longer he kept doing so.

'It should be ... where is it ... " he muttered as he searched. Eventually he managed to pull out a tinderbox. "There you are!"

"You still use that thing?" Laras asked with a scoff. Arran laughed as he knelt down to try and use his seemingly ancient tool.

"This tinderbox sparked the fire that forged the armour we're both wearing," said Arran proudly, "I'm not just going to toss it out."

"Just use my firestarter," sighed Laras. Arran was obviously trying his very hardest, and he finally managed to secure some tiny embers from the clearly worn out tinderbox.

"See? Nothing to it," said Arran before he laughed and sat down on his bedroll. He was tired, that much was clear and his eyes had large bags under them to prove it. He clearly never got enough rest. From the short time that Yara had been with him and Laras she could tell he never slept enough. He would stay up much longer than Laras or herself when it came to guard duty, and if there was anything wrong he never opened his mouth about it. He could crack jokes and make them laugh but he'd never say what was actually on his mind.

"Arran … ?" asked Yara apprehensively, her voice wavering slightly as she spoke. Arran simply made a curious "hm" sound in reply to her. He was too focused on keeping the fire going to respond with words.

"Would you mind if you didn't take guard duty tonight?"

He turned his head towards Yara to pay more attention to his apprentice. "I would mind," he replied.

"But you need sleep too."

Arran didn't laugh. He didn't even crack a smile. In fact, his face was locked in a deadly serious stare. "I can rest later."

Laras decided to chime in with his own opinion. "That's the thing, you never do."

Yara wasn't at all surprised that Laras confirmed her suspicion. Arran's problems hadn't started when he'd picked her up as his student, she'd figured that out already. Arran sighed. He started to say something, but instead Laras cut him off.

"But there's a basilisk right there," Arran said as he gestured broadly at the bridge.

"And who's fault is that?" Laras asked. Arran opened his mouth and shut it again immediately. "I'll stand guard together with Yara," Laras continued. "Don't worry. I won't lose sight of her."

"I think that's a good idea," said Yara. She made an effort to look him in the eyes. She wanted to make sure he understood she was serious, no matter how uncomfortable it made her to maintain eye contact. Arran sighed again but he chose to keep quiet until eventually he gave in and agreed to let them stand guard.

***

"So why is he so stubborn?" Yara asked quietly after Arran had fallen asleep. Laras clearly knew more about their mentor than she did. It seemed only logical to ask him.

"I don't have a clue," he answered in earnest. The answer surprised her. Laras had known Arran for nine years now and not once had he found out why his mentor was so headstrong. "I'm surprised he picked you however."

Yara threw Laras an annoyed and offended glare, though she had no idea if he could see it.

"Not for the reason you think. Let me explain," he said. "You didn't use the proper techniques and no shield, to name two mistakes."

Yara knew what he meant. He was right of course. She didn't use any of the stances and techniques she'd been paying such careful attention to from a distance. She'd chosen for something quicker, something that would grab Arran's attention. It had worked, but she wasn't sure why.

"He must've seen something in you that he recognized or something, because he didn't hesitate in picking you," said Laras. "Which is something he did with me."

Another thing that surprised her. He'd told her how he and Arran met and she had assumed he was instantly asked to join the order, without questioning his decision first.

"I don't know what he saw that made him so determined to bring you along, but I won't question it either," said Laras. With that the conversation was over. Yara stayed quiet as it got darker. Night in autumn set in rapidly and her eyes adapted themselves to her now pitch-black surroundings while the fire still burned behind her. She looked around.

"Is it always this boring?"

"Not always," answered Laras with a small chuckle. "I guess it can be quite bland when there's no monsters swarming you."

"How do you not fall asleep while doing this?"

"I honestly don't know."

They both laughed as quietly as they could. They looked out into the night in silence.

"Remember how you said you wouldn't lose sight of me, but instead we instantly turned our backs towards each other?" Yara asked. She could almost make out a quiet laugh from him.

"You know, both of us standing guard at the same time might not be the best idea," said Laras. "You should rest first. I'll guard you both while you sleep."

"Are you sure?" asked Yara. She turned around to look at Laras. She could barely make him out in the dimmed light of the campfire. There were only some warm embers left to light the campsite. He looked back at her with a hard-to-see reassuring expression on his face. Yara was unsure herself but did as she was asked. She laid down to rest on her bedroll and let the darkness wash over her.

An hour or two later Yara awoke to Laras gently shaking her shoulder.

"Your turn," he said as she shook his hand off. Yara rubbed the sleep out of her eyes and groaned as she got to her feet. By the time she'd gotten ready to stand guard Laras had already crawled into his own bedroll. She looked over to him. He was hard to see in the dead of night but she managed to make out his shape in the dark.

"Sleep well," said Yara quietly. Her words were followed by a yawn she couldn't keep in. Laras had fallen asleep almost the very moment he'd laid down. The sounds she could hear around her all night made sure she wouldn't doze off any further. The simple thought of an impending threat kept her on her toes at all times.

***

The sun crept over the horizon sliver by sliver. Yara could see that the area surrounding the bridge was cleared. The basilisk that'd spent the previous evening sleeping on it had moved and left the way free to pass. Yara immediately started to shake the two men awake. First Arran, then Laras.

"It's gone," Yara said. Arran sat up slowly to look at the bridge ahead of them.

"She's right," said Laras. He'd stood up before Arran could, despite the fact that Yara had woken him up last

"We should get going then," Arran said with a groan as he got to his feet. He kicked some dirt into last night's campfire.

After they had packed up the campsite and gotten back on the horses they continued further east. Looking over the bridge's edge and into the water Yara could see the massive reptile skulking about below the surface. Ashfallow's hold wasn't more than a day away now. After sixteen years of being stuck in castle Hyghwing, Yara would finally get to see the grand fortress that housed the Knights of Ash.

Chapter IV:
Learning the Ropes

Ashfallow's Hold was exactly as imposing as Yara had expected. It had walls that appeared a hundred times her height with towers that stood even taller than that. The castle was built on top of a great hill that overlooked the surrounding area. The road up to the fortress was guarded by a tall gate unsupported by a wall. Instead it was beset on both sides by a steep dropoff. Atop the gate and behind its crenellations stood a guard that looked down upon the path that led to his post. From the stone supports hung two grey banners, each emblazoned with a golden wyvern holding a black sword. The gate itself was made of heavy steel to keep out unwanted visitors.

"STOP RIGHT THERE!" a guard's gruff and old voice sounded from behind the crenelations. Arran looked up as his apprentices calmly approached behind him.

"Who are you?" asked the guard. Arran — now no longer the oldest man in the area — sighed, irritation plastered onto his bearded face.

"Celdric, you've let me through these gates for almost fifteen years," He said, "give it a rest and let us in."

"You still haven't told me who you are!" The guard squinted to get a better look at the man on the ground. Arran sighed and shook his head.

"Arran Stormcleaver, Celdric, I know you're not getting any younger but open that gate," said Arran with a sigh. Yara had to try and not laugh at what was going on, and Arran threw her a quick glare that made her stop nearly immediately.

"You're right, I'm sorry for holding you up," Celdric said as he turned away from the edge of the wall. Not long after the metal gate was raised to let Arran and his students through.

Yara looked ahead and could now see the fortress before her in greater detail. The keep had been built into an exposed rocky hillside. The walls of the imposing citadel still continued around that hillside to wall off every potential entrance. As they approached the gate she could see that the structure looked sturdier than she imagined. They were made of large blocks of well-worn stone that were mortared together so tightly that not even a sheet of parchment would fit between them.

More banners like the ones at the first gate decorated the walls. Yara looked up. At the top of the tower stood a woman with short black hair. She had a wide grin on her face when she saw the new arrivals approach the castle.

"Someone finally decided to show back up," she said.

Arran smiled at her "Hurry up and let us in, Aliss," said Arran "It's late and I've got two very tired teenagers with me," He gestured to the pair behind him to highlight his point.

The sun was low in the sky and the castle bathed in the orange glow of its dusk light when anything actually started to happen. Aliss helped the men atop the gate with opening the heavy wooden doors and lifting the metal grate behind them. The group dismounted and Laras and Arran led their horses to the stables. Yara was too awe-struck to move after she got out of the saddle. She took in everything she could see around her. The citadel was similar to castle Hyghwing, yet it felt entirely different.

"Girl," The voice of the woman from atop the gate snapped her out of her daydreaming. "Do you have a name?"

"OH, it's Yara."

"Well, Yara, you should probably go with them." She had a smile on her face. Now that Yara had gotten a closer look she could see Aliss wore the same armour as Arran did. Yara apologised profusely and looked down at her feet. Aliss laughed.

"You don't have to be sorry, I'd react the same way if I were in your shoes."

"Yara?" Arran called out to her from a distance. She looked at Aliss, who mouthed "go" to her.

Yara obliged and immediately ran to her mentor. She followed him around the courtyard to get an idea of where everything was.

"Those right there are the barracks, they're where the order's members sleep," he pointed at a relatively tall building that had been incorporated into the hillside. She could tell that they were living quarters by the lit candles from behind the small windows in the brick wall. "You ought to go inside and claim a bunk." Arran said to Yara. She dashed in and both Arran and Laras followed her to find their own beds and to get some rest. The next day would be a tiring one, and the first day of Yara's training at the castle.

***

The next morning Yara's eyes shot open. Faint light drowned out by clouds peeked in through the windows and thin curtains and directly onto her face. She scooted over to the side of her bed and sat up, promptly hitting her head on the bunk above her.

"Ow ... " she muttered. Though she would have preferred to shout, she knew to keep her voice down for the sake of those still asleep. She climbed out of her bunk and put on the boots she'd worn the previous day before walking to the door. The rain outside had gotten louder now that she'd stood up. Once she opened the door and looked outside she immediately opted to close it again, as she'd flood the room simply by having it ajar.

"What am I gonna do now ... ?" Yara muttered to herself. She turned around and chose to instead silently explore the building she'd spent the night in. It was quite a large structure in its own right. The bottom floor leading to the outside was mostly reserved for bunk beds, and a hallway connected them to a stairwell. The second floor led to the dining hall, storage, and a few more bedrooms. She found Arran sitting at one of the tables in the dining hall. He was alone, hunched forward over the table he sat at.

"Are you okay?" Yara asked as she approached and sat down with him. She would quickly glance at his face every now and then. For some reason she found it hard to read him. She wanted to blame the beard, but that couldn't've been it. Maybe he didn't want to be read. He looked to be completely focused on his rather meagre meal.

"I'm fine," answered Arran. His voice didn't let on whether he meant that or not. "Sorry about the rain," he said to change the subject before looking up and out of the window.

"At least we're inside and not out there," said Yara. She looked around the room.

"With my luck the ceiling collapses and it starts to rain in here too," Arran said with a scoff. "It'll clear up soon enough though."

"Bit of a shame about the training," she moped as she slumped down and forward over the table. She crossed her arms in front of her as she stared over Arran's shoulder and out of the window.

"We'll go outside when it dries up."

Lightning struck quite close by, and the thundering startled Yara into sitting up again

"Or not ... " Arran said.

"Is there anything to do inside?"

"Well there's things to read I guess? Never saw much use in those dusty old tomes myself though."

"Reading?" said Yara as she looked up, "like what?"

"Like ... " he stopped to think, then raised a finger. "Give me a moment," the wide wooden bench he'd sat on scraped over the stone floor as he pushed it back to stand up. Arran left the room for a little while and Yara waited patiently for him to come back. Not much later he re-entered the room with a book so thick he had to hold it in both hands. Yara quickly retreated her hands from the tabletop before he dropped the heavy tome with a loud thud. Dust sprang off the cover and made Yara sneeze.

"Like this," said Arran.

"That one hasn't been off the shelf in a while," she said as she wiped the cover clean. Elegant calligraphy spelled out the title, "The Encyclopaedia of Dracology by Davio A'tenbrow." Yara read aloud. She remembered seeing a smaller version of this book back in lord Hyghwing's sparse personal library. She'd only ever read its name on the book's spine as her previous guardian would never take it off the high shelf it was on. Considering that she herself wasn't all that tall she could never reach it on her own. He'd always told her that it was an original edition. That it was signed by the author and everything, and that he was very protective of it. Not that she ever believed him, of course, the author had been dead for an era. It had always sounded like a lazy excuse.

"I've got a smaller one with me, but I figured you'd want a more comprehensive edition," said Arran as he opened the book and flipped to the table of contents. "It does have fewer pages than the smaller ones, probably because more fits on a single sheet."

Yara took careful hold of the parchment and began to look through the book. Every pair of pages described a different kind of dragon and each had decorated margins relevant to the animal being put on display. The varying number of illustrations were incredible to look at. Arran took notice of how enamoured she was.

"I don't think I'll be able to pull you away from that for a while," he said, but she didn't respond until a minute or so later.

"Huh? sorry?" Yara had missed nearly every word of what he'd just told her.

"Never mind," her mentor said with a wide grin on his face. Yara stopped and looked up after she'd spent some time immersed in its pages.

"Some of these pages were wiped clean," she said before looking back down. "There's supposed to be something else here."

"Must be the archivists that did that," explained Arran, "some of them are kind of reckless and just blank out pages before putting new species of dragon on there."

"Sounds like a waste to me ... " Yara muttered. She checked the register on the last few pages of the tome. "It says here they're the Alamirian Ash Wyvern ones."

"I figured."

"How so?"

"They might as well be extinct, no point in keeping that information."

"'Might as well'?" Yara asked with a raised eyebrow, her interest piqued by his phrasing.

"There's only one male left, and he's no threat to anyone anymore," Arran clarified. He stood up again, only to move to the other side of the table and sit down next to her. They searched the book together for a little while. Every time Yara came across pages that'd been erased or wiped clean they'd use the index to find out what species used to be there. The only time they couldn't find what animal a page belonged to was when they both found a number for "The Cruel Monarch".

"I think I've seen this page in another book," Arran said. "Most have it redacted or straight up removed because it never really served a purpose."

"What should it say then?"

Arran sighed. No doubt he was happy that she asked so many questions, but Yara was also sure she was exhausting him.

"Well I recall it describing a skeleton, I think it was exhumed for an examination or something," he answered, "not really that important anyway. The dragon on the page was already dead."

"I see why they removed it then," Yara said. She continued to stare at the different pages for a while. As the pair lost themselves in the old book the weather outside cleared, allowing the sun to break through the clouds. Arran looked out of the window.

"Great," he said, "just what we needed."

"What?" asked Yara as she looked up. Her mentor simply pointed to the window. "Oh that."

"Not eager to start?"

"Not that I—I'd just like to keep reading for now," Yara said, pointing at the book.

Arran looked at her and smiled. "Keep going then," he said. The knight stood up from the bench. "I've got some things I need to go and do though."

"That's okay, good luck," Yara replied absent-mindedly. Arran walked away and left his young apprentice to her reading.

***

About a day later Yara found herself outside. It was a chilly but clear day, and she could see all the way to the peak of the mountains that bordered the keep. Arran had dragged her out of the library and to the training grounds after she'd spent most of her morning inside.

"Now as much as I'd want you to stay inside all day to read books and learn more, you can't glean everything there is to our line of work from the pages of an encyclopaedia," Arran said as he stood before Yara. They found themselves on a small, poorly maintained lawn.

"I wanted to have it memorised."

"You'll have plenty of time for that later," said Arran. "I think we should start with some warm-up exercises."

"Are you going to have me flail my arms around?" Yara asked, speaking out of turn.

"Well it'd be a start," Arran answered, perhaps a little incredulously. It appeared she took his comment literally however, as she began to do exactly what she had described.

"Right, I should learn not to answer like that," Arran said to himself. "Stop, you're making a fool of yourself."

"So what do I do then?"

"Some running exercises maybe?" said Arran, "try to warm up a bit without overexerting yourself, stretching and things like that."

He looked on as Yara did as he asked. Despite his lack of direction she seemed to figure it out on her own easily enough. Once they both felt she was warmed up enough Arran wanted to explain something to her.

"As you're probably already aware, there's a wide variety of weapons to pick from," he paused to wait for her to nod, after which he continued, "now the problem is, I only really know how to use one of these," he tapped the sheathed sword hanging on his hip. "Unfortunately I can't really teach you how to use any of the other ones."

"Well, we could both try learning one together?"

"I'm very attached to my swordfighting. I don't think I could learn anything else and not fumble it completely."

"I thought you were the one supposed to encourage me, not the other way around," Yara said, scoffing near the end of her sentence.

"I can teach you how to use any of a wide variety of swords though, and they wouldn't be the worst lessons."

"I think I'll take 'not the worst' then," Yara replied.

"Why don't you get both of us a training sword and I'll take you through the basics again," Arran suggested, and Yara responded by doing so. She came back with two wooden sparring swords and handed one of them to Arran.

"Alright, then we'll begin," he looked at her posture and immediately noticed it was off. her feet were too close together, which made for an unstable stance.

"First thing I noticed: you're approaching the stance wrong."

"Okay ... what do I do to fix it?"

"Part your feet a bit more, make sure that you've got a stable foothold."

She looked at how he was standing, one leg was out in front of him, with his foot pointing forward, while the other was at a right angle and pointed to the side. His knees were bent slightly, allowing for more stability. Yara copied her mentor's stance.

"That's good," said Arran. "Now obviously in the field you can't always stand like this and that's okay. It's important that you get as much balance and stability as you can."

"I understand, I don't think I'd want to fall over."

"Precisely," her entirely serious tone made him snicker. "Now, as for the sword."

She was holding it in a rather limp manner, while her arm looked weirdly tensed up.

"You need to relax your arms first, the tension you're putting on it is going to negatively affect your stamina."

Yara did as he suggested, then looked at what Arran was doing. He had a firm yet relaxed hold onto his sword's hilt. She imitated what he did right away and Arran could see just how rapidly she'd adjusted. It was obvious to him that she was a visual learner, and that her bad habits had come from watching other students make mistakes.

"That's good! you do learn quickly."

"So what now?"

"Well, how about some simple attack forms?" suggested Arran. "I'll block and tell you how to attack."

Yara nodded and Arran began by holding the wooden sword diagonally. She instinctively put both her hands on the hilt of her sword before slashing downward. The use of her other hand was new, likely an addition based on how Arran had fought the wyvern. Arran took note of this as he changed positions.

"I'm going to keep changing how I hold the sword every time you hit, alright?"

Yara nodded again, seemingly too focused to reply verbally.

"If you keep doing as well as you are now, I'll speed up slightly, just so you're aware." Arran took a step back as her sword hit his again. Once more she nodded. Arran had trouble keeping up with her. It was an almost strange level of dedication she had to break through his parries. Following a particularly hard hit the sword was flung out of Arran's hand. He wasn't exactly resisting hard, but he knew at that point that he had to stop her.

"We've done enough for now," he said, and Yara stood down. She was panting slightly, but she at least looked like she'd been enjoying herself.

"That was fun," she said with a subtle smile.

"It was, and you did well, we'll do more tomorrow." Arran got down on eye level with her, "go easy on me next time. I'm old, I don't think I can keep up with you at that pace."

"Oh, did I go too far?" concern commanded her tone.

"No, no I'm fine," Arran replied with a smile, "but I can't do that all the time."

"Okay, I'm glad," Yara said. She was looking at his face, but only to feign eye contact. "Is there anything else on the agenda today?"

"Yes, now that you mention it. I think we should see to getting you fitted for some armour."

***

Balancing on a stool wasn't exactly Yara's idea of a fun way to spend her time. It was mostly boring, really. The only exciting part about it was that she'd get her own suit of armour. At Lord Hyghwing's court she had plenty of clothes fitted for her in much the same way — the occasional dress she'd always outgrown the very next month, or just plain clothes like what she had on now. The stool was a necessity because of her height, and she had to put in a monumental effort to stand still. Every move would make the stupid thing wobble beneath her. If there was one thing she didn't look forward to it was falling and injuring herself.

Ashfallow's Hold had its own armorsmith, Jurgen, who also doubled up as a tailor. He'd initially wanted to measure her himself, but gave his task to Arran instead once Yara had shown to be somewhat resistant to anyone other than him doing it. Arran had explained to Jurgen that it wasn't his fault. He'd informed the craftsman that Yara has trouble trusting people. Jurgen seemed to be content with that knowledge.

"I've seen what it looks like already," Yara said, looking down as Arran measured her arms, "but how much does it weigh?"

"That depends on how big you are, and how much muscle you can put on," Jurgen said, "what do you think Arran?" He changed his focus to Arran, who was too focused on taking his apprentice's measurements to answer.

"Looking at you now," Jurgen continued, "I'd say that you've got some work ahead of you if you want to stop being all skin and bones."

"I can do that, I think."

"And you might want to cut your hair a bit shorter too," he suggested, "it might get in the way."

"Can't I tuck the ponytail into my armour?"

"It might restrict your movement."

"Don't worry," Arran interjected. He smiled and managed to look Yara in the eyes for just a second. "If it gets too long we can always chop off about half."

"But I like my hair like this."

"Kidding, mostly," Arran snickered.

"How old are you?" Jurgen asked. Arran answered for Yara as he noted down her measurements.

"She's sixteen, probably done growing I'd say."

"I think I might get another inch," Yara tried to interject

"Regardless, that's good to know. It means we won't have to worry about adjusting armour for you in the future."

"You think I'll stay this short?"

"Think of it as an advantage," Arran put away the tape measure and ruffled Yara's hair a bit, "they'll never see you coming."

Yara carefully stepped down from the stool, taking care to not trip or lose her balance. She looked at Jurgen, who was focused on the measurements Arran had gotten.

"I'll go and see if we have everything we'll need for her." He left the room and came back a little while later, shaking his head. "I'll need some additional material, other than that, your armour should be ready within a month, maybe a bit more."

"Do you need me for anything else?" Yara asked. Again Jurgen shook his head.

"No, you can go."

They did exactly that, and as they entered the mess hall Yara tried to get Arran's attention.

"You didn't mean that, right?" she asked. Arran looked at her with an eyebrow raised.

"Didn't mean what?" Arran replied with a question of his own as he sat down at one of the tables.

"What you said earlier about my hair I don't know if I want to cut it," she clarified, taking a seat opposite to him.

"No, like I said I was kidding you a tiny bit."

"Oh, because I—"

"I figured that might've been confusing. We can try braiding your hair instead if you'd prefer?"

"I don't like getting my hair yanked around like that. Lord Hyghwing's wife tried once and she kept tugging."

"I'll be sure to be careful and try not to tug if you do want to give it a go," Arran replied. Yara looked off to the side, then back at him with an eyebrow raised. He could tell she was considering it. She got to her feet and with some difficulty picked up her chair before placing it next to Arran. Yara sat down again, her back facing toward him.

"Okay, one try then," she said. It put Arran on the spot a little.

"I can't remember the last time I braided someone's hair. Here's hoping I still have any idea what I'm doing."

First he undid Yara's ponytail before parting her hair into three strands, carefully folding each of them over and under each other repeatedly. It took him a while, and the eventual end-result looked something like a crown braid, though perhaps a little looser than a typical one — a byproduct of both Arran's inexperience braiding and making his best attempt at being careful with her.

"How does it look?" Yara asked. She looked around, itching for something like a mirror to see her reflection in.

"Like ... Well, like I did my best," he admitted. "we'll find you something to see it in. In the meantime though, we should probably find something else to do," he looked to one of the many windows and noticed that it'd gotten darker outside.

"More training?" Yara asked, turning her head to look at Arran. He shook his head.

"It's a bit late for that, but ... " he trailed off while thinking, and his expression changed to a grin not long after. "How do you feel about chores?"

***

In the month that followed Yara did everything Arran asked of her. When they trained or did exercises she followed every instruction to the letter. Her attentiveness certainly paid off on the days she got to train with a weapon, however that wasn't the only thing she had to do. Unfortunately for Yara, following Arran's every word meant she was also saddled with a great many number of chores around the castle. A lot of these chores were just busywork, though occasionally there was a lesson to be found in even the most boring of jobs. Another downside of these chores was that they often introduced her to some of the more unsavoury types in the order.

"Scrub 'em good, girl."

The man that told her to "scrub 'em good" was Grimot. Grimot was a great example of everything Yara expected knights not to be like. He was a dirty, unkempt man who showed no real care for the others around him or their equipment. He was loud and brazen, and he behaved more like a common bandit being given another chance at freedom than a knight with a noble goal. He was a man who would rather let others do most of the work for him, and because Yara was new at the castle it meant that on top of the work Arran gave her she also had to deal with Grimot bossing her around.

Most of Yara's focus was on daydreaming as she scrubbed mud and dirt off of Grimot's boots, which had the unfortunate result of making her work slower. It was obvious enough of a change that Grimot took notice.

"Oi!" he called to get her attention, "you do understand I need these, right? Work faster."

Aside from being rude, he was also impatient. His yelling snapped Yara out of her absent state and made her return her attention to what she was supposed to be doing. "Get another pair" she thought to herself as she scraped caked mud off of his soles. Grimot had been loudly complaining up until that point, but he'd gone quiet now. Yara looked up at him. His eyes had narrowed so much they might as well have been closed.

"*What*?" he hissed, "what did you just say?"

It turned out that Yara hadn't just thought it to herself. She'd said it out loud. To his face. It was embarrassing to say the least. Not realising it was a bad idea to repeat herself, she did exactly that. "I think I said 'get another pair'."

He started to fume now. His unshaven, flabby face was red with anger.

"I don't care if I can get another pair of boots. I want these. You're the newest recruit around, which means you clean them."

"No."

Grimot couldn't appreciate disrespect in any form and he definitely didn't appreciate it when someone he perceived as a child talked back to him.

"You get to complain once you've chased a Mudslipper Wyrm for three weeks. Until then, you clean my boots." He aggressively shoved his finger in her face. "Step out of line again and I'll tell Ashfallow. Him chewing you out ought to get you in line."

Yara put his still incredibly filthy boot down on the ground and looked him straight in the eyes. She chose to ignore his threat. "No," she repeated.

Normally looking someone else in the eyes made her feel incredibly uncomfortable, but Grimot wouldn't budge if she didn't try to intimidate him just a little. He actually seemed to have trouble dealing with her refusal to follow his orders. Clearly Grimot was very much used to being unopposed by those he viewed as beneath him.

"You'll have Arran to deal with if you threaten me again," Yara said. She watched the colour drain from his face. Dropping her mentor's name had worked in her favour.

"Can you at least get the top layer off?" he asked with a somewhat apprehensive and more polite tone than before. Yara calmly obliged. When she was done taking most of the dried mud off, Grimot put his boots on again and left without saying a word. He acted like he was quickly going to forget their whole interaction.

***

"I heard about what happened between you and Grimot," said Laras. Grimot had strung together some sort of story about how rude and insubordinate Yara had been and told everyone but her.

"He deserved it really."

Yara looked down. She did feel a little regret for what she'd done.

"Arran knows as well. It's been making the rounds all around the fortress."

Yara's expression turned to one of worry and she looked at Laras, who had to hide the grin that was growing on his face.

"What'd he say?" Yara asked. She had mixed feelings about the situation with Grimot. She'd felt a tiny bit of pride, but that pride was haunted by a fear of what Arran would've thought of it.

"Oh he wasn't mad at all," answered Laras. He meant to calm her down at least a tiny bit. "He laughed at how Grimot had behaved. If anything he was a little proud of you."

Yara sighed. "That's far more relieving than you might think."

"That being said, he did want you to be a little more careful around people like him," said Laras, "he said he didn't want it to negatively affect your judging with Ashfallow."

"Did he say that?"

"Well, I might just have paraphrased that. It's something I'd still recommend, though."

***

They continued to talk until they reached the training grounds. The small plot was the same one where her training with Arran had begun just a month earlier. Yara saw Arran stand between the target dummies and lean on one of them. Soon she and Laras stood before him.

"I think I should take you through the shield basics this time," Arran said as he looked at Yara specifically. "Laras, could you get her one of the shields? She'll need to get to know how to use one."

"I did see what you did, with the magic barrier and stuff," Yara said, "or is that not what you meant?"

"No, it is," Arran said as Laras walked away to oblige his request. The younger man came back with a shield, one identical to both his and Arran's. The crest of the Knights of Ash proudly decorated its centre. Its edge was sharp near its pointed end, and coated in black steel.

"First things first: put it on your arm."

"How?" Yara asked as she carefully held it by its two widest sides and looked at the inside of the shield. Barring the copious amount of runes she was sure related to the magical barrier somehow, there was a plaque in the centre. Attached to it was a grip for the shield and a belt-fastened leather strap. Putting one and two together in her mind, she grabbed the handle with her left hand and tightened the belt around her forearm. Once she was done she looked at Arran.

"Right, take a proper stance." He waited for her to follow his instructions. "Raise it, kind of like this." He mimicked her pose and then lifted his left arm. His forearm held in front of his chest and head. Now it was Yara's turn to copy him, and as she did her shield projected something in front of her. It felt warm — hot, even — to stand behind it. Her face started to look slightly sunburnt, and it felt that way too.

"Now lower it again," Arran said. Yara gladly obliged. "This shield you've got here, especially that magical barrier, will save you more times than you can realistically imagine right now."

"Really? Does it have to make my face hurt for that to work?"

Arran chuckled. "That's yet another reason why you wear a helmet. And besides, a little bit of sunburn is better than dying a horrible death."

"So what do I do now?" Yara asked. She repeated her stance, took a few different angles, trying to figure out exactly where the protective barrier would and would not appear. "Do I just practise that stance until you think it's enough?"

"Well, actually, I was gonna have Laras throw things at you. You'll have to block them as best you can."

"I hope it's not rocks."

"Ideally he finds something better than rocks to lob at your shield." Arran looked at Laras, who looked a bit put on the spot.

"I'll try and see if there's anything other than those around here."

Once Laras was out of earshot Yara turned to her mentor. "What's the sharp edge on the pointy bit for?"

"Eh ... Well." Arran was having trouble figuring out an appropriate explanation. "It makes the shield into a secondary weapon, you could use it to your advantage."

"I could *punch* someone with it?"

"Not just punch, maim too."

Yara's face went through a series of expressions, from a bewildered "wow" to a toothy grin. "I kind of like that," she said as she eyed the shield. Laras came back not much later, carrying in his arms a basket with a kitchen towel covering it. It stunk something awful, and the waft reached Yara before it did Arran. Her face scrunched up and she waved away the air in front of her.

"What's in that?" she asked, pointing her shield at it. "It's positively rank."

Laras chuckled, "I'm not thrilled about it either," he said, playfully lying through his teeth. Maybe it'd only been the smell he wasn't thrilled about. "It's rotten fruit, I figured that might not upset you that much."

"The only thing getting upset is my stomach." Arran scoffed.

"Great, I'm gonna get pelted with leftovers," Yara said. "It's not rocks, at least. I guess that much is true."

"As long as you hold that shield up, nothing much should hit you," Arran explained, "at least, realistically speaking it shouldn't. Right, barrier up!"

Yara had to think quickly and threw up her shield. Her head bowed down, she couldn't see what was going on in front of her but felt the temperature in front of her go up. The sound of a splat hitting her magical barrier was soon replaced by a singeing and a sizzle.

"How was that?" Laras asked.

Yara lowered her shield, "Good, I think? You can throw more."

"Good, because there's a lot of mushy pears in here," he continued before throwing another pair. Yet again the fruit hits its target with a wet slap and a sizzle.

"How many more of these do we have to go through?" Yara asked.

"Well it depends, do you think you could block a dragon belching fire at you?" Arran asked. He waited for her to shake her head. "Then you keep going. I'm just going to keep watching this and see which one of you gets tired first."

It appeared that Yara could keep it up for quite a while. Her small frame seemed to contain more endurance than either Arran or Laras thought. Only when Laras finally ran out of things to lob at her shield did Yara practically collapse to the floor.

"I think *that* is probably enough," he said with a smile. As he helped Yara get up. She swept her hair out of her face. It had gotten dark in the meantime. It looked like as far as Arran was concerned, it was time to head back inside.

"I could eat a horse," Yara said. Judging by Laras' reaction he was thinking the same thing.

"Couldn't agree more," he said. "Let's see if there's anything in the mess hall."

***

During dinner that evening Yara found her eyes wandering to Arran's sword. She'd heard its name once when Arran mentioned it off-handedly in Laketon. Other than that though, she didn't know much.

"Why is your sword like that?" She asked. Arran raised an eyebrow.

"Like what?"

"Like how it is."

Arran paused for a second, then put down what he was eating and wiped his hands on a napkin. Yara recalled seeing Arran's sword before when he and Laras fought the young wyvern on the road, and during training when he'd taken it out of its sheath. It had piqued her interest when she first saw it. She'd never seen anything like the metal . It was darker than the sky at midnight, yet still reflected as brightly as silver would.

"Skycleave is made of dragonforged black steel, It's one of the many weapons that can slay dragons."

"Did you make it yourself?" she asked, her attention focused almost completely on the sword.

Arran shook his head.

"No, I was ... gifted it," he said with a fake cough. "Not many people know how to dragonforge a weapon. I didn't even know until recently, though it is quite simple."

"How do you make one?"

"You need the heartblood of a dragon and Norvarian black steel. Even if you manage to get those things you still have to bring it to a specific place. It won't work otherwise."

She wanted to ask if she'd be getting one of her own at some point, but Arran stopped her as she opened her mouth.

"You'll get one too, don't worry," Arran answered her question. Yara returned to being silent and eating alongside her fellow student and mentor. She listened to them talk about previous adventures and waited for a lull in the conversation to interject a question, changing the subject entirely.

"Can other weapons hurt them at all?"

"What?"

"Can non-dragonforged weapons hurt dragons?" she clarified.

"I'm sure people have," said Laras. "only they didn't live to tell us."

He was probably right. Brave souls attempting to attack fire breathing reptiles with pitchforks were a kind of unsung hero. They tested the unconventional against a powerful foe. Unfortunately their lack of success was a very clear indicator that their well-meaning but misguided efforts only led to failure.

"We could test it sometime," Arran said. He was joking of course, there was no way he'd try anything dangerous like that. "Until then we should keep it to what we know." He was done with his food and decided to head to bed and his students soon followed. They both bid one another good night before returning to their beds.

Chapter V: Ashfallow

Yara woke up to Arran gently shaking her shoulder. His large hand was placed carefully on her arm.

"I need to leave for patrol later today," he said quietly, "so I wanted to bring you to the main hall."

"Hmmm ... why?"

"There's someone there who wants to meet you."

Yara knew what he meant. Since she arrived she'd been told about being judged by Ashfallow, the leader of the Knights of Ash. She'd heard others around the fortress mention him on occasion too. Usually she only overheard small pieces of conversation where people referred to what they had gone through, though she never caught the full extent of what had happened to them. It seemed that they kept it secret for the most part. Yara assumed she'd never actually seen Ashfallow at the fortress. The name was probably nothing more than a nickname or a title he'd taken up. From what she'd heard she'd started to believe his fury to be like that of a dragon and his prowess in battle more than equal to one. Yara wanted to jump out of bed from excitement. She got out calmly instead, as she'd hit her head on the bunk above hers nearly every day. Not long after dressing herself appropriately she ran out after her mentor. Yara had wanted to meet Ashfallow for the past month and now she actually would. Her excitement seemed to be contagious, as a wide grin had grown on Arran's face as well. Yara was being incredibly expressive about how she felt, more so than she normally would be.

"Don't get too excited," said Arran, and he snickered.

She didn't calm down. The entire walk up the stairs she had a nervous grin plastered on her face. She couldn't wait to see what she was assumed to be a legendary warrior.

The gate to the hall, which stood at the far end of the upper courtyard, was enormous. It looked incredibly heavy and nearly impossible for one person to open, if it even had hinges to open it in the first place. Yara looked at Arran and then back at the door. Her eyes caught a smaller door set slightly off-centre in the larger one.

"You can go in, you'll be fine," Arran said as he pushed the smaller door open without any effort.

Yara entered. The slightly warmer autumn air was replaced by a cold breeze that seemed to have been trapped there since last winter. The inside of the hall was like that of a cathedral. Tall stone arches supported by pillars made the building look imposing. The high walls were lined with boarded-up windows and at the far end of the hall stood a throne. Behind the imposing seat was a gaping hole in the structure, which would've let in warmth under any normal circumstances, but the chill deepened as Yara neared the throne. Light streamed in from the only opening in the building and through the dirty and broken windows. In the corner of her eye she could see that there was a man in the throne at the back of the hall.

Yara was so preoccupied observing her surroundings that she hadn't really registered that she wasn't alone. Finally she focused on him and took a small step back. He was covered in a set of dark platemail. On his head he wore a helmet with a visor that was shaped like a dragon's head. The man's hands rested on the pommel of an intimidating black greatsword with a red gemstone in its crossguard. His concealed face unsettled her. In any other situation she would've been perfectly fine with not looking someone in the eyes. Here, however, it felt disconcerting that she couldn't see what he looked like or what his facial expression was.

"Are you afraid ... child?" His voice was gravelly and deep. The architecture of the room made his voice echo, which in turn served to make him sound old and wise.

"I ... No ... no I'm not," Yara answered, yet she found herself questioning her own response. She was a little frightened, but was sure that the man who led the Knights of Ash wouldn't hurt her.

"That would make you more courageous than most."

The man she assumed to be Ashfallow got up but continued to lean on the sword for support. There were dents in his black armour which he'd likely gained from all the battles he fought.

"Tell me, why are you here?" He pointed at Yara.

"I was ... recruited and brought to Ashfallow's Hold by sir Arran ... "

The man shook his head and laughed.

"No, *why* are you here? Do you want to become a Knight of Ash?"

Yara took another step back. She thought about it for only a second. There wasn't much deliberation that needed.

"My previous guardian told me that I was brought in by a Knight of Ash when I was a baby, and I think I should give something back for that"—she tried her hardest not to stutter—"and I don't think that someone else should end up in my position, this position, where they feel they have to do this."

The armoured man let a hand go from the pommel he held onto and put it to the chin of his visor. It looked slightly humorous to see a human hand put to the chin of a dragon-shaped helm.

"Admirable, I like that."

Despite Yara's attention to detail she only now noticed that Ashfallow's voice hadn't been echoing in quite the same way as hers. She grew suspicious of the man before her. He walked towards her and in response Yara refused to back up any further. She was holding her ground for the first time, determined to find out who he really was. As he got down on one knee he opened his visor, revealing an aged face with a black beard that hugged his jawline tightly and contrasted with his pale, sunken skin. He made an attempt to give her a warm smile but ended up just missing the mark.

"Hello," he said. His voice sounded completely different from how it did before. His face was familiar somehow, yet Yara couldn't recall where from. She was about to ask how he managed to change his voice into the much deeper one from before when a wyvern vaulted in through the back of the hall. It was covered in gilded bronze, black, and ashen grey scales and its great wings pulled it forward into the building. Its sudden movement startled Yara and she had to stop herself from jumping back. The large wyvern crept up behind the knight before stopping and bending its head down to inspect the young girl in front of it. Her first face-to-face encounter with a dragon and it was in the one place she didn't expect it to be. She didn't know what this dragon intended but chose to try and stay calm, regardless of the fact that a giant reptile was inches away from her face.

"You know how to keep the appearance of calm, that is certain," said the wyvern. He sniffed the air in front of him before blowing out hard through his nostrils. The blast of warm air blew Yara's hair back. That was the voice she'd heard — it had come from the dragon, which made it significantly more intimidating. The man before Yara got up from his knee and pushed the wyvern's head away.

"That's enough Ashfallow," he said, "you're scaring her."

"There will be far more terrifying things in her future than me," Ashfallow said as he backed off and settled on the floor. With every word he spoke bared his fearsome, yellowed teeth, each as long and sharp as a dagger.

"Sorry for the trickery," the armoured man said as he looked at the large dragon, "he doesn't like new people."

Yara could sympathise with that. Her eyes stayed focused as her heart raced from the scare.

She looked at where his eyes were meant to be, only to be met by two empty, scarred sockets staring back at her.

"I'm Darav Ebonblade, one of the leaders of the order."

"What about him?" asked Yara, slightly bewildered. She realised nearly immediately that it was a stupid question.

"That's Ashfallow," Darav answered her, "you were here to meet him if I recall correctly."

"**I seem to recall that as well**," replied the gruff dragon as he raised his head. He turned it back to the broken open wall. The red light of the dawn was beginning to fade and though he couldn't see it, it was clear that he yearned to be out there himself.

"Well ... I expected you to be more—"

"**More human?**" Ashfallow replied calmly as he quickly turned his head. It was likely something he'd explained to many others before.

"Yes ... " Yara answered with a faint hope that she hadn't insulted him. She looked down at her feet.

"**Considering how the hunters talk about me, I am not surprised you thought so.**"

"It's not only that ... " she said with hesitation, "I'm not sure I understand why you're even on our side ... " Yara was prone to questions but this had raised even more of them. Her need for answers grew as her list of questions did.

"You are ... confused by this?"

Yara nodded and the dragon tilted his head.

"I see no kinship with those that cannot adapt to changes, they are below me," he said, "many of my kind simply do not understand that rejecting humans and treating them as prey is detrimental to their chance of survival, a thing I deem to be of highest value."

The wyvern crawled through the room and got closer to Yara and his snout found itself directly in front of her again.

"Does that answer your question, girl?"

Yara stood there for a little while and nodded, forgetting for one meagre moment that Ashfallow couldn't see. She looked straight at the creature in front of her and could feel its warm breath against her face.

"Now I have something to ask you," he said, "Are you certain you wish to go through with this path?"

"This path ... ?"

"To hunt my kind," he tilted his head, "are you doing it out of obligation? to underestimate the danger of this way is to fail."

Yara's look changed from one of confusion to one of determination. "Yes, I'm sure. I want to protect other people," she said, "you're right, I do feel like I owe it to the order. I wouldn't be alive without it."

Ashfallow turned his head away from her and towards the outside. He made a rumbling sound with his throat before speaking again.

"Then we have nothing more to discuss." The wyvern vaulted out of the room, spread his wings and took to the air, leaving Darav and Yara behind. The Lord kneeled down again and put his firm hand on Yara's shoulder as he looked her in the eyes.

"You did well, I think he likes you," Darav said, then stood up straight again. He turned around and continued. "You can go now. I have important things to attend to."

Yara understood and immediately turned to leave. Once she got to the door she had to use every muscle in her small body to push it open. Outside she was greeted by Arran and the warm sunlight that she'd left behind before. He'd been waiting for her to return.

"So, you survived," he said as he turned to follow her. "How did he introduce himself?"

"I walked in and the first thing I noticed was the cold."

Arran nodded. "It's always like that in there, continue?"

"Lord Ebonblade and the dragon played a trick on me. Scared me to death when he actually entered."

Now Arran chuckled. "I can't recall whether they've done that before. Lucky you."

***

"I remember when I first met him," said Laras before he took a bite of his food, "when he revealed himself he climbed down from the ceiling like a big, scary bat."

They sat in the dining hall. Arran had to leave on patrol soon and so they chose to spend a little bit more time together. Yara couldn't imagine a dragon hanging upside down from a stone ceiling. She knew for certain it couldn't hold the dragon's weight. Laras often had stories that seemed ludicrous to Yara. At least she found them entertaining whether or not they were true.

"While I'm away," Arran said with a dead serious tone, "you'll have to look after each other, don't let Grimot get the better of you." He walked to behind where Yara sat and ruffled her hair. "Don't do anything stupid, I'll find out."

Yara's face formed into a slight smile. She looked at Laras, who also smiled.

"We won't," he said, "promise."

Arran then turned and walked out of the hall. Laras looked at his fellow trainee and saw that the smile that'd been on her face before had gone, instead replaced with a slight frown.

"You want to go with him, I can see it," Laras said as he tried his hardest to look her in the eyes. Yara shook her head in response.

"No ... I don't know what you mean." She made her best attempt at faking denial. It was a good try to be sure, but unfortunately for her it didn't get past Laras

"You're not the first to be like this." He got up. "Go on, I'll help you out."

Now she allowed herself to let a little bit of excitement show. She jolted up and started running towards Arran. He'd only just walked out of the door when he turned around to see his two students behind him.

"You can't leave without her," Laras said.

"I think I'll have to, you can't come with me every trip I go on," Arran said. He took a glance at Yara and didn't rethink his decision. "No, I really don't think you can."

"You promised Lord Hyghwing you wouldn't let me out of your sight," Yara blurted out. Arran's expression turned from disapproval to sympathy.

"The promise was meant to keep you safe. If you stay here and practise more then eventually you can come with me." he sighed and looked at his older student. "Laras, you can't come either. I need you to watch over her while I'm away."

"I understand," said Laras, "I'll keep an eye on her."

"Don't get hurt when you're out there," Yara said quietly.

"I'll try not to, okay?" Arran smiled at both of them before he turned around and mounted his horse. Laras put a hand on Yara's shoulder, which she shook off near immediately. Arran waved at them from the back of his horse as he rode away.

"Tell you what," Laras said as he leaned his head in Yara's direction, "he's just given me an idea."

Yara turned to him quickly before she looked back in the direction Arran had ridden off in.

"Really, what's that then?"

"How do you feel about horseback riding?"

Chapter VI:
Titans

Arran felt it was somewhat comforting to be on his own for once. Getting to spend time with his apprentices had been well worth it of course. That being said, every now and then he did enjoy his fair share of solitude. He'd left Ashfallow's Hold just a day or two prior and was approaching the city of Rivertop.

It was located just northwest and opposite to Laketon and bordered the same body of water. On a clear day anyone standing at Rivertop's southern gate could see the spire of Laketon's cathedral towering over the city. Arran had decided to head to Rivertop after overhearing a conversation between two travellers he crossed paths with. According to them a monstrous creature had been stalking the wilds of western Abonia and Presten County. Apparently the creature could spit mist to confuse its prey before striking from the fog. It had certainly piqued Arran's interest when he heard them say it. There was always the possibility that it'd been made up to scare visitors away from the area. There didn't seem to be any harm in investigating regardless. After all, it'd simply be another day's work for him.

Notice boards were a common sight outside of towns and villages. Occasionally Arran would take a quick peek at them to see if anything interesting was pinned up on one. Most often the answer to his curiosity was no. However there was the rare case of something small popping up. Even if it wasn't a job for him it could still draw his attention. Something unintentionally funny such as a pamphlet sharing local misfortune. More often than not it was something like a small bounty on a fox that'd been stealing hens, or requests for aid with a non-dragon monster that'd been terrorising the town.

This time around Arran nearly rode past one such board. It'd been hidden behind the thorny vines of a raspberry bush and most of the notices were obscured. After carefully pushing away some of the bramble Arran could see what was hanging on the board. He'd hoped to find anything that could tell him more about the creature he'd heard about. One of the sheets of paper had a contract on it written in now faded ink. It described something all too similar to what the travellers had mentioned. Farmer's notices had remarks about how they needed help with their fields in the early morning due to the fog. Guards alerted people to disappearances of both cattle and peasants on their notes. Whatever was happening here was a widespread problem and it meant he'd have to get involved. Arran set out to find someone who would know more. Perhaps he'd be able to help out.

A little searching eventually led him to a guard captain. A stout man in stature, he was only a little taller than Arran. His presumably flabby cheeks went hidden behind a moustache and mutton chops. He recognized Arran as a Knight of Ash from the sigil on his saddle and called out to him.

"Thank the saints you're here." Not a hint of sarcasm was in his words. "Were you sent to help us?"

Arran was a bit surprised that he was so welcoming. "Uh ... not exactly," he replied in an unsure tone. "I was passing through and came across some notices. I figured I should ask someone for more information."

The guard's gaze shot around nervously. "We've had those notices up for a good while now, as you could probably tell from the ink. Most people don't even stop and think to help us."

"Well I'm here now, aren't I? Just tell me what you know."

"You've already read all the notices. As far as we're aware it comes from the south."

"Anything more specific than that?"

"We think it might be hiding in the river most of the time, but that's all I could tell you."

Arran raised an eyebrow. He'd asked for specifics but this did nothing to answer his question. "Any reason why you might think so?"

"Because it reeks — the monster stinks like a bog in midsummer," the captain answered, "you could catch the scent with a disembodied nose and its original owner would smell it."

"You've come close to it?"

"Only once, and I wish I hadn't."

Arran tugged on his reins a little to stop Reed, his horse, from trying to graze.

"Well I'm sorry to say, but you might have to get close a second time," he said as he looked at the man on the ground. "I need you to bring me to where in the river you think it might be. I suggest we move quickly." He looked the captain in the eyes. "That dragon isn't going to get rid of itself."

***

Yara and Laras found themselves outside the fortress the day after Arran had left. Laras had wanted to begin teaching Yara how to ride a horse right away, but he'd had trouble getting his hands on a horse she could actually get onto.

"This is Helena," said Laras, pointing to the deep grey mare standing next to him. Yara calmly walked up to her and patted her on the nose.

"Hello, Helena," she said. The horse blew out of her nostrils. Laras watched Yara walk towards the saddle and make her first attempt at climbing into it, but her inexperience caused quite a scene.

"You have ridden a horse before, right?" Laras asked, his head held at a slight angle.

"I ... have," Yara said with a grunt as she struggled. The horse she was repeatedly attempting to mount wasn't impressed and kicked at the dirt.

"Would you like some help?" Laras said, a wide grin plastered on his face, "I'd be glad to—"

"I'm fine," Yara managed to blurt out before she fell to the ground. She stopped herself from letting out a yelp as she fell and opted instead to yell out "ow!" at the top of her lungs when she'd crawled onto her knees. Laras ran to her to try and help but she shook her head and held up her hand to stop him.

"Less fine now," she got up and rubbed the side of her body where she'd hit the ground first. "I guess it has been a while since I did this on my own," she admitted.

"If you'd like I can give you a little boost." Laras walked up to and looked at her.

Yara looked at the saddle, then at Laras, before turning back to the saddle again. "Yeah that'd be nice."

Laras cupped his hands and squatted down slightly. Yara put her right foot on his hand and the other in the saddle's stirrup.

"Ready?" asked Laras before he saw her nod, "alright, one, two ... " he raised Yara up a tiny bit which finally allowed her to get in the saddle. Laras stood up straight, then he put his hands on his hips and looked at her with pride.

"Hey!" he shouted with an elated tone. "It took you a little while but you got there!"

Yara giggled softly. "I think I remember a little of what I have to do."

"Good, that means you're already further ahead than I was." Laras walked to the horse's head. He bound a lead to the bottom of the headcollar and held onto it loosely. "Just follow my lead."

"It's not like I have much of a choice."

Laras snorted. "You're not wrong." He began to walk slowly, and Yara and Helena followed him. "From what I've seen you're a quick study."

Yara nodded. "I've always been told I am," she said as she inspected her reins. "I thought it was because I was taught a lot really quickly, which meant I had to try and keep up."

"You don't think so anymore?"

"I don't know. Even now that there's less to learn at a time I'm still going at the same pace."

"If anything it's a good thing." Laras turned a little to look at Yara. "The faster you learn, the sooner you'll get to go out there."

After walking a little further they came to a clearing not too far away from the fortress. Laras stepped into the centre and kept Yara and her horse at a relative distance. "Now let's put that talent for learning to the test, shall we?" he said to her. "Let's start with something a little more calm."

***

"You said it was here?" Arran had kneeled down to inspect the ground more closely. They had arrived at a bend in the wide river a short distance away from the city.

"Here's where it stinks the most."

"Mhm, with good reason too." Arran picked something up from the ground and got back on his feet. He held the object with only his index finger and thumb and far out in front of him.

"What's that?"

"Dead flesh, the rotting kind." Arran openly presented it to the guard captain. "It's definitely not fish."

"What is it then?"

"Well I can't be too sure but to me it looks like it came from a dragon." he pinched his nose as he dropped it on the ground. It hit the mud with an audible splat. Once more he was glad he wore gauntlets for these kinds of things. "I think you're right. It's here."

"So what's next, do you just wait ... ?"

"Next I lure it out. If you have any ideas on how I could do that they'd be more than welcome."

The guard scratched his sideburns and looked around. "One of my men reported it attacking fishing dinghies before." He spoke a little absent-mindedly.

"If we got in a rowboat or something that might work." Arran's previously pointless scanning of the area had now turned into a search for a dinghy to push out onto the river. Just on the bank not too far away laid one such boat. The guard ran for it and Arran soon followed.

"You suggest one of us gets in it?" Arran asked as he saw the other man pick up an oar.

"I mean it's not going to row on its own." The guard captain was about to get in when Arran grabbed his arm.

"If anybody is going to do so, it'll be me. I have experience with these kinds of creatures."

"With all due respect sir knight, I'm a guard. Laying down my life for this city is what I do," he said. "You stay on the shore and make—"

"Fine, we're both taking the boat then," Arran interrupted, "you row and I'll watch out for it."

The guard nodded as if to say "fair enough" and the two men worked together to push the boat into the water. Once it was far enough, the guard rowed it away from the shore, which prevented Arran from getting in.

"I'm sorry sir," he shouted to the knight standing on the riverbank, "You'll do far more good not being eaten alive than I will." Arran was in disbelief as he stared down the guardsman rowing away from him and onto the river's current. He followed the boat on foot and kept a close eye on the water's surface. He had to resist the urge to pinch his nose again once he got to the rancid smelling section of the riverbank. The water's surface began to shift and change slowly as if it were being forced upwards. Arran noticed and instantly shouted at the guard, who started to row for dear life, away from the river's centre and directly toward the shore. From below the subtle fringe between the air above and the water below rose a spiked back, followed by a triangular, wide, beaked serpentine head on a short neck. It unleashed a hellish shriek before it attempted to crush the boat. Its waterlogged, heavy body crashed down on the fragile dinghy, and it raised one of its wings out of the water to grab onto the small vessel. The guard had gotten close enough to the riverbank to jump out and run the rest of the way. At the same time Arran stood at the ready with Skycleave in one hand and his heater shield in the other.

He looked at what was emerging from the water through the narrow visor of his helmet. The monster vaulted its way out of the river and onto dry land. It then opened its beaked maw a second time and let out another ear-piercing scream. The beast reeked as badly if not more so than the small bit of shore it stood on. Arran expected it to spew fire at him when it lowered its head and opened its beak, however instead it created a wall of mist around itself, much like what he'd overheard.

Arran could hear the dragon skulk about the thick fog before it took its chance and lunged forward. Fortunately he managed to narrowly dodge the attack and cut into the creature's shoulder. Instead of it bleeding like a normal living being would, a heap of clots and rotting flesh spilled out onto the ground with a chorus of disgusting splattering. Arran had to resist the urge to open his visor and retch at the sight and stench. The decomposing creature's reaction contrasted his, as it didn't seem to notice that it'd just been cut into by a dragonforged weapon. The monster used its large, tattered wings to jump away as it continued to leak more filth.

Arran's thoughts raced. What he'd previously thought to simply be an ordinary dragon turned out to be something completely different, something he wasn't necessarily prepared for. Undead creatures weren't typically something he'd deal with. Normally that remained reserved for actual experts on fighting the unliving. He looked around. He was still surrounded by the heavy banks of fog that the monster had made.

Arran only knew of one definitive way to kill anything that had been brought back from the dead: removing the head and then burning the body. He needed to wait until an opportunity arose where he could decapitate the monster. It came up behind him and attacked with another terrible screech. Though he attempted to dodge he could feel the creature knock into him, pushing him onto the ground. Quickly Arran got to his feet and took a moment to observe what he was fighting. Its appearance became more clear now that he'd gotten a proper look at it. Pieces of its wet scaly skin flaked off with every movement it made and it looked like almost nothing was holding it together. It had been dead for a while, that much was true.

Arran charged forward and cut deep into the animal's neck. Its milky white eye rotated in its socket and stopped to stare at him. Arran stared right back into it, not betraying a single hint of fear on what little of his face the beast could see. He had to turn away as soon as he pulled the sword out and before he'd get covered in an avalanche of bile and filth.

Once again the undead dragon appeared to be preparing to spew a new cloud of mist. Arran scrambled to raise his shield in time in case it wouldn't be what he was expecting. It was fortunate that he did, as the monster instead belched a spray of scalding hot water at him. He raised his shield and the heat of its magic barrier evaporated the already boiling water. It made a gurgling sound as it stopped, and Arran could see it looking down at where the water had spilled from its neck. Then, the focus of its gaze changed back to him. It must've eventually realised that its attack was doing fairly little, as it changed its tactics immediately.

The undead dragon leapt forward and clasped its jaws around the shield just as Arran raised it. The tip of the monster's beak came dangerously close to his visor as its massive teeth closed in on his arm. Arran tried pushing his arm just a little further, just so he could have his barrier activate and bisect the monster's maw. He looked back and forth between the undead monstrosity and his sword. In a risky move he undid the strap on his shield, let go of its handle, and jumped to the side of the creature's head. Here he took Skycleave in both his hands and brought the razor sharp edge down on the dragon's neck. It yelped out of surprise and let go of Arran's shield, flinching and jumping backwards. Arran's black blade dug deep into the monster's neck but didn't go far enough to sever its head entirely. He raised his sword a second time and brought it down once more. The undead creature's head was hanging down limply, only kept together by lingering tendons and decayed strings of muscle. More disgusting drek poured out of the opening as it grew with every slash. The beast kept shrieking with the same consistent tone in spite of this.

Arran struck one final blow and severed the head. Its neck spasmed wildly as its body gave out and the two pieces fell to the ground with separate sickening thuds. Arran's side was covered in the sickly green and red mess that had spilled out of the monster. His heavy breathing was audible even from the inside of his helmet. The knight dared not open his visor for fear of catching more of the disgusting stench that arose from the corpse.

The guard captain had stood a short and safe distance away to watch the fight. His curiosity must've peaked when the dragon's sounds had abruptly halted, and because it looked to be over he made his approach. He nearly walked into the hunter as he had tried finding his way through the now dissipating fog.

"Did— did you—"

"Burn it as soon as you can." Arran brushed past the guard captain, tired and finding an urgent need to return to Ashfallow's Hold. "Destroy the body completely. You can't risk it coming back somehow."

"What was it even?"

"It definitely wasn't alive, I know that much." He was being short with the guardsman, but he had no time for niceties. He needed to go back and warn Lord Darav.

"So what do you propose we do?"

"Like I said," replied Arran, his voice carrying an annoyed tone, "Burn it. I've got to go report this." He neared his horse. Finally he could take off his helmet to catch some fresh air. "I trust your men know how to set a fire?"

"Not for something this big. I'll ask the local pyromancer for help with this ... situation."

"Good luck."

"As to you, Sir Arran."

***

Another day of horseback riding laid ahead of Yara and her substitute mentor. The previous day she'd gotten a little practice with riding at a calm pace and some simple trotting, but other than that they hadn't gotten much done. Most of the day had been spent getting a hang of the basics, such as making sure she didn't fall off. Laras had taken his own horse with them and led Yara and her new equine friend to the same clearing again. This time she only needed a little help getting on Helena's back.

"Are your feet in the stirrups?"

"Yes," sighed Yara. He'd ask her mundane questions much like this one all the time. Even though she knew he meant well it often made the experience of horseback riding quite tedious.

"Good, today I thought we should pick up the pace a little," Laras said in response, "does galloping sound good to—" he stopped himself when he saw someone approaching in the distance. Whoever they were, they were in a hurry. "Or we can go see what that's all about."

"What?"

"Over there," he pointed at the rapidly approaching figure. Yara then caught sight of them as well.

"I think that's the better idea."

Laras ordered his horse to run at full speed and Yara mimicked him with only a little difficulty. Soon they both approached the person that'd been moving so quickly, and upon getting closer they could tell it was Arran. One of his sides was caked in drek that reeked like rotting flesh.

"Arran!" Laras yelled out to his mentor. "What are you doing back so soon?"

Arran's response was to slow down his pace but he didn't say a word.

"Arran?" Yara rode up next to him.

"I have to get to Darav."

"Why?" Yara asked.

"It's important."

"How—'

"Never mind how important it is, it just is." Arran cut Laras off.

The pair followed him up the hill and into the fortress above. Arran looked around before he got down from his horse.

"Have you seen him today?" he asked Laras and Yara. Only the former replied.

"No he hasn't been outside the hall since you left."

Arran didn't really respond to that. He simply ran towards and up the tall stone stairway to access the higher courtyard. Both Yara and Laras followed him. Once atop the steps Arran was panting, but he continued to run towards the large hall regardless. When he burst in through the heavy wooden door Darav's gaze shot up from the documents on the stone table before him and towards Arran, Yara, and Laras. Ashfallow was at the back of the room. Though he lacked eyes, his head also turned to face Arran. It seemed like they had been deep in conversation about something when the knight had suddenly entered.

"You're back soon. Too soon, even," said Darav. He made an attempt to sound calm. "I assume you have a good reason for that?" He spoke through gritted teeth.

"One very good reason."

"Then by all means, share it," Darav said as he put one hand on his hip.

"One word," Arran said. He looked at Ashfallow, who had tilted his head in curiosity, much like how a dog would. He recoiled in disgust at the pungent odour of rotting flesh that Arran had carried with him all the way from Rivertop. "And I think he knows what I mean."

Darav looked at Ashfallow as Arran pointed to him. "Well, spit it out, or are you both going to continue being cryptic?" the lord asked impatiently.

"**He appears to be speaking of ... a titan,**" Ashfallow said that last word with horror. He could tell what Arran meant purely from the stench.

"Mind elaborating?" Darav's annoyance only deepened.

"**Undead dragons,**" Ashfallow continued with that same horrified tone that was now joined by disgust. "**Mere husks of what they once were in life, a worse fate than even I endured.**"

Darav looked back at Arran. "Did you manage to kill it?"

The knight nodded. "They die the same way as any other undead thing. Cut off the head," he said. "I assumed destroying the body would help too."

Darav turned back towards the large stone table. "Then we should prepare all of our members for any encounter with a ... what did you call it? A Titan?" He said as he continued to poorly mask his anger. "Now all of you leave, I need to write to my brother."

Everyone except Darav left the room. Once the door closed they could hear him shout in anger inside, followed by the clattering of metal. Laras walked ahead a little bit while Yara stayed by her mentor's side.

"We're probably going to have to move your training to the road." He grabbed her attention in one fell swoop. "If there's more of these things we'll need as many people as we can get to get rid of them." Arran looked down at her, but she didn't return his gaze, avoiding eye-contact. "Besides, you'll learn more in the field anyway."

"So when do we leave?" she asked hopefully.

"A few days I think," he said, "right after I get this stink out of my armour."

II

Chapter VII: Patrol

Yara sat high on Helena's back. The sword Laras had used previously was now stowed on her saddle. Now that Arran had made him his own, the proverbial torch had been passed down to her. Yara and Arran had been on patrol for nearly three weeks now, though this had only been her second excursion after becoming a knight in training.

Shortly after Arran had returned bearing news of undead dragons she'd gone with him to find and destroy them. She'd used the time spent on horseback to get better at riding, purely so she could keep up with him on every patrol.

Just as her first patrols had started they noticed something strange. The amount of dragons they'd come across had dwindled sharply. Neither Yara nor Arran could really think of a how or why. Arran told her that he would've liked to believe that it was because of them and their order, that they were doing a good job, but realistically he knew that wasn't true. Yara instead theorised they were recuperating, taking somewhat of a break from their warring with mankind. Most patrols didn't lead to anything big. Usually they would stumble upon a drake harassing farmers or cattle herders. Much of what they'd come across hadn't been anything either of them couldn't handle together. They'd run into a dragon only once, and it had turned into her first kill. She'd wanted to keep one of its horns after the fact but lost it shortly after she got it.

Yara looked around. Since her training began she'd started to notice that she had a certain attention to detail that others didn't, which made her excellent at the kind of tracking the Knights of Ash had to do. Right now, however, she couldn't find anything extraordinary. Snow covered pretty much everything and left little for her to pay attention to, leaving her staring at the ground with mild disinterest as she looked for quite literally anything to break up the monotony. Yara looked towards her mentor, who sat hunched forward atop his mount. He wore a hooded, yellow winter cloak to protect himself from the cold, and his helmet hung from the side of his saddle. As Yara had grown more attached to him the distance between them when riding on horseback had shrunk. Yara didn't want to presume, but she hoped this meant he was growing more trustful of her. She rode up closer to her mentor, who was focused on the ground in front of him to help Reed avoid any missteps in the snow.

"Arran?"

He looked up when he heard Yara call his name. There was a curious expression on his face. "Yes, Yara?"

"Can I have the book again?"

"Again?" He asked, "you'll wear it out if you read it any more," He slowed his horse by a pull on the reins before rummaging through his saddlebags, mumbling to himself as he did. He pulled out a thick book with a brown leather cover and handed it to Yara. Carefully she removed one of her gauntlets and opened the book with fingers that trembled from the cold. Yara navigated through the pages like she had done many times before. The detailed illustrations of the dragons and their descriptions were what kept her interested. As she flipped through the tome she came across names she'd started to recognise from the times she'd read the book before. She always ended back up on the same two pages.

Unlike the larger tome at the fortress, this copy had retained its chapter for the Alamirian Ash Wyvern, Ashfallow's species. It was one of the only pairs of pages that had no information on how to kill the dragon they described. Instead that section of the chapter had been replaced with an interview, which consisted of a lengthy conversation between the author and Ashfallow. She read through it again. It painted an interesting picture of Ashallow's motives. His entire life appeared to revolve around surviving, outliving all other dragons simply out of spite. Yara was so invested in the book that she hadn't noticed that Arran called her name.

"We're almost at the next village so don't get too deep into that book again."

She looked up from the manuscript and towards her mentor, who had turned to look at her directly. She hummed and nodded to let him know she understood. Yara closed the book and put it away in her own saddlebags as she focused on following Arran.

The village they entered seemed to be interesting the moment they arrived. One of the barns had been ripped to shreds, while a smaller house nearby showed marks of recently doused flames.

"This seems fresh," Arran said as he climbed out of his saddle to inspect the site. Yara soon followed and quickly set foot on the cold ground. They both looked around to try and find any signs of what happened, though in their haste to investigate they forgot that the village was still inhabited. One of the townsfolk walked up to them and tapped Arran on the shoulder as he inspected the burnt wooden floor.

"Excuse me sir knight, but to what do we owe your visit?" the woman who asked sounded like she was attempting to be polite. Yara realised they must've looked like squatters to any passer-by. Arran turned to the woman. She was somewhat elderly and dressed in a thick coat to prevent herself from freezing

"My apprentice and I are on patrol, hunting for dragons in the area," said Arran, "your little hamlet here was simply of interest to us."

Yara thought it was odd that the woman looked surprised when she answered. "Why's that, sir knight?"

"A barn ripped to shreds and a burnt down house, seems quite obvious. Do you recall any dragon attacks?"

She thought about what he asked and answered with a decisive no. "It must've been a storm, lightning probably struck the house," she continued, changing her tone to be quite short when being polite hadn't worked the way she would've liked.

"Really?" Arran raised an eyebrow. "We're sorry to bother you, then, thank you for your time."

"I don't mean to be rude sir knight, but we really don't need your help here."

"Don't worry, it's likely we won't be here for long regardless," Arran said.

The woman then turned to leave. She seemed satisfied but refused to thank him as she walked back to her house. Once she was out of earshot Arran decided to turn his attention to Yara.

"I think she was lying," He said.

"How come?" asked Yara, curious about where this suspicion had come from.

"The fire that burnt down this lovely little cottage here was aimed. It was directed by something," explained Arran, "and if we take a look at the barn ... " he walked over the crisp, one-day-old snow that coated the ground. It was arranged in such a way that you could see a massive upturn of earth where the barn used to be. "This was a crash." He was focused on the ground to try and find any clues about what had made its emergency landing here. Arran crouched down to get a closer look.

"I'll get the book," said Yara before she walked back to her horse. Arran kept looking, and occasionally Yara saw him disturb the pristine white snow to look under it. After some time searching he stumbled onto a small puddle of frozen reddish-brown liquid.

"That's odd ... " Arran said as he wiped away the snow that covered most of the frozen puddle. Yara could see he'd uncovered something new. Shards of something which almost looked like ice — cold blue, yet clear like glass. "Are there any in there with a breath attack that forms icicles?" he asked without looking up at her.

"I'm sure there are ... what'd you find?" she asked. Arran carefully picked up one of the delicate shards and showed it to his student, who examined it with care.

"I may have seen a sketch of something like this in the book." She hastily searched through the pages. There was one chapter which yielded a plausible result: the Northern Frost-Scale Wyvern, one of the pages she'd skimmed earlier that day. "I think it may be this one," she turned the manuscript to show Arran the pages. It depicted a sketch of a limber, pale white wyvern with scaleless skin. It stood tall on its hind limbs, with its large pair of wings raised up.

"Not too intimidating," said Arran.

"That's how it looks during the day," Yara went on to explain, "at night its skin is covered in a thick layer of impenetrable ice, which only melts in direct sunlight."

"That sounds interesting," said Arran as he scratched his bearded chin, "what makes you think it's that?"

Yara pointed to another part of the page which detailed how it fought. It described the peculiar ability to control the local weather, a power which would apparently grow with age. The next paragraph laid out its breath attack, a blast of frost so cold it could burn skin like fire. Arran mouthed the words as he read them.

"I can see where you're coming from, but to be sure we'd have to melt one of these ... shards ... "

he said in response, "and it doesn't look like it's clearing up anytime soon."

The sky had been inundated by grey clouds even since before they arrived in the village. Both Arran and Yara had assumed that these clouds were perhaps remnants from the snowfall of the day before.

"So what do you propose we do?" Arran asked. Yara, caught off guard by her mentor's question, but immediately started considering her options. They could stay in the village and wait out the weather until it cleared, or they could scout out the area surrounding the hamlet. Perhaps there was something else they could find that could lead them to the creature. She thought of the possibility of a storm hitting or getting kicked out because they overstayed their welcome. Her mind drifted off and Arran gently shook her by the shoulder to pull her out of her deep thoughts and into the real world again.

"Huh?" she murmured.

"Your proposed course of action, Knight Yara?" he hid a smirk when he addressed her with the title.

"We should ... we should scout out the area to see if we can find anything more," she said. Her insecure tone shifted to a decisive one when she became convinced that her choice was correct. Arran nodded in agreement.

"Shall we get going then?" the knight asked as he mounted Reed. Yara agreed, climbed back onto Helena and followed Arran out of the village.

***

Arran pulled on the reins to stop his horse in its tracks and Reed neighed as his head was pulled back. He had been looking down the entire time to search the ground, and spotted another frozen puddle of red merged with mud and molten snow.

"Yara, hold."

She pulled on the reins and waited.

"The same as in the barn ... " Arran muttered to himself as he inspected the frozen puddle. He'd gotten off his horse to look more closely at the object of interest. Around it were more of the strange shards they found in the barn. "It's wounded."

"What is?" Yara asked curiously, though she realised only after Arran answered her that it'd been a stupid question

"Your wyvern. Judging from the size of the pools we find and the ice around them, it appears to be bleeding heavily into its ice shell before it finds its way through small cracks and openings," explained Arran. He'd turned around to face her briefly before he returned to inspecting the ground.

"But how? Its armour should protect it during any and all fights," said Yara.

"Perhaps whatever it was fighting found an opening." Arran turned his head swiftly. He looked from the ground back at where they'd come from. "It might've gone further north."

The dark clouds in the sky had broken. It wasn't snow that had started to fall but rather a downpour of rain. Ice cold rain. And it was right behind them.

***

From the sky fell an immensely powerful, cold downpour that under any other circumstances should've been a blizzard. The rain drenched Yara and Arran's coats, and the freezing temperatures made them shiver.

"This definitely isn't a natural storm!" yelled Yara through the sound of torrential rain, likely afraid that Arran wouldn't hear her. He understood what she said quite adequately however.

"I definitely hadn't thought of that," he grumbled sarcastically. "It's at times like this that I wish I knew how to use magic." He looked ahead and through the torrent. Somewhere in the distance he saw a glimmer of ice reflecting a tiny bit of sunlight that'd managed to break through the clouds. The ice must've been at the opening of an overhang or cave. Finally something to keep them dry. Arran made Reed gallop, while Yara followed him closely and the two of them found refuge under the ridge.

"Why is it raining? It's a northern winter for Saint's sake," Arran said as he removed his drenched cloak. He looked outside to search for the dragon that was hunting them.

" ... the more powerful the dragon, the more control they have over the weather ... " Yara repeated quietly to herself. She was silent for a minute before asking her mentor a question, "power comes with age ... right?"

"I think it does?" replied Arran, unsure of his own answer, "should be living age though, I don't think it could create a storm this powerful if it was a titan," He peered out of the overhang and through the fog and rain. The water that hit the ground froze almost immediately from the surrounding cold.

"If it made this storm then it should be in the clouds," said Yara after she stood up and walked towards the edge of the shelter, "so what should we do?"

"We wait ... " he answered as he looked down at her. The knight turned his attention away and to the sky.

Not too long after they had found themselves a place to hide, a howling roar sounded in the distance. Finally the creature had finally given out and had to land to recuperate. Now that their foe was out of the clouds, they had another problem. It was using its self-created storm as cover. Luckily, that cover wouldn't last for long. It couldn't control the clouds from the ground below.

Under the overhang Arran had managed to recover some dry wood from his saddlebags and used Yara's tinderbox to create a small campfire they could use to warm up. Arran heard another distant roar and sat up straighter.

"It's coming ... " he said aloud as he took up his helmet and put it on. The shield he usually kept under his cloak was now firmly held in his left hand. Yara stood up and took a stance similar to her mentor's. Much like him she was fully armoured, though not as well armed. Her only weapon was the broadsword Arran had handed her.

Amidst the weakening yet still heavy rain a figure had become visible, and as it came closer it was easier to see the dragon in its entirety. Just as described, its skin was completely covered in a thick layer of icy armour, and a beard of icicles hung from its lower jaw. Water dripped down from them as it pushed its short head through the cavern opening, forcing Arran to take a few steps backwards. The creature saw him and uttered a single word.

"Prey ... " it said with a strained voice. Immediately it lunged at Arran, who hastily raised his shield just before its jaws could lock around him and pierce his armour, just about missing the angle where his barrier would activate. The beast turned in an attempt to flank its target.

"Yara don't let it—"

"So ... the prey speaks ... " the dragon took deep and laboured breaths between its words, "not many do ... they just ... scream ... " Its voice, though old and weary, still held an arrogant and snide tone. The dragon attacked Arran again with a delayed jump forward. Its jaws clamped tightly onto Arran's shield and kept pushing forward to try and bring him off-balance.

"Pathetic ... " the wyvern released its grasp to speak before it bit down again.

While the beast was preoccupied with Arran, Yara had been looking for weak spots. She'd taken the dragonforged broadsword from its sheath at the start of the fight and started checking for cracks or spaces in the mass of ice on the creature's back. Fortunately, she found one. The neck had open spaces to allow the dragon to move more easily. It was the perfect spot to jam her blade into. She ran towards it, took hold of one of the spikes on the creature's frozen back, and stuck the sword right between two of the plates. Its tip sunk into the dragon's flesh easily. However, when Yara saw it had barely progressed further than that, she decided to stamp on it with one of her feet as she held onto the spike she had grabbed before.

Now the creature felt the sharp blade pierce its scaleless hide and responded by reeling back as it shrieked in pain. Yara's hands slipped off the creature's armour as it bucked and she fell onto the cold ground. Arran managed to get up, with his shield in his hand. He ran to protect Yara from any attacks the wyvern might throw at her. She scrambled to get up. The fall had bruised her a bit, however she seemed to do just fine otherwise.

"Can you stand?" Arran asked worriedly, his eyes fixed on the dragon. He hadn't seen whether she'd gotten up again.

"I think ... Yeah, I can ... " Yara groaned as she got on her feet. "What do you need me to do?" She figured that there would be time to be in pain later.

"I want you to — " he was interrupted when he blocked an attack with his shield, "take Skycleave and be ready to stab it."

He heard a short clatter and then the sound of steel being dragged over stone as Yara picked up the sword. She held it in a way in which it poked past his shield and through its barrier. The wyvern clawed at Arran with its wing, a blow narrowly blocked by his timely response.

"It is rare for prey to fight back ... " it said calmly before charging at them, its head impacting Arran's shield, "Normally I expect them to ... lay down and accept their fate." The creature yelped and recoiled when Arran went and swung his shield directly at it. It then raised its head again. Both Yara and Arran expected it to spew ice at them, but instead it bit down onto the shield, intending to push Arran onto the ground a second time.

Instead of that however, Yara managed to find an opening to push Skycleave through. The dragonforged sword penetrated the soft inside of the dragon's maw, sending spurts of its deep red blood out from the wound. It recoiled in pain as Yara pushed the blade through the back of its head. Then, as quickly as it closed its mouth, she pulled Arran's sword back out. The wyvern yelped in pain one last time as it stepped backwards before collapsing to the ground, slowly bleeding out through the wound in its maw.

"Inspect it for any injuries we're not responsible for, there's got to be a source for the blood we found," Arran said to his student, who started searching the creature. She ended up finding the source of the blood. Underneath its left wing shoulder was a festering, infected wound. The flesh rotted away slowly as Yara looked at it.

"I think I might've found it," She said with audible disgust, turning away to let Arran see.

"That's a claw mark from another dragon," said Arran as he pointed to three deep gashes at the heart of the wound.

"Which one are you thinking of?" asked Yara.

"Well, considering the ... content of the wound," he pinched his nose as he looked at the decaying mass. He could swear he saw vermin crawl around in it, "I'm going to say it's an undead one ... "

Yara turned to Arran with a dissatisfied frown on her face. "So the first proper sign of a titan and we noticed too late. Great."

Though he didn't agree verbally he certainly felt the same way about their predicament. He quickly looked away from the corpse and walked back to the campfire. To his dismay he discovered their little tussle with the wyvern had kicked dirt and snow into it, killing what little fire they'd managed to cultivate.

"That's worthless now ... " Arran mumbled as he poked at the campfire's remains, "we should wait out the storm. It should die down now that that thing's dead." He looked over at the corpse and saw his student messing with the dragon's head. She looked up at him, her ungloved hand firmly gripping one of its teeth. She didn't turn to look at what she was doing as she pulled it out.

"What are you doing?" asked Arran with an eyebrow raised.

"Taking a memento."

"You really shouldn't do that."

"Why not?"

"It's bad practice," said Arran, "if you do that with every dragon you kill, you'll run out of space."

Yara looked at the tooth she held in her hand, "can I at least keep this one?"

"Go for it, you just have to pick and choose which ones you take."

She nodded and put it away in her saddlebags.

"I should probably cut its head off. If that rot spreads it might turn it into a titan," Arran said. He picked up Skycleave from where Yara had left it and began working on cutting off the dragon's head.

Chapter VIII: Words for a King

It took them just under a week to get home, and when they finally did it was to a surprise Arran wasn't particularly happy about. The king was there. He stood waiting at the entrance next to Darav, his brother. King Valos Ebonblade of Anglavar. There was a name he knew well, too well for his own liking. Valos and Darav had the same hair and almost exactly the same face. The two brothers could easily be mistaken for twins if it hadn't been for the fact that they were separated by five years. Strangely, and for reasons unbeknownst to anyone other than the royal brothers themselves, it was the prince — ironically the younger of the two — who looked the oldest.

Arran and Yara approached calmly, stopping their horses just shy of where the king and his brother stood. Arran made a slight bow to Valos from atop his horse.

"My liege," he said to the king in a deadpan manner. Yara didn't even look at Valos. Both dismounted their horses and Yara looked on in confusion when Arran presented himself properly by bowing before the king a second time.

"I see that they forgot to teach her etiquette during her upbringing," Valos said.

"Forgive her, your highness," Arran replied, "she has ... difficulties interacting with people she doesn't know." He diverted his attention to Yara, who must've only just realised who she stood opposite to. She made a slight, awkward bow.

"Now, as you both were away you cannot possibly know the nature of my visit." Valos said now that his need for proper etiquette had been satisfied.

"That is correct," Arran interrupted him unintentionally. Recognising his mistake he immediately shut his mouth, opting instead to turn around and begin unpacking his saddlebags. "And I would not dare presume what that nature would be." He used the privacy that turning away gave him to roll his eyes.

"As you might remember, the celebration of the Ebonblade victory is upon us again, in less than a week's time."

"It's a little hard to forget, your highness."

"I would like you and your two students to accompany me and represent your order," Valos continued after he'd let Arran answer him.

"Well, we are kind of in the mi—"

"I'm sure it can wait. Now, please, pack anything you might need, for we will be departing immediately." the king interrupted. He turned to walk away but his brother didn't follow him, instead he stayed with Arran, who gave him a tired and annoyed look.

"Did you *have* to tell him I was here?" asked Arran, "I distinctly remember us departing on the worst of terms."

"I couldn't exactly refuse"

"You know what I think of him, and he knows it too!"

"He's the king, Arran, do you know what might happen if I tell him no?" said Darav with a resigned chuckle. "He might declare war on me."

Arran sighed and walked away with Yara in tow to look for Laras. Arran wasn't going to let his former apprentice get out of it if he couldn't.

"Laras? Laras! You're coming with us," he shouted to get his attention. The young knight turned around, eager to hear what Arran had to say.

"What? What did I do this time?"

Arran shook his head.

"Nothing wrong, I hope," he said. "Definitely not anything I know of. You've been assigned to the same mission as us."

"What mission?" Laras' excitement was visible, and it only grew when he heard those words.

"Royal festivities."

And just like that his excited grin turned to a frown. They were all going to have to suffer together.

***

Barely even a day's rest and they were back out into the world again. Neither Arran, Yara, nor Laras were looking forward to this occasion. Being dragged around essentially as glorified display pieces by king Valos wasn't what any of them would consider to be a good time. Naturally, the king was with them, yet again dressed in unassuming garb.

Laras sat up straight on his saddle as he admired his new sword. Yara looked at it from the back of her own horse.

"What'd you call it?" She asked as she studied its wavy edge.

"The sword?" Laras looked up from it and at her.

"I mean … is there anything else you've named recently?"

"Well, uh, no."

"So tell me, what'd you call your sword?" Yara repeated her question.

"Drakeblight," Laras answered as he held it up to Yara a bit more.

"Drakeblight?"

"Drakes are the things I keep running into, it felt appropriate."

"Have you actually killed any?" Yara asked. She had to hide the grin that'd started to grow on her face.

"Of course I have, why?"

"Oh, well I just … you know, haven't seen you actually kill anything."

Laras frowned. "That's not— I'll show you sometime."

Yara wanted to say she'd take him up on that, but instead she decided that she didn't want to change the topic. "What's it like, having your own?"

"It's great. Feels much lighter than the broadsword you're saddled with," he replied.

"Can I try it?"

"It won't be as light for you. I don't know what Arran did, but it made my sword basically impossible to use for anyone other than me."

"I wanna hold it anyway," Yara said. She made sure she was riding directly next to him before he extended the hilt down to her. Carefully she took hold of it and compared it to what she remembered both the broadsword and Skycleave to be like. Skycleave had been the lighter of the three, but Drakeblight made her wonder how she could even hold it up without Laras' help. He took it back just as carefully as he'd handed it to her.

"You'll get your own soon enough," he smiled at her, "just don't nag Arran about it, I would've had it a little before we picked you up if I hadn't."

"It took you about nine years, right?" Yara asked. Laras nodded.

"It did, but again, I wouldn't stop bothering him about it. Best to not bring it up too much."

Yara snickered, "I'll try not to."

***

Arran rode next to king Valos, but rather than pay attention to the monarch he was looking back at his apprentices. He'd tried to eavesdrop on their conversation and caught something about Laras' new sword. Arran's gaze shifted to his own weapon, which was stowed on his saddle. His mind started to wander until the king's words shook him out of it.

"How do you get used to it?" Valos asked a bit abruptly.

"Get used to what?" Arran replied absent-mindedly.

"Dragon hunting, I mean. How do you get used to killing things larger than life?" the King repeated himself, "you went from finding their continued existence preposterous to slaying them for a living. I mean, I'm sure that for the common people it can't have been an easy adjustment either, but you *do* directly involve yourself with these creatures now."

Arran hadn't really thought about that before, and he found himself stammering as he thought of what to answer with. "Pardon the pun, but killing them really sort of 'grounds' the idea of a dragon. Really, at this point it's a lot like any other job."

"Well, I guess so. I wouldn't know, would I now?" Valos shrugged, as if his interest had faded the moment Arran had answered him. It appeared he was far more interested in talking about himself. "I remember my last dragon hunt, the only one of course. No doubt it was the first of many for you, though. Imagine where we'd be if we'd never gone on that hunt. We'd never have to deal with that gold-scaled ingrate." he pointed over his shoulder as if to gesture at Ashfallow's hold, and sighed. "I almost miss it. Since then it's just been politics and courts."

"Sounds thrilling," replied Arran in a cynical tone. "Spare me the details on how you got used to it."

"Truth is, I didn't," said Valos, "it's easy enough, really, but the constant political malarkey and endless amounts of social gatherings are really not for me in all honesty."

"Doesn't surprise me, you weren't that type fifteen years ago either," said Arran as he looked ahead, "you always preferred brute-forcing everything."

"You're right. It was only after Delvor was gone that I had to get into the actual politics. Dividing up his former lands proved to be a nightmare," said Valos, "I'm a conqueror. Give me strategy, give me warfare, anything but drinking wine with a Lord from Yilgra to discuss trade routes," he stopped for a second and sighed again, "this, now this is life — one like yours, on the road, fighting for people." He cocked his head and looked at Arran.

"I figured you'd think something like that," replied the knight.

"You disagree? Would you rather sit inside all day prattling on about political issues?"

"Is that not what we're doing right now?"

"Well no, we're outside. But the sentiment remains, you'd rather do anything other than this, no?"

"I would, but I'm sure you remember that choice was taken from me. I have to live with the consequences now." Arran said, his tone dripping with spite as he glared at Valos. He'd wanted to specify that the consequences were for the royal's actions, but figured that he'd already understood as much. The king looked away, willfully ignorant of Arran's intent.

"Well, I suppose that war took something from all of us," he said. "However, I'm glad we both lived to see a world after it."

"I'm not sure I always agree."

"Really? Even now? Judging by the girl, it seems to me that you decided to follow my advice after all." The King pointed at Yara and Laras with his thumb.

"What advice?"

"To get over it and have another child."

Arran's eyes widened as he heard those words leave Valos' mouth. He looked at the king, trying to hide just how angry that phrase had made him.

"I have to assume that's what this is. Even if it isn't, you have to admit you're proud of them," The king continued.

"Well, yes, but—"

"Then quit your whinging and bask in that achievement instead," said Valos, intentionally domineering, "if you're not going to be proud of your service or your blood, at least be proud of the impact you've had on the world," he failed to reach Arran when he attempted to pat him on the shoulder, "I am, if you'd like to hear a personal example." He changed topics just as easily as he'd done countless times before. "My daughter."

"Your daughter, huh?" Arran started to lose interest in the conversation even more rapidly than he had before.

"Meya's proven to be more than a worthy successor. She's a real prodigy in warfare," he said, beaming with pride, "not even I caught the hang of leading armies as quickly as she has."

"You can't be serious, you're teaching her to fight your wars for you?"

Valos shook his head and laughed. "No, no of course not," he said, "I'm teaching her how to fight my wars *with* me. After all, my brother can no longer be my Drakeheart, and I have no eldest son to take his place," he said, "my father did it with me. I've chosen to continue what my grandfather started with my only daughter instead."

Arran couldn't believe what he was hearing, and for once his glare didn't go unnoticed.

"Speak your mind, I can't do anything against you without my brother throwing a fit, and he has the human-eating dragon on his side."

"Are you sure you want to push your *only child* into a life like that?"

"I fail to see how it's any different from taking an orphan from her home and raising her to fight fire-breathing serpents," Valos' voice started to sound mildly agitated as he attempted to point out the hypocrisy he perceived in Arran.

"The difference here is that I let her make that decision herself, as opposed to it being some family tradition."

"Are you seriously about to tell me that you wouldn't have taught your own child to fight dragons?"

"I ... my apologies, your highness, I didn't intend to cause an argument," Arran started to backpedal as he realised that at this point, arguing would hurt him more than it would help.

"Apology accepted," the king replied smugly, leaving Arran to mope in silence.

***

Castle Hillguard stood just about a day's distance away from Ashfallow's hold. Arran had always found the building to be quite imposing, even though when he'd visited it, it'd been nothing but a ruin. He was surprised to see it restored at first, but when he thought about it his surprise dwindled. It made sense for Valos to want it restored. After all, what kind of a king would he be if his palace was a ruin. The king had transformed its towers, which had previously been either filled with holes or just completely gone, into a pristine work of modern architecture. The large courtyard they entered, once covered in vines, moss, and all manner of overgrown plants, now looked to be the most well-groomed garden on the island.

Arran looked to the large doors straight ahead of the gate. There he saw a woman he wasn't particularly fond of — Alynn Ebonblade, Valos' queen. She looked back at the group that'd just arrived, but appeared focused on her husband.

"Splendid, simply wonderful. I'm glad you've arrived." She embraced him once he got down from his horse. "You have to see the ballroom. Our servants have worked hard to make it perfect for tonight," she added after turning her attention to their three guests.

She looked closely at Yara, Arran, and Laras, who were tracking mud and dirt over the recently polished tile floor.

"Apologies for how brash this may sound, but your attire simply won't do. Don't you have anything more appropriate?" she asked with a thinly veiled tone of disgust.

"My queen, I can't recall the last time I've been to an event like this, let alone participated in the festivities," said Arran.

"Oh it's hardly public," the queen said, "however you and your students will be pleased to know that we've prepared for your travesty of a wardrobe." She addressed Yara directly. "I would've expected a girl like yourself to enjoy parties such as these. You do at least know how to dance, don't you?"

Yara nodded, but that appeared to not be enough for queen Alynn.

"With your words, please. Do you know how to dance?"

"Yes, your grace," she replied quietly, "but—"

"See, she will do absolutely fine," the queen interrupted. She turned up her nose at them. "Go upstairs and change out of those rags, please, you're dragging muck all over my freshly polished floors."

Yara and Laras turned around to the wide staircase behind them and began to climb it. Arran wanted to follow them but was stopped by Queen Alynn. She snapped her fingers to get his attention before he could go any further.

"Is that *really* your new apprentice?" she said with a fake offended tone once Yara was out of earshot.

"Yes, your grace," he replied, confused as to why it would even concern her.

"Don't you think she looks a little unfit for training?"

"With all due respect, your grace, it was her decision," he wanted to say more, particularly in reference to her own daughter, however he opted not to. Offending the royalty would probably ruin the night before it even started.

"And you know this how, exactly?"

"I asked her when we met," Arran replied with a shrug. Whatever he had left to say would be more rude than anything said previously, and so instead he opted to walk away, leaving the gobsmacked queen behind him.

***

Yara and Laras returned to the ballroom after they'd changed out of their armour and into more comfortable clothing. It still wasn't the ballroom outfits they'd been provided with, but at least now it was less cumbersome to walk around. The issue of their boots dragging mud around was something they'd solved by simply stamping it out on the floors of their rooms and throwing it out of the window.

The large, tiled ballroom floor was completely immaculate. It was so clean, in fact, that Yara could almost see her own reflection in it when she looked down.

"Can you imagine the amount of people this can hold?" Laras asked as he feasted his eyes upon the massive room. It had been decorated in a fancy Yilgran style. Banners with the Ebonblade crest, a blackened blade and a bow with a crown above the sword's pommel hung from the walls, and intricate chandeliers were suspended from the ceiling.

"A lot, I think."

Laras laughed, "thanks for pointing out the obvious." The source of his nervosity was that he,

Arran, and Yara had to represent their entire order to nobles from all over the islands. The others might do fine, As far as he knew Yara would be accustomed to fancy gatherings, and Arran had more than enough experience to know what he needed to do. Laras however would be described as "jumped-up" by anyone above his station. He'd risen above where he'd started in life and had no idea of what he was supposed to do. As he thought of what could go wrong a single obvious thought popped into his head. "I don't even know how to dance," he stated as he continued to observe the large and open room.

"I think most of it will just be standing around and talking," Yara shrugged, "but if you want I can try to help you figure it out?"

Laras looked at her.

"I've lived in a Lord's castle most of my life, even as his ward I had to learn how to dance," she said with a smirk on her face and a snicker in her voice that she definitely tried to hide, "even if I barely ever enjoyed practising,"

"Are you sure? You don't have to, really."

She nodded to reassure him, "I've never liked big crowds or gatherings, but I can at least try to have a little fun," replied Yara as she intentionally avoided looking him in the eyes, though occasionally she'd make contact to try and read him. She took the lead as she instructed him, and she gave him criticism on his footwork as they moved.

***

Arran was watching Yara and Laras from one of the balconies overlooking the ballroom. The exterior wasn't the only thing which had changed. During his last visit the skull of Angalir's previously last known dragon had decorated the ballroom, but it was gone now. He was snapped out of his thoughts about where it could've gone when the queen joined him.

"It's sweet," said Alynn as she walked up next to him. The knight had to resist telling her to leave him alone. He didn't want to draw her ire given how he had last left things with her.

"Your grace," he greeted her with a slight bow of his head.

"It's commendable that she's so willing to help him in spite of his … lowly beginnings. I assume the comradery is of high importance for your order?"

Arran had to stop himself from rolling his eyes and throwing a biting remark back at her, but his mood changed and he had to hold back a smile. Laras had nearly fallen over and taken Yara with him to the floor. Arran watched as she scolded her companion before breaking into laughter.

"I had one question actually," the queen said, "since I am not well-versed in the ins-and-out of your order — does your title actually mean anything?"

"Excuse me?"

"Oh, pardon me. I meant your title as a knight," she clarified, "you see, I've been referring to you as a knight. but I don't recall my husband ever granting you or your order formal knighthoods."

"Most of our members have symbolic titles. We're not really knights," explained Arran, "as for myself, I was knighted after the battle of Silvergrass Hill, at the end of the war."

"Ah, so tonight is a personal anniversary of yours?"

"Of sorts, yes," he answered quietly, intentionally neglecting to mention the fact that he'd lost that knighthood nearly immediately.

"Speaking of anniversaries, I've had our tailors prepare the three of you with custom attire for the event."

"Did you now?"

"Your order's crest is on it, though I never understood why my brother-in-law picked such an ugly one," she said with distaste commanding her voice. "A wyvern, bleh, we have enough of those already," she stopped herself and laughed, "then again, it's not like Darav has any sense of taste."

"Were you made aware ahead of time of who was coming?" asked Arran, "I'm surprised you have those ready for us."

"A carrier pigeon was sent ahead and I gave the order immediately," she replied, "making any sort of clothing goes rather quickly when you have an army of seamstresses at your disposal."

There was a pause in the conversation before it occurred to Arran that there was something he might want to know.

"Will Lord Draehal be here?"

The awfully specific question threw the Queen off by quite a margin. "But of course, why do you ask?" She answered, "His house and family played a major part in making this celebration possible every year."

"I'm aware, I thought it best to make sure he was invited," said Arran, "he and I weren't on the best terms, following the cause for tonight's celebration, and it'd make for an awkward reunion."

"Well I don't think you'll have to worry about bad terms with him. After all, he's begun to dement quite heavily," she said. "I doubt he'll remember anyone he's spoken to in the last five minutes, let alone however much time you've spent refusing to talk to him."

Arran threw a piercing glare at the Queen as she snickered. She quickly caught onto his malignant stare.

"I'm sorry, I simply can't help but laugh. It really is quite sad, of course." She adjusted her expression to be perhaps a little more solemn.

"By all means," the knight said through gritted teeth as he turned away, "if you'd excuse me, I should take my leave and change for the evening."

"Quite so," answered Alynn. Arran could feel her gaze burn on his back as he left her to go and change.

Chapter IX:
Too Many People

Evening had come quickly. The candles that lit the halls of castle Hillguard gave off a warm, orange glow, contrasting its rather cold daytime appearance. Yara walked down the steps together with Laras. He was dressed in one of the tunics he'd been given and Yara had exchanged her own clothes for the ash grey dress. Stitched onto both their formal clothing was an elegant pattern in golden thread resembling a wyvern.

Trying the dress on had been a fight in and of itself. The waist had been a little too tight for her and only after a good deal of fiddling did it finally fit. Arran was in a similar tunic to Laras, though the golden wyvern had been given more detail to distinguish the two. The wyvern had been given the sword normally seen on the order's crest to hold in its claws. Arran had shaved his face for the occasion, his rugged grey beard giving way to a striking, straight jawline. By the time Yara and Laras got downstairs, Arran had already immersed himself in the crowd, where neither of them could easily find him. Instead, both went on their own tour of the ballroom.

***

Even though she'd preferred to have stuck with Arran, Queen Alynn had practically dragged Yara with her before she could even find him. She'd been so adamant in fact that it'd made Yara feel perhaps a little uncomfortable. She took every opportunity she had to look for an out, but so far none had presented itself yet. She'd gotten stuck waiting at the edge of a group of nobles talking to her royal highness and thought that maybe this was her chance. Unfortunately for her, the queen noticed.

"Oh, right of course. I've forgotten to introduce you all to one of our esteemed guests," Alynn said. "Where did she go … " She clicked her fingers when she found her. "Girl, would you please come over here?"

Yara turned and made an attempt at a curtsy, or at least what little she could remember of one.

"Tell our guests your name, girl," Alynn said. Yara wondered if she was being polite, or if she had just forgotten.

"My name is Yara," she said, "it's an honour to meet you, my lords, my ladies." She tried her hardest to be courteous.

"Looking at her now you'd almost forget that she and her companions spend all day in the muck," one of the Lords said.

"Hush, Clement, I'm certain that's hardly her choice," said a lady, likely the man's wife judging by how she spoke, "I can't imagine how much of a relief being here must be for you," she turned her eyes to Yara with feigned sympathy.

"Oh no, actually. Her mentor *assured* me that it was her own decision." The queen butted in.

Yara felt the need to defend Arran at that. "I'm quite comfortable out there," she said, quickly adding a correction, "my lady."

"Really?" the lady's eyes went wide. Another noblewoman decided to interject.

"But how do you stand it?"

"Well I—"

"Out there in the cold, in the rain? Gah, you'd have to be an animal to not retch at the thought."

"Tell me, girl," another Lord spoke with a deep, stern tone. "Don't you think it's somewhat odd to teach a girl any of the myriad of things I'm sure they must be stamping into you?" he asked, "I could understand an absolute tower of a woman, but you? Are you really suited to it?"

"I like learning the things my mentor, Arran, teaches me," Yara answered, "I don't think being suited to it matters."

He genuinely looked appalled at what she said. "Are you certain?" he asked. "There's plenty of other things for a girl like you to be doing."

Yara looked down. She could almost feel his gaze burn on her skin. "I can't think of anything else I'd rather be doing."

"Well, uh-," he stammered.

"Not only is it disgusting, but I imagine it's highly dangerous. You're all skin and bones, likely to shatter like glass if you tripped," another noble said. Yara looked down again. These questions were starting to get on her nerves. She felt irritated, but had no clear way of expressing that without possibly injuring any of them. She raised her right arm and flexed it to show them that she'd already put on muscle underneath how skinny she looked. The queen seemed equally appalled by the direction of the conversation. She made her way through the small group and towards her guest.

"That's quite enough out of you," she said to the nobles standing around Yara. "Perhaps we should find you some other people to talk to."

And so they went, hopping between different groups, each with ultimately the same questions. Finally Yara found her opportunity to sneak off and disappear. She wanted to be anywhere else. There was too much noise. Too many people.

***

Arran took comfort in the fact that he was allowed to carry his sword with him, though the only occasion where he'd need it would be to show it to his fellow guests. He rested his hand on the hilt whenever he could to give himself a sense of security.

He used his time in the spotlight to ask questions pertaining to titan sightings. Reluctantly he stayed near King Valos, by the king's royal request of course. The King wanted to keep an eye on his personal guest.

Different Lords and ladies came to speak with both Arran and Valos, either to make small talk that none of them really cared for, to catch up on business, or to simply meet the King for the first time in forever. When they came to speak with Arran he mostly received questions or even uncivil remarks about the Knights of Ash. At this point in his career he'd come to expect it from anyone with higher status. To many of those who'd never encountered a dragon before the order was deemed as a waste of time and crown resources.

Unfortunately the people he asked about titans appeared about as knowledgeable on the subject as they were on daily life outside their walls. Nothing of note was gleaned from these conversations, and after a barrage of constant rude queries and comments Arran noticed an elderly gentleman carefully making his way through the crowd, with assistance from a younger woman. Arran knew who he was looking at: Lord Illian Draehal. He was slightly hunched forwards, his silvery hair combed back, and he had a kind but ultimately confused, perhaps even disoriented look on his face. Arran looked away to make sure that Lord Draehal wouldn't recognise him and started to look for king Valos. Once he'd found the king in the middle of a rather large crowd Arran informed him that he was leaving to get some air. The king looked as if he was going to stammer a command at him, but closed his mouth before any words left it. Valos nodded to his guest, who left the ballroom near immediately.

***

Laras wouldn't see the end of the night before having his own avalanche of questions thrown his way. There was only one thing these nobles found interesting about him, namely the fact that he used to be a farmer. They didn't really seem to care about anything other than the things he got up to before becoming a Knight of Ash. He was cornered as a group did everything short of interrogating him.
"What kind of farm did you live on?" A young noblewoman asked.

"I don't see— "

"Were there animals there?" She interrupted him as she stepped closer to him.

"Get back, young lady," another noblewoman said. "You wouldn't want his filth to rub off on you, would you?"

"Hey, that's not fair," Laras said.

"Well you are a farmer's son, are you not?" that same noblewoman said. "Frankly I find it surprising that you think a reminder of your station to be offensive."

"What kind of animals did you work with, exactly?" A nobleman with his nose stuck up in the air asked him. "If you worked with those, of course."

"My father farmed horses."

"At the very least he dealt with noble animals."

"Wouldn't you rather know about what I currently do?" Laras asked. "That's why I'm here, after all."

"Oh you're one of those dragon hunters right?" the younger noblewoman from before asked. "How did you go from farm boy to dragon hunter?"

Laras opened his mouth. He wanted to explain why, but realised before he could say anything that it was just a thinly veiled excuse to get him to talk about his life prior to the Knights of Ash again. Instead he excused himself and took his leave. He was going to look for someone, anyone more invested in his present than his past.

***

Yara sat on her own at the edge of the bustling dancefloor, with her knees to her chest and her arms wrapped around them. Her loose hair hung in front of her face. She'd never had trouble with small crowds, but she hadn't anticipated how difficult it would be for her to be in a place with so many people. Yara looked up when someone approached her. It was Laras. He appeared to be making an effort to stay calm for her sake.

"Are you doing okay?" he asked in a genuinely concerned tone.

"No ... " she replied softly. "I knew there'd be people, but I thought I'd be fine. As you can see, I'm not."

"Was it all the questions?"

Yara nodded. "They kept asking why a girl would want to do what we do, and they wouldn't listen when I answered them."

"Hmm, well," said Laras as he sat down next to her. He rested his elbows on his knees and looked at his friend, "I know that the queen would be livid if she saw you like this."

"So..?"

"So ... how about we get out of here?" he suggested as he gestured at the mass of people occupying the hall. "I'm willing to bet you'd enjoy not being around all this for a little bit."

Yara got up slowly. His idea didn't sound bad at all. "I think so too," she said. Laras stood up and waited for her to follow him before leaving the ballroom together.

Being removed from the crowd did calm Yara down by quite a margin, and looking around the building to admire the architecture turned out to be a helpful distraction. It was like all the stress left her when she could obsess over every tiny detail.

They could hear the sound of their own footsteps more clearly the further away they moved from the ballroom. Another sound similar to that of their own shoes on the tiled floor approached from a distance. Both Yara and Laras wanted to hide from whoever was coming their way, however decided against scurrying off when the person making the sound came into view. Arran had taken his own time away from the crowd in the same place as them. He almost looked surprised when he came across his students.

"What are you doing here?" he asked when he saw them, "you should be in the ballroom enjoying yourselves."

Yara looked down to avoid eye contact with him and Laras scratched his arm nervously.

"Well, I was doing fine," Laras said, "but Yara wasn't."

Arran turned to Yara and his expression changed from concern to sympathy. He squatted to get down on her level but she continued to avoid looking him in the eyes.

"I hadn't realised crowds like that might've been an issue," he said soothingly, "I'd assumed you would be fine."

Yara scratched her arm, "I wasn't sure myself. I thought I could handle it," she appreciated the thought regardless.

"I wasn't looking forward to going either, but it would've done me good if I'd known I wouldn't've refused for just me," Arran scoffed. "you're feeling better now, right?" he asked, wanting to make sure that she was alright before he went back. Yara nodded quietly and Arran got back up, walked past them, and both Yara and Laras began to follow him.

"Oh, you don't have to come with me, explore as much as you want." He then looked directly at Yara. "I'll make sure the queen won't be looking for you."

The pair of students looked at each other before either replied.

"We won't be gone for long," said Laras. Both him and Yara then turned and ran as fast as they could in what they were wearing. There was a wide grin on Arran's face as he watched them bolt away.

***

The rest of the celebration passed by quickly as the evening progressed. Yara and Laras did eventually return to the ballroom, though in order to avoid getting overwhelmed again Yara opted to stay near Arran. This seemed to help at least a little bit. A staged fight that was more like a play was put on to entertain the guests. The fight made Arran react incredibly fanatically, particularly about the mistakes both participants were making.

To close out the festivities a large dinner was orchestrated, which fortunately went off without much of a hitch. Yara and Laras gladly participated in that part of the evening, to the dismay of Queen Alynn. She had to watch Yara eat like she'd never even held silverware in her hands before and she couldn't do anything about it. As time passed the mass of people dwindled in numbers until only a few remained. Arran and his two students had returned to the King and Queen's side near the end.

"I trust your evening was a success?" asked Queen Alynn, "managed to curry any favour with the nobles?" her eyes switched between her three guests. In her hand she held a glass of wine by its bowl. At the same time Arran held his own glass by the stem, showing perhaps more sophistication than he'd usually let on. He looked at it as he continuously swirled the ruby wine inside.

"You could say so, though these things are still not my 'forté' as our southern neighbours say," he sniffed his wine first before taking a small sip. The Queen looked at him and quickly corrected how she held her glass, as though she'd only just remembered.

"And you?" she pointed at Laras with her pinky finger. "How about yours?"

"Mine, your grace?" he asked in response, "uneventful, really. Yara and myself spent most of the evening away from the crowd, admiring the building and such."

"Really? 'admiring the building'," she scoffed loudly, "what's there to admire about a collapsing pile of bricks."

Valos sat up slightly in his chair, as though he wanted to rebut what she'd just said.

"I mean no disrespect, your Highness, but I've never been in a castle like this before," Laras replied.

Queen Alynn shook her head before she took one quick glance at Yara, who sat with her shoulders slumped as she looked down and quietly tapped her fingers together. She looked exhausted. The Queen didn't say a word to her, which did not go unnoticed by either Arran nor Laras, though it appeared that Yara herself was a little too disconnected and tired to notice. Laras pulled at his collar.

"This is getting a little tight." he looked at Arran, who knew he was implying that he wanted to leave. "I think I'm going to get changed." He stood up and tapped Yara on the shoulder, and she looked up at him. "You want to come with me?" he asked.

Yara didn't say a word but instead answered with a nod.

Arran was now left alone with the two nobles, a situation he knew wouldn't end well. He put down his glass and scratched his shaved chin. He missed the comforting, familiar feeling of his facial hair.

"You know—" the queen started, but Arran cut her off.

"I understand that you believe she's strange, that she doesn't follow etiquette and such," He said a bit snappily, and King Valos, who had been dozing off in his chair, noticed and immediately sat up again. It almost looked like he was going to stand up to Arran, but instead he stayed where he was. Valos wasn't the one on the chopping block, and Arran knew he only cared about himself.

"She's simply not like you. In fact, most people aren't. You ought to learn that before you put up that facade of yours." Arran gestured to her glass. She looked to her husband, who'd slid back in his comfortable chair like what his guest had said didn't matter.

Arran stood up and walked out the room, right after his students. He stomped through the hallways and towards their assigned rooms, where he found Laras in his own chamber, removing the tunic with difficulty. Yara was in the next room over, simply sitting on her bed focused on her hands as she fidgeted with the skirt of her dress. Arran sat down next to her and apprehensively put a hand on her head. When she didn't shake it off he leaned sideways towards her.

"Feeling a little better now?" he asked at a near-whispering volume.

"Think so," she spoke with a quiet tone as well, using as little words as she could. Arran moved his hand from her head to her shoulder.

"Hey, I had an idea."

Yara looked Arran in the eyes. Knowing how hard this was for her, especially while exhausted, he chose to make full use of her attention. "We could leave tonight. Get away from this stupid place, sound good?" he gave her a gentle smile and Yara nodded to agree with him. "Right then, I'll go tell Laras, you go and get changed now, okay?"

Yara nodded again to answer him. Arran stood up to go and tell Laras. Soon they'd ride out again, back to where they came from.

Chapter X:
The Cruel Monarch

The blunted tip of a steel sword was thrust hard into the makeshift shield Arran held up. The wood creaked loudly when the tip of Yara's weapon collided with it. Arran could feel the recoil of her attack. In the scant few months she'd had to train she'd already improved quite a lot. His pupil had quickly learned how to deliver powerful blows and her progress was showing.

"Come on, again! You're not going to get better if you can't keep that up!" he taunted. His verbal jab resulted in the sword being thrust into the shield yet again, with more force behind it than before. She took a step back after attacking to catch her breath.

"I'm going to break through that thing if we keep at it like this," she said, refusing to hide her frustration.

"Exactly! Just what you should be doing."

"But that's not the point of a sword, is it?"

Again it dug into the centre of the shield. Arran had a wide grin on his face which Yara couldn't see.

"You're right, but you won't be fighting against anything with a shield will you? keep at it!" He said. Encouragement had proven to be the most efficient way to motivate her. "The things you'll be faced with are going to be tougher than what I'm using now," said Arran, "they'll have razor sharp claws, fire breath, a powerful bite, and a tail to hit you with. Unfortunately for us those aren't things you can easily parry if at all," He stopped to inspect the damage Yara had done. There, at around the middle of the shield, was a massive dent she'd caused, "look at that, and that's with a blunt sword."

Yara gave him a nervous little smile and focused her gaze on the shield. Arran then continued to lecture her.

"All you can really do about that is try and cut through it, which we fortunately have the tools for," said Arran, scratching the thin, itchy start of his new beard.

"Isn't there more for me to practise though?" Yara asked.

"Outside of what we're doing now? A few minor things," Arran replied. "Why do you ask?"

"It's getting a bit repetitive. I know repetition is useful and all, but it's getting a bit … boring, I think."

"If you want I can try and spar with you?"

"There's not anything else involved in fighting dragons you can show me?"

"Nothing you wouldn't get bored of."

"Then I'll try sparring, sure."

"Get us some training swords and we can begin."

Yara turned around, ran towards the weapon rack and came back with a second blunt blade. Arran thanked her and continued to direct her further, "we've done this before, remember?"

Yara nodded.

"And you also recall what we do every time we train like this?" Arran wanted to make sure she did. Inadvertently harming her was the last thing he wanted.

"I think so?" she answered, "don't rush into things, right?"

Arran nodded, "you did remember, good, assume a ready stance," he said, "and try not to hit me on the fingers again."

They started slow. Arran held his blade in a defensive position and Yara swung her sword at his leg, which he easily deflected.

"This is a consistent issue I've noticed," he said, "your movements are very telegraphed, obvious even. Try to distract me first. That way you'll be more sure to get a hit in."

"I think you mentioned something like that before," there was a hint of something else in her voice, something a little more sly. So far Yara hadn't been the best at hiding anything subtle in her words but this had slipped past Arran. She swung the blade to his left side and Arran blocked it a second time. Another swing, blocked, followed by another, and another. Arran noticed that his pupil was getting into a sort of rhythm. Her gaze was focused, though he couldn't tell exactly what on. When he parried another leftward swing he stepped back and chose to say something, "if you end up in a fight somehow I don't imagine they'll just be defending like I am," he got ready for another strike, "you need to try and be less predi—"

At that very moment she swung again. At first it looked like an easy block, but then Yara's sword shot to the right like a snake's tail mid-swipe and flew in towards his waist. In a show of immense self-control she stopped herself as she was about to hit him.

"I wasn't done talking," he chuckled in disbelief, "though that *was* impressive."

"Thanks," Yara replied half-heartedly. She shuffled awkwardly with her feet as if she felt uncomfortable with taking compliments, "I tried to think quickly, I think."

"I appreciate knowing that you do listen to me, even if it looks like you're dozing off half the time."

"I don't get enough sleep," she said sarcastically as she held back a yawn, "I have to find *some* time for it."

"Keep at it like you are now and I'll teach you how to sleep on horseback," said Arran as he laughed to himself. "Actually, hold me to that, you'll find that useful."

Yara resumed her battle ready pose. Now it was her turn to block Arran's attacks. Arran swung to her left. Parried. To her right. Deflected. His next strike nearly got her. The knight put both hands on the hilt of his weapon, and tricked her by trying to swing to his left, but he then turned his strike downwards diagonally, not too dissimilar from what she'd done with him. She quickly raised her sword and grabbed onto its blade with her free hand. The blunt sword pressed hard into the leather of her glove.

"That's a good reaction time, good use of your hand too," said Arran, grinning with a hint of pride. He released the pressure he put on her and lowered his sword when he heard Aliss' voice shout his name. Arran looked around to find her, spying her standing not too far away and waving him over.

"Have you done your physical exercises today?" he asked, not looking at Yara as he did.

"I think so."

Arran then changed the focus of his gaze, "have you done them twice?"

Yara shook her head. "No, wh—"

"Do them a second time. Aliss wants to speak with me," he said, pointing at her over his shoulder. Yara looked annoyed and like she wanted to object, but nodded dejectedly and followed his instructions. She took his training sword from him and returned the weapons to where she got them before she began her exercises by stretching. Arran walked away and Aliss greeted him as he neared her. He had to look up at her as he made his approach

"You called?"

"Well not specifically me. The big guy in the cave needs your help."

"The dragon?"

Aliss nodded. "I can spar with your student if you need me to?"

"No she's already got something to do," said Arran "Besides, I doubt she could reach you."

"I can crouch down," Aliss said playfully.

"I appreciate it." Arran laughed. "Thanks for the heads up."

She put her hand on his shoulder as he wanted to pass her. "Good luck, I imagine he'll be as stubborn as ever."

***

"The cave" she'd said. Arran had only ever been in the cave once before, for his own judging.

At the time the hall above had been in disrepair and thus unavailable. He still felt it was redundant after being one of the people to discover Ashfallow was alive in the first place, but he wasn't Darav. He wasn't going to argue with a dragon about its logic. This grotto was the wyvern's home. It was the place where he rested after hunting, and it was also where he stayed when he wasn't occupying the hall atop the hill. The inside of the hill was made of a hard black rock and a dark, glass-like crystal. It was because of this that the inside of the mountain seemed to eat any light that entered it, even the warm, orange light of a torch made barely any difference. Despite this darkness it was never cold. Whether that was because of Ashfallow or from some other unknown source remained a mystery.

The lack of light had never really been a problem for the blind wyvern that dwelled within the cavern, but for humans that had to visit him it presented somewhat of an obstacle.

Luckily, Arran had the foresight to bring one of the torches kept at the entrance with him. Even if it didn't illuminate the entire passage it would be enough to see a little bit in front of him. Through the cavern opening was a narrow and roughly cut staircase which ran deep into the bowels of the hill and each of Arran's steps echoed as he descended it. The walls closed on him somewhat with every step forward, until at a certain point it grew wider again. The echo of his feet hitting the stone steps grew more distant, until he eventually walked into a broader, large cavern. Far away from where he stood there was an opening which let a tiny amount of light bleed in. Unfortunately it was too little to see by.

Arran heard a quiet rumbling quite close to him, and as he held his torch forward he illuminated Ashfallow's black, gold, and grey snout. The dragon emerged further from the shadows with every step Arran took.

He'd never quite liked Ashfallow, and he wasn't thrilled about being stuck in this cave with him again. "You wanted to speak to me?" he asked apprehensively, intending to throw the torch on the ground in front of Ashfallow to illuminate him further without getting closer. He stopped himself when he heard the sound of a shallow puddle splashing as he put another foot forward and realised that water had collected on the cavern floor. Between the rumbling of Ashfallow's breaths Arran could hear water drip down from the ceiling.

"I did indeed ... " said the wyvern as he got up, **"I have grown tired of Ebonblade, he is slow, he refuses to destroy the weeds by their roots."**

"I'd prefer it if you spoke in fewer metaphors and more clear sentences."

The dragon let out a soft hiss.

"You are in my home, Stormcleaver, you are only here because I allow it," Ashfallow's deep voice echoed in the dark cave, **"now, will you listen to what I have to say?"**

Arran nodded. "Go ahead."

If an eyeless dragon could look even faintly satisfied that'd be exactly the expression Ashfallow would have on his face. **"On my last hunt I struck down a dragon much younger than myself, it was injured and I could smell the stench of its putrid wounds from far away. It was frightened and it had searched me out, it told me about our foe, the one who made my sole goal to spite him."**

"Who exactly?

"The Cruel Monarch. He appears to be looking for me." Ashfallow grumbled as he clawed at his vacant eye-sockets. **"He is the one who blinded me. The monster has earned his title."**

Arran only had a rough idea of what dragon Ashfallow was talking about. He knew this "Cruel Monarch" to be a somewhat important historical figure, at least by human standards. The most notable thing about it was that it was dead, killed by a man Arran knew he was descended from.

His father hadn't let him forget it when he was a child.

To Arran's knowledge a titan had to have died recently in order to live any sort of coherent un-life, otherwise they'd end up like the one he'd dealt with at Rivertop.

"I figured we'd had a titan problem, but I don't understand how *he* could be the source," The knight asked, his tone filled with slight disbelief "I remember being told that he was resurrected by ... a witch," he chose that last word carefully, "but I'd assumed that he'd died after she was killed."

"**It would seem that assumption has been proven ill-made,**" said Ashfallow, "**I am quite certain. I know where he will be and I want you to hunt him down. You have faced a titan before, and so you have the most experience with this.**"

Finally the dragon had said something agreeable to Arran. He refused to show it, but he was more than glad to be the person to clean up that mess.

"I wouldn't call myself "the most experienced"," said Arran in an attempt at humility, "but if you think I'll do, where will I be going?"

"**Grenhil. Up against the mountains,**" said Ashfallow as he took a step back, turned around, and began to dig at the dark rock which surrounded them. As he clawed at it a piece chipped off. He knocked it towards his visitor with the wrist of his wing. The sound of the piece of rock hitting the puddle echoed through the cavern.

"Take this with you," said Ashfallow. Arran picked it up. The fragment was as sharp as a knife and slightly translucent in the warm light of his torch. Even if it hadn't been wet it would've reflected like glass.

"Obsidian?" He had to avoid cutting himself on its edges as he looked closely at what he'd been given.

"Ashen glass," Ashfallow corrected, **"strike your blade with it and the sound will call me to you."**

"Why would I need that?"

"That is not for me to decide," The dragon turned around and moved towards the edge of the shelf in the cavern he rested on, **"I suggest you hurry,"** he added. The dragon deliberated as Arran turned around to leave, but he spoke before the knight could exit, **"bring the girl, she could learn more in the field."**

"I'll try not to disappoint," Arran felt it strange that Ashfallow had assumed he wouldn't bring his student, but chose not to comment. Instead he turned and left the dragon to its own devices.

***

When Arran returned to the training ground he could hear his student audibly counting as she did push-ups. "Alright you can stop," he said, watching as she stopped exercising and turned to face him.

"You want to continue sparring?" she asked excitedly as she got to her feet.

"No, we need to leave again," Arran said with a sigh. He'd enjoyed being in the same place for a little while. Yara didn't need to say anything to show that she felt the same way as he did. Her face was locked in a frown.

"Not my decision. It was the big lizard's idea," he said as both himself and his protegé walked towards the barracks.

"The big lizard"?" Yara said. A smile grew on her face.

"Ashfallow," said Arran absent-mindedly.

"You call him the big lizard?" she'd started to laugh now.

"Is that not what he is?"

"Well, I guess he is," Yara said, "I wouldn't say that to his ... face? snout? head? Anyway, did he tell you where we were going?"

Arran couldn't help but grin at the child-like barrage of questions, "northward, and it's best we left quickly."

***

Normally the north-east of Anglavar wouldn't be as cold of a region as the rest of the country, but as they gained altitude and entered the mountain vale above they were met with a surprising change in scenery. A cold wind managed to brush past Yara's face and send shivers through her entire body. The mountain city of Grenhil lived up to the title. Built on a grassy foothill its proximity to water had attracted many people to come and live there over the long period of time since its founding. Though normally building a city that close to a mountain range would be a defensive hazard, for once it seemed to have worked as a natural fortification.

Arran and Yara mounted the ridge that would bring them into the vale itself. They looked down and could see that a crowd of people was pouring out of the front gates.

"Are those ... people?" asked Yara as she peered down into the dale.

"Looks that way. They're fleeing, and fast too," said Arran.

One look to the sky above the city told them why. Flying high above the city's spires was a winged beast, a dragon by the looks of it. Neither Yara nor Arran could make out any details of the creature. They both hastily commanded their horses to gallop down the path. The dirt road gave way to cobbles and they again gave way to more solid pavement the closer they came to the city. People screamed in fear around them as they sped past. Elderly and ill started to fall behind as the two dragon hunters rushed through the crowd and towards the danger so many sought to flee.

The monster above cast a dark silhouette over the city. The way it roared stuck with them. It was a mixture of howling and belching, ending in a raspy rumble. They assumed that the creature had perched itself high atop Grenhil's tallest spire, but neither Arran nor Yara could see it from the narrow streets below. Only when they reached the cathedral square did they manage to get a good view of what it looked like.

Atop the towers of the fortress above sat a vile green dragon, covered head to tail in rotting scales. From what they could tell in the pale moonlight its hide was coloured like the leaves of a sick tree. Its mighty, tattered wings spread open to blot out the moon's light. This massive wingspan produced an imposing silhouette across the streets and houses of the city. The back of the great monster's head was adorned with a crown of horns twisted and curved into several shapes. The monster's maw started in a pointed, bird-like beak, behind which a fearsome set of teeth went hidden. Two of its horns above its brow and the one above its nose pointed forward, meant to skewer its opponents. The powerful roar it produced sent shivers down even Arran's spine. He could feel it in his gut that the monster's gaze was fixed on him.

Arran jumped out of his saddle, shooed his horse away, and started to run down the main street towards the city's keep, his shield in one hand and sword in the other. Yara followed him but unfortunately lagged behind a little. She had no idea what had overcome him so suddenly. As she looked up, she saw the dragon on the donjon tower above jump down onto the walls. Its four legs gave it stability as it crawled and yet it still used its wings as a way to keep balance. It vaulted to the roofs of the tall houses closest to the castle walls. Bits of its decaying figure tore off with every movement, however that didn't seem to bother the monster in the slightest. Its beaked maw was locked in a rotten, toothy grin as it jumped down from the roof and onto the street. It folded up its wings as it came ever closer.

In the back of the monster's throat a flame of white and deep purple cultivated, nearly ready to be let loose on any of the living that remained. Arran raised his shield as he approached to protect himself from the fire.

"I don't believe I have met your sort before ... " the dragon spoke with a deep and ragged voice. It came across as conniving, "have I finally drawn the traitor's ire?"

"You mean Ashfallow?" asked Arran.

"Is that what it calls itself now?" the beast asked as it looked at Skycleave. It laughed in a mocking manner, "You think that weapon could do anything to harm me?"

Arran instinctively raised his shield when the dragon spewed forth purple fire from its open jaws, and his barrier spread open to deflect the flames. Yara came up behind him, her own shield raised to catch any embers which passed him by. The beast halted its assault and took two steps back. It inhaled through its nostrils twice, then blew out loudly when it saw that its prey had remained unharmed.

"I suggest you run, I doubt even that barrier would hold against a second volley," the titan stopped speaking to vault back onto the top of the row of houses it'd jumped down from only moments before. Arran ran towards and inside of the same building the titan had just ascended. Yara followed him in.

"That's not a dragon," she said with heaving breaths. Both her and Arran were panting from the sprint.

"You're correct, that is a titan."

"Did you know?" Yara asked with almost a bit of disbelief in her tone.

"I realise now that I probably should've told you," Arran answered. He then focused on looking for a back door out of the building.

"Did he tell you who I was?" The hoarse voice crept to Arran's ears from the roof above, "or did he want you to find out for yourself?"

Its words were followed by the sound of shingles being dislodged and falling onto the street below, where they shattered into thousands of pieces. The titan's steps proved too heavy to leave any intact and in place.

"Keep walking," Arran whispered to Yara when he sent her into the alleyway first. With every step they had to avoid the debris being knocked down from the roofs above.

"Of course you already knew who I was … "said the titan above as he stepped onto the roof of the opposite building. Yara rushed through the alleyway and into another building. Arran could almost hear the vile grin in the way he spoke. "I would not expect the traitor to be truthful with his lambs before he sends them to be slaughtered, lying is, after all, his greatest quality."

The streets were covered in debris from the roofs, and Yara and Arran had to carefully navigate it to avoid stumbling. Arran ran further through the alleyway and into another house, while his pupil followed close behind.

"the witch spoke of you to me, about leaving you be," the titan continued. "I would hate to disappoint her."

With every step they got closer to the church square, a large open space like that would be the best place for them to fight. The beast above sniffed the air to try and find where they were.

"I have caught the scent of your blood before I believe ... " It spoke with an apprehensive tone, like it wasn't sure what to think. It was the first time Arran had heard the arrogance waver in the titan's voice. The titan leapt from the roof onto the side of the large cathedral and slammed its tail into its walls, making some of it collapse to the streets below. It used every limb including its wings to haul itself onto the clocktower. Once it had perched itself at the top the beast looked around what it perceived to be its newly conquered domain. It spewed its flame down toward the now empty houses and set them alight, illuminating the streets and church square and bathing them in its purple light. Yara and Arran hastily ran to the city's centre. The coldly coloured inferno made buildings collapse and crack under their own weight. The beast roared again before it jumped down from the spire.

"So what will it be ... Knight of the Ashen Fellow," he spat out with disdain, "will you lay down your life to fail at slaying me?" it grinned with the sort of arrogance only a dragon could have.

Arran raised his shield in a defiant manner, seemingly uncaring that it might do little to protect him. Yara stood next to him, following his lead. Both of them were as prepared to fight the titan as they could be. He nodded at the undead dragon. It lashed out at them with its tail. The sound it made was like a whip cracked in the air before it collided with Yara's shield. It pushed through the magical barrier in front of it, scorching the rotting scales of its tail, knocking Yara onto the ground as it collided with her. She attempted to get to her feet on her own, but felt the pain rush through her as she stood.

Arran ran forward with Skycleave in one hand and his shield in the other to get in front of her. The beast clawed at him but the knight barely managed to dodge it. It then snapped at Arran with its powerful maw. Instinctively he put his barrier between himself and his monstrous opponent. Its jaws clamped tightly onto the barrier's side and the tip of the creature's beak came dangerously close to Arran's visor. The titan's fierce bite bent it out of shape with the force it exerted. Its glowing azure eyes glared at the man and it released the grip its jaws had on the shield. Not that it mattered to Arran, as he'd managed to get close enough to the beast to stab the titan just below its shoulder. It flinched and reeled back. Though it appeared to hurt the monster it didn't seem likely the wound would have any greater effect.

"I know why it stings," it said with a hiss as it reared back its head. Arran was speechless, bewildered by the fact that his blade had made the creature feel even the slightest bit of pain. Previously he believed that to be impossible, knowing that only decapitation would kill a titan.

"The weapon was forged of my ichor," he stated calmly, "though of course, you knew that ... blood of Dorum," he said triumphantly as his suspicions were confirmed, "I am Nimhailc, the Venomous Tempest, The Cruel Monarch," the titan spread out its wings to the furthest extent to display its full figure in an animalistic attempt at an intimidation display. Its entire body was illuminated by the moon's light and the purple inferno burning around them. Arran's attempt did appear to have a single effect: the creature's left wing had trouble opening as wide as its counterpart on the right.

Arran dreaded the thought that he was right about what he had been faced with. He'd known to be careful when he spoke with Ashfallow. Yet here he stood, facing the very dragon killed to make the sword he wielded.

"Despite your best efforts you will fail here today," Nimhailc's maw formed into a vile grin, "but I must thank you for informing me that the traitor yet lives. Tell him I will be coming for him. I have no other reason to let you leave here alive," Nimhailc smirked with his near lipless maw. He let out another scraping howling roar before he took to the air to fly far away from the city he'd attacked.

Chapter XI:
Dragoncrown Peak

Both Arran and Yara were out of breath. Yara felt a pit in her stomach at seeing the large undead dragon flee, and judging by his face Arran felt about the same way she did. Arran had sheathed his weapon and Yara followed his lead. They were fortunate enough that none of the burning buildings had collapsed down onto the city's streets, or worse, onto them. The flames had started to subside as they took their leave. Yara watched as Arran changed his focus to a pile of rubble and began to search through it.

"W— What exactly are you looking for?" She stuttered, still a little shaken from her encounter with a titan, let alone surviving it with only a few bruises.

"I'd normally wait, just as I did with Laras ... but ... " said Arran. Yara saw him drag up a cache of resources hidden under the rubble. A hand poked out between the collapsed beams and walls, as a macabre way of letting them know these materials wouldn't be used anymore.

"It'll have to be a rushed ceremony," Arran muttered to himself.

"Sorry, what?" Yara asked.

"It's a figure of speech. I meant that I'm getting you your weapon early."

Her eyes lit up. "You're not joking, are you?" she asked, a little suspicion undermining her excitement. Arran shook his head as he tossed aside several ingots of varying but clearly unimportant metals.

"Nope. There's someone I need to ask some questions, but before that I need to get you your own weapon." He sighed as he cast away several more metal bars. "I just need to find some ... " His voice petered out slowly when he saw what he was looking for, as if mentioning it had made the sought-after material appear to him. "There it is!" he exclaimed as he picked up a lengthy bar of what he was looking for, the same black steel he'd bought in Laketon for Laras. Arran turned to face his student and smiled as his eyes remained fixated on the ingot. "Before we go climbing up a mountain path." He looked at Yara. "You do know how to keep your balance, right?"

***

"You've been extra quiet," said Arran as he tore off a piece of bread and offered it to his student. On their journey to Dragoncrown peak they'd taken a break, now sitting around the campfire they'd made for the night.

"More than usual?" Yara poked at the fire with a stick, more so than she usually would. Arran looked into the flames as well as he chewed on the piece of bread he'd previously offered her.

"I think so. Though I suppose you're normally like that," he said. "That's got me wondering though ... "

"About what?"

"Have you always been quiet?"

Yara looked down. "Not really," she said. "Lord Hyghwing just sort of pushed that on me ... I was always too loud or too active, I had to sit still and be quiet. I think he didn't really care about what could help me and focused more on what he wanted instead."

"Is that related to why you're uncomfortable with eye-contact?"

"No, that's always been there. Lord Hyghwing didn't like that either though."

"No wonder you wanted out of there," said Arran, "I can understand feeling awful that nobody listens to you."

Yara turned to look at him, "I have a question — two questions actually ... though I'm not sure if you'll answer them," she said. Arran looked at her.

"Go ahead?"

"First ... " she considered her words carefully, "what did that titan mean with 'blood of Dorum'?"

Arran shifted where he sat. "It's nothing," he said, "it refers to someone descended from Sander Dorum. He's the man who killed that titan the first time around. It's not really that important."

"It was important enough for him to mention it," said Yara.

"Important to him, sure. That was the man who killed him, after all. I've never known a dragon not to hold grudges but it doesn't really matter to us. He'd want us dead regardless."

"I guess that makes sense. I think I'd be mad at the person who killed me, too." She looked at him before swiftly moving on. "The other question on my mind was ... " She paused and started stammering a little. "Well ... why did you become a dragon hunter? Laras told me you didn't talk about it with him, so I got curious."

Arran didn't say anything. It looked like he had lost himself in thought as he continued to chew. Silence fell between them for a good number of slowly passing seconds.

"I suppose I should tell you—"

"You don't have to — I understand that you didn't want to tell him," Yara cut herself off mid-sentence.

"No, I think I should," he said. "Keeping it to myself for this long is bound to become unhealthy."

"It's oka—"

"I'm a bastard," he said rather bluntly, "an illegitimate son of house Draehal."

Yara wracked her brain trying to remember what she'd learned about that while she still lived at Castle Hyghwing. Draehal bastards were famous — or infamous, rather — for quite a few things, including the last war Anglavar got into.

"Like Delvor?" she asked. House Delvor, the family that had divided Anglavar, was founded by one of these. They'd managed to somehow capture a dragon at one point, but lost all their power in a single night when it got out and burnt down everything they had built. "You're a Cleaver?" she added apprehensively. That was the name she knew had been forced on the Draehal bastards. She studied Arran's bearded face closely as she awaited his answer.

"Not exactly." He put his hands together and looked at them. "I was legitimised, but I ran away regardless. After that I was mostly fine. Did pretty well for myself, until the war happened."

"The Anglan-Delvor war?"

Arran nodded. "Following Silvergrass Plain I had a ... falling out with his royal highness. Cost me my title as knight and my family name. When I got home the life I built was gone. I felt like I had nothing left."

"What happened?" asked Yara.

"A courier brought me a missive after the battle ended. It said my Isa and our little girl were gone." He stared down at his hands as he wrung them together. "I don't really know how to describe how it felt — empty would be the only word that fits. I didn't feel angry. I don't even think I felt sad. That went on for months. I needed something to do, anything really. Then a knight of ash blew into town, looking for work. You met her at the fort, Aliss, the tall woman with the black hair."

"I remember her," Yara replied.

"She found me instead of a dragon to hunt, and now I'm here. It took some getting used to but … It's not the worst, not anymore."

"I'm sorry," she said quietly, "I shouldn't have asked you, that wasn't my place."

Arran shook his head and wiped away a tear that'd run down his cheek. "It's alright," he said, a little wavering in his voice. "It's natural to be curious, so you have nothing to apologise for. Besides, it's not like you knew how I would react."

"Are you sure you're okay?" Yara asked, her head tilted to one side.

"I'm not, but that's fine," a slight but pained smile grew on his face, "I suppose I will be." He stood up. "Now get some rest," he said, on his face was that same warm smile Yara had gotten used to, "There's still a bit left to go."

She nodded and bid him a good night before she laid down in her bedroll and made an effort to get as much sleep as she could.

***

The next morning Yara awoke early. Her eyes shot open at the sound of a fox's call in the near distance. Across the trees and fields around her laid a thick layer of fog. She looked at Arran, who sat quietly at their rekindled campfire.

"How long have you been awake for?" Yara asked, her voice was a little groggy from just waking up.

"An hour or so," he replied.

He was lying. Even Yara with her below-average social awareness could tell that he was. Arran avoided looking at her. Instead he just sat at the fire and warmed himself to it.

"How long have you really been up for?" She repeated her question more sternly this time.

"I ... didn't sleep. I couldn't anyhow," he relented, "we needed someone to stand guard anyway."

"I could've done that as well," said Yara, slightly annoyed. Most of her annoyance found its source in concern for her mentor.

"It's fine, really." He smiled at her "I've gone without sleep for longer than this."

"Just because you've done worse doesn't mean this is right," Yara huffed. She was frustrated that the progress she'd thought she'd made the night before had seemingly melted away during the night. There was no real point in trying to poke at it now, and so instead she got up and started to pack.

***

Dragoncrown peak was a solitary mountain, though it wasn't too far removed from any ranges. The mountain itself was enormous, taller than Yara could've imagined for a peak standing on its own. On its northwestern side it was incredibly steep while on all other faces of the peak it was steadily less so. Its surface was rugged and layered, almost like that of a dragon's horn except eroded by wind and rain.

Arran pointed to a precarious staircase that'd been carved into the mountainside in a now long-distant past. It was long and winding, with narrow steps one could easily fall down from.

"That's what we need to go up on," he said as he nudged Yara with his elbow. At the foot of the staircase stood a small shrine of sorts with a pair of hitching posts. The shrine had a sign on it that read the mountain's name.

The wind blew hard enough to bend the treetops just a little. Arran removed his gauntlet and put his finger in his mouth before he stuck it in the air. "Climb's going to be rough."

"How can you tell?" asked Yara. She couldn't see how a little wind resistance would make the ascent all that much worse.

"Some of the steps are either quite brittle or completely gone," Arran answered. "Besides, it's a bit brisk." He grunted as he took his materials from his saddlebags and stored them in a rucksack he'd also packed away. He looked at Yara. "It's gonna be a long climb, you're sure you're ready, right? Didn't forget anything, did you?"

Yara nodded, then shook her head.

"Right, best get going then," said Arran, and he put a foot forward onto the first step. Yara followed him immediately and stayed close.

Up the old and decrepit stairs they went. Yara counted every step in the staircase, including those that she could barely stand on. Arran had been correct about its state. In fact, saying that it was falling apart had been a generous understatement and Yara had to watch where she put her foot down with every step forward. Winds blew hard against them both as they climbed further up the mountain.

The sound of their steps began to change to the crunch of snow being crushed underneath heavy boots as the peak grew ever closer. The staircase grew less steep and eventually they ended at the entrance to a cavern which at a quick glance resembled a ribcage, with stone monoliths nearly connected in the centre to form a slightly open ceiling. Near the back of the flat area, built against and slightly dug into the side of the mountaintop was a forge. A forge that was cold, like no fire had raged within it for years. Yara noticed that the floor they walked on was made up of ridges and rings, almost like the cross-section of a tree or a horn. There stood an anvil of a blue-hued black metal close to the forge and on top of it laid a hammer of a similar steel. Its head had been decorated with markings which resembled dragons of some kind. Yara noticed a trough filled with some sort of dark red liquid, making her wonder if it was some kind of special oil. Arran walked closer to it and ran a hand over the forge's edge. His steps echoed against the ceiling.

"It looks ... dead," said Yara with apprehension as she observed her surroundings. Arran nodded.

"It always does, I said the same thing when I first saw it," he said "It wouldn't make sense to keep the forge lit forever, though at the time I didn't know better of course."

"So how do we light it?"

"There are several ways — either with the first flame of a hatchling dragon, or the sparks that fly off of black steel when it clashes. According to some of the things I read a long while ago, the blood of a stone dragon should also work." Arran paused as he unsheathed his weapon, "seeing as both our first and our third choice remain anywhere between hard and practically impossible, we can only really do the second one."

"So we have to fight, then?"

"We don't have to, I could just run one sword along the edge of the other, but I'm willing to spar if you are," Arran said, "that does mean that there'll be no holds barred though. You're going to have to mean it."

"I think that'd be fun," said Yara as she unsheathed her broadsword, and she smirked, "don't get angry with me if I miss the sword."

"I won't, just ... try not to?" He tilted his head.

In that moment Yara realised they'd forgotten something. "Hang on, our helmets are still with the horses, aren't they?"

"Didn't I ask you if you'd forgotten anything before we climbed up?"

"You did ... I thought we wouldn't need them and they'd just weigh us down" Yara said. "Should we go get them?"

"No, the wind might blow us off the path and down the mountainside, we'll just have to be careful," he said. Yara wasn't thrilled about fighting without her helmet, but climbing down the mountain path would probably be more dangerous, let alone exhausting.

Arran defaulted to a defensive position, contrary to Yara, who immediately chose to attack. Following a parry he struck forward himself and forced her to jump aside. The disparity between the length of their weapons meant that Yara had to resort to dodging more than blocking. She swung her broadsword at Arran and attempted to perform a similar diversion to the one she had succeeded in their previous sparring match. Arran had prepared himself this time around however, and he caught her swipe with Skycleave. The black steel shrieked as the edges slid along and caught on each other, followed by sparks from the collision.

"That's it, right?" shouted Yara excitedly through gritted teeth. Their swords disconnected again. Arran laughed and shared in her enthusiasm.

"Almost!"

The forge was still cold however. These few sparks hadn't been enough to heat up the coals.

Arran swept forward again but Yara jumped back just in time to avoid being hit. Instead of

Arran's next attack being followed by a parry, Yara lunged forward. Her mentor's quick attempt at blocking her attack missed the edge of her sword. Instead Skycleave's tip hit the right side of her face. It cut from just under her right eye to her lower cheek, and only when it reached the edge of her jaw did she manage to distance herself from the sharp tip.

Arran noticed what he had done a little too late when blood started to run down from the wound. Yara dropped her weapon and reached for her face as she let out a whimper lined with profanity. The sharp pain had caught her by surprise and in response Arran dropped his sword and rushed over to help her. He quickly inspected the wound and he was visibly relieved to see that it wasn't deep.

"You're okay, right?" he asked.

"I'm fine," said Yara quietly as she wiped away the blood that had seeped out of the cut. She smiled slightly to hide that she was still in pain, "just part of the job, right?"

"Well, no, not this way usually ... " Arran mumbled. "You're lucky I didn't hit your eye." It sounded like he wanted to play it off as a joke, but that was likely more for his own comfort than for hers. "I'll just light it on my own," he said. He picked up her sword and brought it over to the forge before turning to his rucksack. "This'll sting a bit," Arran said as he walked back, a bottle of spirit and bandages in hands. He got down on one knee and began treating her injury.

"That was a bad idea," Yara said through gritted teeth as her mentor cleaned her wound, "I should've never suggested it."

"Mistakes happen, it's better you learn from them now than later," Arran said. Yara watched as he studied her face, probably intending to find the best way to bandage up the wound. The bandage she ended up with was almost like an eyepatch, just much lower. Once Arran was done he started to gather the materials from his bag, depositing them all next to the forge. He picked up Skycleave and ran its edge alongside that of the broadsword. The sparks it produced rained into the dry, cold coals, which were set ablaze the moment they were touched by even the slightest bit of heat. The black steel, which Arran had laid in the forge before, began turning more and more red as it heated up.

"So is this all there is to it?" Yara asked. "Do you just climb a mountain and make a sword?"

Arran chuckled. "No, we'll need the heart of a dragon to quench it with."

"But we don't have one of those." She pointed out as she used her wrist to wipe blood off her jaw.

"We'll get to it, don't worry," said Arran, and he looked at her, "and I'll get a healer to look at that as soon as we can."

He looked into the fire and at the black steel, which had become white hot in the flames, taking on the colour of the sun at dusk as it disappears below the horizon. Arran removed the metal from the fire and laid it on the anvil, where he took up the hammer and began to work away at the steel. It sang when the hammer's head slammed down on its surface, and with every hit the shape of the blade became more apparent. Arran quenched the steel in the trough, then put it back in the fire to heat it back up. He wiped the sweat off his brow and showed Yara the hammer.

"See that mark?" he pointed at the dragon carved into its side. "Dragons are quite good at hearing, and when I hit the anvil with that side it rings out to any of them that are nearby. They'll be eager to try and stop us." He paused, looked away from the forge and towards the grey clouded sky "You'll just have to take care of the problem while I work."

Yara kept her eyes focused on the hearth, where her mentor removed the steel and repeated his previous process. Her thoughts raced. She'd never actually fought a dragon on her own before, and she certainly didn't want to in an enclosed space like this. They could simply leave. Get her to a healer for the wound on her face, kill a dragon together, and then come back with its heart. Maybe if she asked him really nicely Arran would do the killing for her.

But then she realised she wouldn't have to do any of that — around her neck she wore the perfect solution to her problem: the vial with dragon blood in it. She'd all but forgotten about it since she got it. It had just been a trinket really, and now it was going to save them a lot of trouble.

"W— wait! don't use the hammer," Yara blurted out as Arran was in the middle of bringing it down again, "remember that vial you bought me?"

Arran looked up, "the one from the market? What about it?"

"There's dragon blood in it, remember?" she said, "why don't we just use that?"

"That's good thinking, we can give that a go," he said as his gaze remained focused on his work. "Pour it into the trough when I tell you to."

Arran pulled the blazing hot metal out of the fire. Yara sat down on the floor and watched from a distance. Every time that Arran took out the metal and hit it she had to cover her ears, as the shrill sound it sent out caused her to flinch. It went on like that for what felt like hours. Arran seemed to work the metal perfectly, like he'd done it hundreds of times before.

"Do you think it's ready?" Yara asked after she felt like she'd waited enough. Her eyes were fixed on the work being performed before her, to the point where she'd forgotten how long something like this might take.

"It should be ... " said Arran as he brought down the hammer again, "open the vial and empty it into the trough."

Yara removed the tiny cork that'd kept the small tooth-shaped bottle sealed tight and dumped its contents into the oil. The deep crimson red blood trickled out until only small droplets clung onto the vial's edge.

"Put a little of your own blood in it before you grab a crossguard and hilt," he said as he picked up the tongs to quench the metal one final time.

Yara looked up at him and then down at the trough. She was lucky enough that the cut on her face had yet to close. She wiped a little blood off of her face and let a single drop fall from her fingers, directly into the mixture of oil and dragon blood. Yara then walked to Arran's backpack and began to look through it. She could hear the black steel hiss as it was lowered into the mixture.

Yara found a straight crossguard and a previously prepared hilt in the backpack, which she then quickly handed to her mentor. He combined the separate parts and completed the weapon. The blood-forged sword gave off a faint crimson glow as Yara grabbed the heft with both hands. The sword was shaped similarly to Arran's own — a long and narrow blade with a pointed tip, meant for piercing through a dragon's thick scaly hide. Much like Arran and Laras had told her about their own weapons, it was unnaturally light and she swung it through the air like it was nothing.

"Have you chosen a name?" asked Arran after he dusted off his hands by slapping them together.

"No ... I haven't yet," replied Yara quietly, still looking at her new weapon.

"You had all that time to think of a name and didn't?" Arran said. Yara could tell he was joking, if only barely.

"I'm pretty bad at naming things, and I was too focused on watching you work," she said, "I don't know if I've really earned it."

Arran raised an eyebrow when he heard that. "You feel like you haven't earned it?"

"It's just a bit early, I think," said Yara quietly. "I haven't really worked for it."

"You've worked very hard, and if it helps *I* think you've earned it," Arran said in a genuine tone. Yara shook her head in response. He squatted down a little to get on eye level with her and put a hand on her shoulder in an attempt to be reassuring.

"I think you'll do great things with this weapon. You don't need to doubt yourself at every step you take." She gave him a half smile, and Arran ruffled her hair as he laughed. "Now it's time we keep going, can't stay here now can we?" he got up, "besides that, I'm freezing."

Yara agreed, and they carefully climbed down the mountain path.

Chapter XII:
The Visit

Buckets of water came down and made it hard for Yara to see the world around her. That which she had managed to catch a glimpse of was, in a word, bland. The ground was flat, no hills like she was used to. Often the road bordered, if not sank directly into, the land's stinking bogs. Even for spring it was cold here. This had been one of the few things she'd expected of a county bordering on the Havstormer sea.

Veerdam was the capital of Nedervar, that much Yara did know. She looked up and at the towering walls built high atop one of the only hills in the country, and bordering on its only cliff-face. In the distance the roar of the ocean clashed with the torrential downpour of the rain. Though they appeared tall from afar, the city's fortifications ultimately looked rather lacking as they got closer. Regardless of that fact, Veerdam was known as one of the most easily defended cities on the island, if not in the known world. Not even the royal family's army could easily take the city, as had been proven during their last and only attempt at conquering it. Yara remembered being told about the three-year siege. Looking at the city now, it seemed like a waste of time.

Suddenly Yara and Arran both had to pay more attention to where they were going. The unstable dirt path gave way to a paved one. Pavement was maybe a bit of an exaggeration — really it was a collection of wooden bridges to cross the treacherous marsh surrounding the city.

"Is the weather always this bad here?" Yara asked, shouting to avoid her voice being drowned out by the rain.

"I'm inclined to say yes!" Arran laughed, "I'd always assumed that's how this place ended up so soaked with water."

Normally Yara would give Arran the space he usually wanted, but in this downpour she opted to ride closer to him. "Who are we visiting anyway?" she asked as she kept her eyes on the slippery, mud-covered, wooden path.

"Well, really it'll just be me who's visiting," he said in response.

Yara looked him directly in the eyes, and for once, he was the one to try and avoid her gaze. "I didn't think you'd be meeting this person alone."

"I don't want you to talk to her. She's not exactly what I'd call a good person," Arran explained, "you'll be buying us provisions and picking a place to spend the night." Yara used the pause that followed to think about what he'd said.

"When you say 'not a good person', what do you mean by that?" She asked, her words breaking the silence. Arran sighed.

"Truth be told, I don't think you should know," he said bluntly, "she did something terrible, and now she's paying the price for it. Anything else you wanted to ask?" his response was quite irritated and Yara picked up on how quickly his mood had changed. He continued to avoid her gaze, and looked around before fixing it on something that protruded out of the mud. Yara wanted to ask what he saw but as soon as she opened her mouth to say something Arran raised his hand to shush her.

"They're barricades, they look sharp too."

"Are they new?" Yara cocked her head. It was hard to see through the rain pouring down on the mud, but the thing Arran had seen was definitely there. He nodded, but told his student to be quiet when they reached the city gates. The guards, recognising the armour they both wore, threw them a glare. It wasn't the same type of glare they had gotten used to. These guards didn't just look at them as if they were a waste of money. No, these men had a malicious stare on their faces as Yara and Arran passed them.

"I don't think we're all that welcome here," whispered Yara. Arran nodded.

"Agreed, a lot less welcome than I remember being a year ago anyway," he said, "best we keep our mouths shut about it while inside the city."

Veerdam was packed to the brim with both houses and people. Some buildings shared a place, others were stacked on top of each other. The residents did anything to fit their homes and livelihoods inside of the walls, to the point where they were nearly spilling out. Outside of the main street you could barely ride your horse through the city. Despite the fact that Veerdam was a maze you could always tell how to get to the palace. Elegant signs made of wrought iron could be found at every intersection, and they always directed towards it.

"Are we heading for the palace?" Yara asked after she took notice of the signs.

"I am, yes." He looked at her. "They keep their prisoners close to the Lord-Steward."

"Steward?" Yara frowned. The word confused her. "I thought counties had Lords."

"Nedervar isn't a county. It's a vassal, and it has stewards for its own four counties, and a Lord-Steward. He's who's in charge around here," Arran explained. Yara looked at him with an eyebrow raised. "That's vassals for you, it doesn't make sense to me either."

They reached the central square of town, King Willem's Square. The statue depicting the king for which the square was named stood at its heart and they passed it on their way to the palace. As they came to the end of the square they stopped. Arran turned to Yara and handed her a coin pouch in it before climbing out of his saddle.

"You know what to do, right?"

"Find a place to rest and get provisions," she replied calmly and he smiled at her.

"You're learning," said Arran, "come to the gate of the palace after you've finished. I'll see you once I'm done."

***

The palace's antechamber fed directly into the main hall, where Arran simply let himself in. While wandering around he studied the grave markers which had been carved into the stone floor. No matter how many times he'd been there he'd always felt it was morbid to walk over top of real dead bodies. He read the dates and names of important Nederan people who were buried directly underneath, whether as ashes or full corpses.

Much like how he'd done the previous times he'd visited, Arran found a set of stairs which led out of the hall. As he walked through the hallways which led him to where he needed to go Arran took notice of another change since his last visit.

None for house Ebonblade, or house Draehal, or any others. there were only those belonging to the four counties of Nedervar. Arran could figure out what this meant on his own, but he knew better than to say his conclusion out loud.

Not long after he'd started his stroll through the halls did he look to his left and see an open door. Arran could hear talking coming from inside. He entered the Steward's Hall, where Lord Thijmen Kolder was engaged in conversation with one of the six other stewards of Nedervar. Kolder was a tall, though certainly not skinny man, who was wearing bronzed armour with tassets in the same colour, as he always seemed to be, no matter the occasion or time of day. His bald head was flanked on both sides by two large ears. From experience Arran knew that telling him a joke would bring no change in his always incredibly stern expression.

The steward, speaking in his native language, stopped himself as he took notice of his newer guest.

"Sir Arran," Steward Kolder nodded at him, rolling his R's. His accent was thick, and it always took Arran a minute to get used to it.

"Lord Kolder," Arran bowed his head slightly

"I trust you didn't come here just to interrupt an important conversation?" Kolder asked, his face locked in a frown. Arran shook his head and put his hands behind his back.

"No, I came here to visit ... the prisoner."

Lord Kolder looked at the man he was speaking to before, nodded, and then looked back to Arran before beginning to walk out of the room.

"Follow me," he grunted as he walked past Arran at pace, "is there any particular reason you need to see her now?"

"I'm afraid that I can't really share that with you."

Kolder let out a disapproving "hm" as he led his guest. As they made their way through the hallways, the sound of the sea crashing into the cliffs below became louder and louder. The corridor intersected in a T with another built along the outside of the palace. These halls led to a bridge which spanned the distance between the palace and a precipice out in the sea. The pillar housed the prison he visited on an annual basis. Their feet splashed in pools of water that'd collected on the bridge.

Soon they came to a heavy, metal door, similar in colour to Arran's sword. He heard Lord Kolder say something in his native language to the men guarding it.

"You can go inside," Lord Kolder said to Arran as the two guards he'd spoken to opened up the door. Arran was about to step through when the

Lord-Steward grabbed him by the arm. "Remember, don't bother lashing out at her if that's what you're planning to do, there's no point to it."

Arran nodded. "Believe me, I know." He stepped forward and into the cell.

The draft disappeared as he heard the door slam shut behind him, its clang echoing through the room for just a second. Only a little light was cast through the door's tiny, grated window, and as Arran got out of its way he could see more of the room. His eyes adjusted to the dark that remained, and he could see the person he was there for.

At the centre of the cell was a frail, small figure, who if she stood would only barely be taller than himself. She sat with her legs crossed, on top of a cushion she'd made out of the skirt of her dark robe. Her long, dirty, white-blonde hair hung down her back, and she tilted her head upwards just a little, letting out a long sigh.

"Hello, Arran," she said, turning to him slightly.

"Eleyna." He only responded with her name, no greetings of any kind were warranted if he had anything to say about it.

"A year already?" Eleyna said. Chains rattled as she got to her feet and turned to him. Her eyes, muddled by a layer of milky white overtop her once vivid green irises, stared directly into his.

Arran noted that her expression was calm, without contempt or any ill will, unlike previous times he'd visited.

"About a year, yes," he said, "I hope the guards have been ... better since the last time I visited."

Eleyna shook her head and pointed to her chest, where three large, gaping gashes slowly oozed blood. "They see these and remember what I am," she said with a hint of lament in her tone, "why are you here?"

Straight to the point, that's how he remembered her. "I'm looking into a dragon, one that's been causing a certain amount of trouble."

"Oh, well that's par for the course for you, isn't it?" Eleyna said, an eyebrow raised in both curiosity and scepticism, "why, pray tell, would you need the help of a woman who hasn't been out of her cell for nearly fifteen years?"

"Because you might actually know something about this one."

Eleyna scoffed. "Good one," she said, "when I was free — or alive, even, there was only one dragon on Angalir, and you work for him."

"What if I told you it's not exactly a dragon I'm after."

Her eyes narrowed. "What game are you playing?" she said, and for a second she stopped to think, "unless you mean ... "

Arran nodded. "Yes, I mean that the titan you created is still around, as undead as it was when you died."

"It didn't die when I did?" Eleyna cocked her head. "Isn't this a bit cruel? I'm already in prison, what's the point in lying to me? Are you trying to see if you can break me down?"

"I've never tried to in the past, why would I start now?"

"I don't know? Why don't you just track it down, cut off its head, and be done with it? Why ask me anything?"

"I've met it, stabbed it — it didn't feel anything, other than a sting maybe," Arran explained, "if there was going to be anyone who knew how to hurt — or even kill him, it'd be you. Besides ... " He deliberated for a second. Should he say it?

"Besides what, brother-in-law?" she asked, reminding him why she believed he was the only one to ever visit her. Arran, realising he'd already misspoken, chose to finish his thought.

"This might be a way for you to atone for what you did."

Her gaze turned from astonishment at learning Nimhailc was even still undead to a deathly glare. She would've lunged at him out of pure rage had she not been chained to the floor by her ankle.

"I'VE BEEN IN THIS CELL 'ATONING' FOR WHAT I DID FOR FIFTEEN EXHAUSTING

YEARS!" she shouted, "I've 'atoned' enough for one lifetime, let alone the apparently infinite one I've been given! Don't you *dare* lecture me on how to take responsibility for the things I did. I've had nothing else to think about."

Arran had winced even before her reaction. It was warranted, that much was true. Still he couldn't feel the sympathy for her that he knew he really should. She'd killed a large number of people and created a monster. That's why she was there. Eleyna's rage gave way to tears as she turned her back to Arran and slumped down to the floor.

"Nothing else, except your visits, or my sister, or ... or Aliss," she said, sobs sending shocks through her body, "does she even know I'm here, that I'm ... 'alive'?"

Arran, unsure what to say, looked down at her. He knew he shouldn't have provoked her like that but he'd done it anyway.

"I ... I don't know how she'd feel if she knew."

"Why don't you tell her?" she looked back at him, staring daggers through her tears. The question gave him pause.

"I suppose it never felt like my responsibility. Really someone like Darav should be the one to do it, I think," he answered, knowing that it wouldn't be satisfying for her to hear that, "but if you think it I should, the least I can do is try," he expected to be shouted at again, but all he heard were her quiet sobs.

"Leave," she said, "I— I can't stand looking at you. If you really think I can help, you can come back tomorrow."

"I'm sorry," Arran said as he knocked on the door. With a clang the mechanism shifted, and the heavy metal moved to allow him through.

"No you're not ... " He could hear Eleyna say just as the guards shut the cell behind him.

***

Yara squeezed herself past the large crowds and through the busy streets. Though she usually hated how small she was, she found comfort in knowing that it also helped her get through big groups of people easily. Before now she'd managed to get her hands on some provisions — more of the same dried meat and bread they always had. Now all she had to do was find them a place to stay. None of the signs had any writing on them, which Yara thought was odd initially, until she realised most people here probably couldn't read. They were all elegantly carved. She saw one with loaves of bread, another with some nondescript meat, and of course plenty of others she passed by. They all began to blur together until she finally found what she was looking for —

a large sign, with a hearth and what she assumed to be a rooster.

She stepped out of the now calm spring rain and into the warmth of the inn's lobby. By the looks of it the place also served as a tavern during the later hours of the day. She already took notice of the group of men who sat close to the hearth on a set of comfortable couches. They revelled in their drinks as they played dice. In the back right corner of the inn's main hall sat a bard fine-tuning his mandola for the copious amount of songs he'd be playing and singing later that day. A woman, who looked to be a traveller not unlike Yara, sat at a table with a grimace on her face as she listened to the bard pluck his instrument.

Behind the counter stood the innkeep cleaning a mug. He was a very ugly man, looking like he'd walked head-first into a wall when he was a child. His face looked like he was already very tired of his work day.

Yara realised that this establishment really wasn't for anyone her height. Her head barely reached over the counter. She cleared her throat and the man turned his attention to her. First he spoke in Nederas, his eyes still focused on the tankard he was cleaning before. Yara, who felt it a bit awkward to tell someone she didn't speak their language, didn't respond verbally. Instead she resorted to gesturing to try and get it across. Only after looking up did he see what she was doing.

"Anglan?"

"Uh, yes."

"Well, do you need something? Or did you just want to correct me on my language?" He sounded irritated and slightly hostile, but by the sound of his accent he didn't appear to know much Anglan.

"Well ... I'd like to book a room for two."

"Two pyrite and one silver," said the man in a contemptuous tone. He didn't appear to care that she was on her own. Yara dug into her coin pouch and took out what he'd asked for, laying it down on the counter. The innkeep picked up each coin and held them up to the sunlight that streamed in through the window. Once he figured he'd been given real money he pointed her to the stairs.

"Up there's your room. Here, this is how you get in," he said, handing her the key. He then turned away to talk to another patron who'd entered just after Yara. Both of them spoke in Nederas, meaning Yara couldn't tell what they were talking about. They occasionally glared in her direction.

The key had a small circular chip attached on a little chain, displaying the number of her and Arran's room. Yara walked up the stairs she'd been pointed to, through a narrow corridor, and opened a small door directly to the left of her. The room couldn't've been much bigger than a broom closet, but it had two beds and enough space for all their things. It wasn't much, though she hadn't expected much for how little she'd paid.

Yara dumped her own bags in the room, locked it after she walked out, and proceeded to get back out onto the streets. She brought nothing with her but her armour and her newly forged sword sheathed at her hip. Thinking about it made the reddish scar on her face sting and itch a tiny bit. Even though they'd seen a healer for it, she'd requested to keep the mark as a reminder. Something like that wasn't quick to let you forget to wear a helmet.

***

Much like at castle Hillguard Yara found herself wrestling with the same issue: crowds. The number of people wasn't necessarily the issue for her, the problem was that every single person there *had* to make noise. For some reason all of them felt the need to talk, or yell, or make any kind of sound at all. If they'd all been quiet, she would've been fine. In order to comfort herself she rested her hand on her pommel. It wasn't much, but that feeling of security in her sword, *her own weapon*, did just enough to calm her nerves.

Fortunately the crowds thinned as she approached the castle, and instead she was met by a pair of guards standing at its gates. They looked down on her. Their orange and blue gambesons looked rather motley, like they'd been patched up several times. The one closest to her, on the right of the gate, rested his hand on the head of a comically small axe. It looked more appropriate for splitting logs. He had a nervous look in his eye as he focused on Yara.

"Halt!" The other guard, a tall, lithe man resting slightly on his halberd, raised his hand. He spoke Anglan, meaning he must've made a guess about where she was from based on the armour she wore. Though perhaps a bit small it still resembled that of any other Knight of Ash.

"State your business?" he asked, his eyes switching between his fellow guard and Yara.

"I'm here to wait for my mentor," she said. The watchman who'd been tightly gripping his axe looked to relax his arm a little.

"He went in here?" he asked, jerking his head toward the palace.

"He did."

They looked at each other for a moment, and then the tall one spoke up. "You'll have to stay where we can see you. No sneaking off, yeah?"

Yara nodded, but now she was the one getting suspicious. What reason could they possibly have to be scared of a sixteen-year-old girl? Even if she knew how to wield a sword, she'd still stand no chance against them in a real fight. She walked backwards and away from them, until eventually she turned around to lean against one of the houses opposing the palace. She slid down against the wall to sit on the ground.

Yara kept a close eye on the two men guarding the gate, who very likely were doing the exact same thing to her. She played with the idea of sprinting past them and into the palace, or running off to try and find another way of getting in. Ultimately she knew none of that would work, or it would and she'd get hurt. Simply entertaining the thought was enough to keep her occupied until Arran exited the palace.

It wasn't long after she had arrived that he came out of the front gate. The two guards, who appeared to have been dozing off, stood to attention as Arran passed them. He saw Yara sitting on the cold floor and immediately walked over.

"How'd it go?" Yara asked, "did you learn anything? Can we kill Nimhailc?"

Arran looked almost relieved to hear her questions. "No, nothing yet," he said with a smile, "did you have more luck?"

"I think so," Yara answered, "but it feels like everyone here has it out for me. Did I do something wrong?"

Arran shook his head. "No, but I think it's related to what we saw outside of the walls," he said, "regardless, if we're lucky we won't have to be here for longer than two days."

"That's not a lot at all," said Yara, "I think I can put up with it until that's over."

"It all depends though."

"On what?"

"Whether I make a complete fool of myself again tomorrow."

***

Early the next morning Arran stood at the gates a second time. Yara had wanted to come with him the day before, which is why he'd left today without waking her up. He didn't want Yara and Eleyna to interact. Something about that simply didn't feel right to him.

For some reason unknown to him the guards had kept him out. The pair who'd stood at the gates yesterday had been replaced by two men who looked like they'd both been cast in the same mould — tall, broad, and wearing uniforms which looked well-maintained and new. Arran had tried to communicate to them that he was to be let in, that he had someone to speak with, but they either wouldn't hear it or couldn't understand a single word he said. So there he stood, directly opposite to the two men, with his arms crossed as he waited. He hoped someone would come along and let him in.

Eventually a man whom Arran presumed to be a knight, donned in silvery platemail high atop his golden, black-maned horse approached the palace gates. Once he got close enough his squire, who followed on his own, smaller mount, helped him out of the saddle. The knight didn't wear a helmet. His striking, handsome face went paired with short, dirty-blonde hair. Arran felt like he recognised the man. The guards addressed him in some terms Arran couldn't understand.

The armoured man looked around, noticed Arran standing there kind of sheepishly, and asked him something in almost perfect Anglan, "are you waiting for something?"

"I have a meeting with someone inside, and it's rather urgent."

The man looked back and forth between Arran and the guards. "Will they not let you in?"

"They will not, good sir."

He barked something in Nederas at the guards, who seemed to shrink in their armour, like toddlers getting scolded by a parent. They quickly raised their halberds and let both Arran and the knight through.

"So what is an Anglan doing all the way in Veerdam?" the knight asked as he walked forward, keeping his gaze fixed on what lay ahead,

"There's a prisoner here that's somewhat important to me, I'm visiting them," Arran responded. He didn't want to divulge too much to this random person, no matter how helpful they'd been.

"Ah, family, eh?" the knight joked, "well, if you want my advice, Ashknight, get out of Nedervar as quickly as you can."

Arran's face turned from a stoic expression to one of mild astonishment, but the moment he looked at the knight's face he knew to hide his surprise.

"I'm not telling you this because of some loyalty to your King, but I appreciate the work you do—" he paused as they passed a guard and entered the palace "— and it'd be a damn shame to have a good man be slaughtered for what his Kings did."

Arran couldn't help but let out a nervous chuckle. He found it somewhat comforting to know that there were still reasonable, if not kind people in Nedervar. The knight put a hand on his shoulder.

"Thank you, sir knight," said Arran.

"The name is Rens," he said, "If Wouter is still alive, send him my regards when you return to your fortress."

Arran nodded to let him know his request was heard, and then they let each other get to their business. Arran walked out of the main hall and through the corridor, back to the cell spire he'd left the day before. The sound of roaring waves slamming against the cliffs increased in volume yet again as Arran approached the dungeon tower bridge. A guard carrying the keys to Eleyna's cell followed him along the overpass.

"Was she fed and given a new cell, like I requested?" Arran asked, but the guard gave him no response, either because of a language barrier, or because he simply didn't care. Arran had asked Steward Kolder the day before to treat Eleyna perhaps a bit better, that the tiny cell and short "leash" she was kept on was too harsh. He'd only been met with apathy and a rather dismissive "sure, I'll get someone to do it".

The walk still wasn't that long, and when they got there it was still the same cell she was in. The guard Arran had brought with him opened the door and almost pushed him in. Yet again it closed behind him with the same loud clang as before.

"Oh, so you did come back," Eleyna said. She sat on her knees, facing away from the door again.

"Were you expecting me not to?"

"Not after yesterday."

"If a few harsh words could stop me I wouldn't ever have come here."

"The guards talked about moving me to a different cell, that you'd told Kolder to feed me."

"Judging by the fact that we're back here again, I'm going to guess you didn't get anything," Arran said dejectedly.

"No, I didn't," Eleyna turned her head to look at him. "But you did try, and that was good of you."

"I figured that — "

"I also overheard my night guards talking about their previous posting at the gates."

Arran raised an eyebrow. "Why would you mention that?"

"You're not here alone," She stood up. The chain, still attached to her ankle, rattled with every step she took. "Why didn't you tell me about her?"

"Tell you about ... my apprentice?"

Eleyna nodded. "They talked about how she looked. Light blonde, brown eyes." No mention of the scar on Yara's cheek, "Did you ... is she alive?" She sounded almost hopeful. Arran realised who Eleyna meant. He saw the look in her eyes go from a panicked hope to disappointment when he shook his head.

"No," he answered, "I would know."

"You should bring her to me, let me see her. I might see something you didn't."

"I don't think that's a good idea."

Eleyna's gaze was fixed on Arran's face as she studied it before abruptly switching topics. "Is she helping you in your hunt?" she asked, bringing the conversation back to the purpose of his original visit.

"She is," Arran admitted, "which is another reason I'll need anything you can tell me. It's not just me doing this. Do you remember anything that could help us?"

"I don't remember much about the day I died," Eleyna said honestly, "I tried to block it out, which I think you can understand."

Arran nodded. "Anything at all would be great."

"I remember Valos' murderous eyes as he stabbed me. I remember that wyvern was there ... and ... " she deliberated for a second, "what was the name of that sword you, Darav, and I dragged across the country looking for allies before the war really got started?"

Arran's stomach dropped. "You mean Tyranny?"

"Yes, that one, I think I remember Darav using it. There was a lot of pain too."

"Yours?"

"Well, probably," Eleyna said with a morbid chuckle, "in Nimhailc too. It stabbed him and I ... he screamed. I think that's the only time I've ever seen him feel real pain. The only time I can remember feeling his pain."

"So you're saying Tyranny could do it?"

"I think any of the original three could, but if Tyranny is the one available to you ... I don't see why you'd use anything else."

Arran wanted to turn to leave. He'd heard exactly what he needed to. The sword Darav always kept so close, the thing that'd ensnared him — of course that would be the thing to destroy a titan like Nimhailc, a weapon that would devour its victim.

"The least you can do is thank me," Eleyna said, "it's not like I get much else here."

"You're right," Arran said, "thank you."

"You're welcome, Arran," Eleyna grabbed his arm as he turned to leave, "and thank you, too, for being willing to right the things I made wrong."

"Of course, El."

III

Chapter XIII:
Trailing a Titan

"There I sat, crouched behind a fallen tree, my friend Erik squatted down behind its stump just a short distance away. Our armour caked in mud. Anglan archers had us pinned down," the soldier said as he sat up in his seat at the back of the inn's common room. He took a break to drink from the tankard he held in his left hand, using his right hand to gesture, as it was missing its thumb.

"I can recall how my mate pointed to me before nodding. He was slightly ahead of me and closer to the enemy. I shook no at him but alas, in a foolish effort he ran out. Arrows whistled through the air before they hit him in the head, stomach, and in the centre of his unmentionables," He chuckled uncomfortably as he pointed to his groin.

The soldier noticed a young girl at the back of the crowd with pearl-blonde hair bound in a crown braid. She'd audibly giggled at the idea of where the arrows had hit Erik. He shook his head and got back to his story. The soldier remembered it like he was still there. The stench of dead bodies all around him, and flat open fields turned into bubbling mud bogs. Besides the stink of corpses another smell had filled the air: that of soiled trousers. He could recall his friend's body the most out of any, or at least, how it looked just as he'd died. The glazed-over eyes of his comrade still pierced through him.

"The Anglans with their longbows had gotten down from their perch. Started looking for survivors I assume." though he didn't want to mention it, he remembered nearly soiling himself as they came closer. "Then from far away I could hear a howl. A howl that soon turned to a screech. I remember it getting louder and louder. Its wings were like ragged leather as they slammed hard against the air, and I could swear its stench got more potent as it approached. It howled a second time, and now that it was closer I could hear its rumble reverberate through the air and I could feel it shake my bones."

"What happened then?" a bystander asked. If the former soldier's story hadn't been so grim the narrator would've smirked.

"The Anglan men had seen the creature first, but they wouldn't live to tell the tale," he said. "I saw them scatter and run in horror before a monster swooped down just above me. This thing looked like a dragon, but it acted nothing like how I'd expect one to. There was no grace, it wasn't some magical experience. The only thing I felt was terror."

A man in armour with short, dark-brown hair coughed loudly, and the soldier stopped himself. He raised an eyebrow before continuing his story.

"Nah, this thing was nothing like what I'd always hoped to see. A single blast of its purple flames burnt up the Anglan men looking for me. I only managed to get out because I found a spot to hide myself. We may not have been on the same side, but it's a damn cruel death, that. I could swear that thing was laughing when it killed those men." The soldier realised that people had started to lose interest and he chose to conclude his story. He saw that the blonde-haired girl who'd laughed had gotten up and left the room, while the man who he'd heard cough had begun to approach him.

"Excuse me sir? I'd like to speak with you outside," the man asked after the crowd had returned its attention to whatever they were doing before. The soldier looked at him with confusion. He thought for a second, then nodded and got up to follow him.

They stepped out into the warm but misty late spring morning. The soldier walked ahead of the man who'd invited him along until they reached the stables. Here the girl with the blonde hair he'd spotted in the crowd before stood waiting. She rested her hand on the pommel of a sword that hung from her belt, a sword that almost looked too large for how small she was. Instantly the soldier felt less safe.

"We were listening to your story back at the inn," said the girl. She had an accent that was like a strange mix of northern and southern Anglan, and a scar on her right cheek, only a month old by the look of it.

"We'd like to know more," the man that had brought the soldier to the stables asked. He put his hand on the soldier's shoulder and tightened his grip.

"More?"

"Yes, more. You wouldn't happen to remember where this battle was, would you?"

"A-are you scavengers? Grave robbers?" he replied with a shake in his voice. The girl sighed.

"We hunt dragons." She pointed over her shoulder towards a heater shield hanging from one of their saddles. The middle of the shield carried heraldry he recognised, that of the Anglan King's personal dragon hunters. "That dragon you talked about in your story — we've been looking for him for a while now," she continued, "do you have anything you think could help us?"

"Well, I ... the battle was a day south from here, but I don't believe that thing would still be there."

"So you saw him leave?" The man cocked his head.

"No—"

"Then again, if he hadn't left I don't think you would be here now," the hunter said as he scratched his lightly stubbled chin, "any way for us to easily recognize where this battle happened?"

Johan nodded, "it won't be easy to miss how much it stinks," he waved away the air in front of his face, "feels like I can smell it from here."

"Thank you," the girl said as she turned around and walked to her horse. The soldier wanted to breathe a sigh of relief, however when he tried it turned into a hiccup as the other hunter grabbed his arm.

"Better not tell anyone we were here," he said, "really, for everyone's safety," he then slapped the soldier on the back and left alongside his companion.

***

"A day from here," Yara repeated to herself after they had ridden a short distance away from the town and inn.

Laras tilted his head in her direction, "I'd wager we're getting better at this intimidation thing," he said, chuckling to himself. "Even if we haven't been at it for that long." He was right, of course. Their search had only been going on for just over a month.

"I had no idea I could be so scary to people; I'm tiny! and a girl to boot. How could I ever hurt anyone?" she said with all the sarcasm she could muster, bursting into laughter immediately after.

"Well, I don't think it was just you," Laras said with a grin, "you couldn't have done it without me."

"I'll give you that much," she conceded.

Though it hadn't been much of a conflict compared to some of the wars of old, Nedervar had finally done what it'd wanted to for centuries: it seceded. They'd declared their independence about a month ago, around the same time that Yara and Laras split off from Arran. Their declaration was immediately followed by black messenger pigeons being sent to all the Lords of Anglavar, including, of course, the king. He'd received his first, and now there wasn't a battle Valos didn't personally command. No matter how great Nedervar's natural defences were they simply stood no chance to fend off the conqueror-king.

The war benefited more than just Valos' bloodthirst however. Scavengers of all kinds, including dragons, found their own value in the battlefield. One party took part in the chaos more than most, however, and it just so happened that that party was the one Yara and Laras were tracking down. The Cruel Monarch took advantage of the confusion of battle. The soldier's story was just one of many. However, few ever led to any real leads. They were glad that just this once, it led somewhere that could prove interesting.

***

Just on the border of Nedervar and Anglavar is where Yara and Laras found the battlefield that the former soldier had told them about. Just about a day after they'd left did they arrive at the scene. The field was littered with the dead and abandoned weapons of war.

"Can't see any beasties," Laras observed, "you'd think scavengers would've shown up already."

"I can see a few," Yara said, pointing to a fair number of corvids enjoying themselves tremendously as they squabbled over the dead bodies. "Definitely no Nimhailc though."

Laras nodded. "I wasn't expecting to see him, but we should still be able to find where he's been, I think. I doubt scorched earth or burnt trees will be too hard to find."

Muddy earth clung tightly to their boots and sometimes even sucked them in as they walked. Like Yara had pointed out, carrion fowl like crows and ravens had turned their attention to the battlefield soon after the fight had ended. There wasn't much left to scavenge for the stragglers she'd seen, though it was rather morbid to catch a glimpse of a crow pecking at a dead man's body, or even plucking an eye from its socket. She'd faced a titan before this point, but the sight of a bird taking apart a human face made her feel queasy.

Normally dragon tracks wouldn't be too difficult to find, but the upturned earth here certainly didn't work in their favour. It felt like the ground was constantly shifting, trying to hide what happened there. Yara squatted down to take a closer look at the soil. They'd walked through this area before, at least that was how it felt. She dug two of her fingers into the soil and brought those up to her face. Yara hadn't noticed it before, but now that she got a closer look she could see one side of it was scorched black by fire. She smelled the dirt, confirming her suspicions. As she got back to her feet and wiped her hand on the tassets of her gambeson she started to look around more. Only now did she notice the minute difference in colour between the dirt she stood on and what surrounded that spot. She was directly in the middle of the cone of fire.

"I think I found it!" Yara shouted at the top of her lungs. Laras rushed over as well as he could without getting stuck and falling face-first into the mud. He looked a slight distance to the right of her, then pointed to something sticking out of the ground.

"You could be right." He raised his arm to wave her over. Once Yara reached him she saw what he'd found. The corpse of a man who looked to be wearing some kind of Anglan colours. The body had been incinerated, making it hard to tell where the poor man had hailed from. However little of his armour that remained resembled barely anything, but the blackened, thoroughly scorched skeleton housed inside was enough to tell that this had definitely been a person at some point and not some scavenger's haul.

"Maybe we should go look for people who live nearby," Yara suggested, "maybe they'll know something. They may've seen Nimhailc."

Laras shook his head. "Nah, I doubt anyone's in the area. Living close to a border in wartime is just asking to be raided." he stopped to stand up straight again. "Either they fled before the war got started, or they're already dead."

"So it's a dead end, *again*," Yara said with frustration.

Laras nodded, then shrugged his shoulders. "Looks that way."

"Saints, we have terrible luck, don't we?"

"Well I wouldn't—" he cut himself off. Yara had already started to walk back to Helena, her shoulders slumped. Laras had initially followed suit but stopped dead in his tracks when he heard an arrow snap below his feet, followed by a rib cage cracking under his weight. Yara could hear him audibly curse behind her.

"Something wrong?" she turned around. Though she'd asked with genuine concern she couldn't help but form a tiny smirk on her face.

"No, I'm fine." His reply was so obviously sarcastic that even Yara understood what he really meant. "Yes there's something wrong! I just stepped on a corp— hang on." Laras cut himself off again as he crouched down. "This wasn't one of the soldiers."

Yara raised an eyebrow and slogged through the mud to get to Laras. He was right. This man wasn't a soldier. He didn't bear a coat-of-arms, and his leathers weren't in any particular colour. Most importantly, the fact that he wasn't a burnt-up husk was the biggest giveaway.

"He looks like he only just died. If we'd gotten here earlier we might've been able to talk to him," Laras murmured. "A scavenger, you think?" he said as he looked up at Yara.

"Him? Definitely. The archer? I don't know," Yara replied. She took a closer look at the fletching on the arrow Laras had snapped. Coloured green and red, she recognised the colours as belonging to one of the northernmost

Anglan houses, though she couldn't remember exactly which one.

"Right well I doubt that his body rolled or slid in at all, so judging from the arrow's angle our shooter should be ... " Laras looked around before pointing to a hillock not too far away from them.

"The colours in the fletching, do you remember what house they're for?" Yara asked, hoping he could fill in the gaps in her knowledge.

"Can't say I do," Laras answered as he shook his head. "You're the one who grew up with that sort of information, not me."

"That's right, I just can't place it." Yara's face shifted to a dejected expression like the one she'd had before.

"Think we should go and find out?" he attempted to get her spirits up again. Yara nodded. "Right then," he said. "After you."

***

"See these bootprints?"

"What? No?" Laras had to squat down next to Yara to get any inkling of what she was talking about. Once he got closer to the ground he could see what she'd meant.

"Wait ... Yeah right there ... " he said after he took a closer look. The tracks were hard to see, likely made by a person wearing light boots and carrying very little weight. They followed a barely visible line that would be difficult to follow under any circumstances. How Yara did it was a mystery to Laras. They both set out to track down wherever the person to whom the prints belonged had gone off to.

"You've got great attention to detail," Laras said to her, "most people wouldn't have caught that, let alone keep seeing it after the fact."

"Thanks." Yara gave an awkward smile in response to the compliment. "Details ... things like that just sort of stand out to me." Her gaze stayed fixed on the wet ground before her.

"Tree," Laras warned her in a deadpan tone. He was about to pull Yara aside when she avoided it on her own.

"I know ... " her reply was absent-minded and quiet. She stopped walking. "Wait, can you smell that?"

"The field or something else?"

"Something else, something nicer ... "

Though it'd taken him a little longer Laras now caught the scent as well. It was warm, like a hearty dinner after a long day of work. Laras could feel his stomach rumble a little. "You're right, it is nicer," he said. "a bit like ... roasted game?" He wanted to say more, but Yara cut him off. She nodded without looking at him.

Just a small distance away sat a man hunched towards a fire he'd made. He wore a gambeson dyed black and brown, the royal colours. A cloak draped over the log he sat on depicted a red hare with dragon wings standing on its hind legs. It was heraldry from one of the northern counties. Next to him on the ground lay a quiver with barely any arrows left in it. All of the remaining shafts had red and green fletching. Right next to that quiver was an unstrung recurve bow, likely what he'd used to hunt. It didn't look like it had enough pulling weight to have been the weapon used to kill the scavenger.

He sat there eating a rabbit he must've shot just a bit ago. Yara looked Laras in the eyes. Quietly she unsheathed her sword, nodded to him, and then slowly stepped forward through the bush. The moment that the man took notice he raced to take up a longbow — a proper war bow — he'd hidden behind his seat and nocked an arrow with terrific speed. His right shoulder bulged with muscle and made him look like a hunchback

"Another step and you'll find this shaft right between those big brown eyes of yours," he said. His voice commanded a stern tone emphasised by his northern accent.

"Who are you?" Yara asked. She stood deathly still. One of her hands was raised, while the other was still firmly grasping onto her sword's hilt.

"Why do you care?" He pulled back the string of his bow with only three of his fingers on his right hand. The other was open, balancing the bow against the space between his thumb and the rest of his palm.

"We're looking for something — or someone if you want to look at it like that," she replied. "Last we heard it was seen at that battle back there."

"You're scavengers?" The man pulled back his bowstring further, "you're not convincing me to not kill you."

"Not scavengers, we're—"

At that moment Laras burst out from behind a tree to the man's side and tackled him to the ground. The arrow fell from where it was nocked.

" ... dragon hunters," Yara finished her sentence with a sigh and put her fingers to the bridge of her nose. She was hoping Laras could've held off for a little longer.

"If you're dr— Agh!" the archer grunted, "dragon hunters, what are you doing chasing a deserter?" He struggled heavily as Laras restrained him.

"Deserter?" Yara cocked her head as she sheathed her weapon. "Why would we care about you deserting?"

"We're not here under the King's orders, if that's what you're worried about," Laras added, "any information on what we're looking for could be helpful. you wouldn't mind telling us who you are, would you?"

"I'm ... my name is Egbert," he said. "I ran away during the battle."

"Have you ever done that before?" Yara asked.

"No, as one of the better marksmen in the King's forces I wouldn't."

"What was so different this time around?" Laras followed up.

"First I need to know if you'll be turning me in," Egbert asked with a waver in his voice. He continued to struggle.

"We don't really have any reason to, but we can, if you don't help us," Laras said with a smirk. He meant to bring that across as a joke but failed.

"There was something flying overhead, something big."

Yara's ears perked up. "Something flying overhead?"

"Yes, that's what I said, didn't I?" Egbert said sarcastically. "The sound it made — deafening. When it spat fire and the purple flames blossomed out I'd seen enough, I had to run." He stared at the ground before him. "That fire was as beautiful as it was horrifying."

"We've heard that before from a good number of survivors," Laras said.

"So why are you asking me?"

"Because we're dragon hunters, and we're hunting the thing that attacked during the battle," Yara answered him. "We've kind of hit a dead end so we're hoping you can tell us where you saw it go."

"East I think," he said quietly before looking up, "that's all I can remember seeing before running."

Laras let Egbert go and helped him to his feet. "Told you we wouldn't turn you in." He smiled and dusted his former prisoner off. "Sorry about roughing you up a bit." He turned towards Yara. "We ought to go."

"Enjoy your meal," Yara said to the archer as they left, realising only after that she might've come across as perhaps a bit mean-spirited.

"So what do you think we should do? Other than go east, I mean," Laras asked Yara when she had caught up to him.

"Find a pigeon fancier and get a letter to Ashfallow's hold," she said, focused on the ground, "Arran should know we've got an actual lead."

Chapter XIV: Tyranny

"I can't believe I have to keep saying this: the answer is, has always been, and will always stay NO," Darav shouted, exasperated by Arran's insistence. He continued, "I am not letting you anywhere near that sword, I *refuse* to give it the satisfaction."

Arran had fought with Lord Darav over this issue since the moment he'd hastily rode through the gates of Ashfallow's hold a month ago now. He'd rushed back to the castle as soon as he learned of Tyranny's importance. Every time Arran had asked Darav to borrow the sword he'd been denied. The entire time Arran had been there Darav refused to stop being a stick in the mud.

"Darav, she wouldn't lie to me, you know her just as well as I do."

"That's exactly why I don't trust her. I'm surprised you even can after what she did! She's a criminal, and I will not be reduced to listening to criminals."

"Listen to what you're saying," Arran said, "you're irate. She used to be your friend just as much as she was mine."

"I don't care, Arran, she murdered people and caused this titan problem in the first place."

"You can't blame her for something she didn't know would happen."

"I can and I will!" Darav's eyes were wide, his bearded face red with anger, "don't you dare tell me what to do. I'm your Lord, your prince even, *I'm* the one in charge."

Arran stood with his arms crossed and a stern expression on his face. He could only think of one thing: the way Valos had treated him fifteen years ago. The thought escaped his mouth, and Arran couldn't tell whether it was intentional or not. "You're acting like your brother."

Silence fell. Darav's expression shifted from rage to indignance. He opened his mouth to try and say something, but closed it again soon after.

"I didn't think that would actually get you to reel yourself back in," Arran said, perhaps a little too impressed with himself.

"Don't pat yourself on the back too hard, you might break something," Darav said as he turned to his throne again, "you're right to point out that I'm being irrational."

"Finally, I get you to admit to something." He breathed a sigh of relief.

"Quit pushing your luck. I haven't changed my mind," Darav said sharply. "You *know* I can't let you use it."

"You're afraid it'll eat me up inside like how it did with you, I'm assuming that's why."

Darav nodded. "And like it did with my grandfather, and everyone else who's ever used it. Knowing what you've already been through I don't think that's really fair to you."

"So what do we do then?" asked Arran, "Skycleave won't do anything to Nimhailc, and judging by the letter I got from my students they've caught onto his trail. If anything we should do this quickly to get it over with."

"You can try going back, ask Eleyna if she knows of anything else?" Darav suggested, twiddling his thumbs as he spoke, "could go to the Spyre and ask for any records on ancient titans."

"If you're expecting me to sift through a library for an alternative to the most obvious answer available, then you don't really know me all that well," Arran said, his head cocked to one side, "I don't know of any other option. Eleyna said something about needing a weapon that would devour the soul of its victims, and that's what Tyranny usually does, isn't it?"

"It's not had much to 'devour', so I don't know. I've never used it to kill a dragon."

Arran didn't say it out loud, but he did think of Darav as a victim of the sword. A side-effect of being the wielder was that all the wielder's worst attributes — in Darav's case his anger issues —

would be amplified as it slowly devoured every bit of strength they had. Judging by the faint glow in the red gem at the heart of Tyranny's crossguard it was happening right now. Arran figured that that was why Darav had lashed out like he'd done earlier.

"As much as I'd like to get to Eleyna again to ask her, I doubt that with the war going on I could get anywhere near the palace. I'd get apprehended on sight, or worse."

"Right, the war." Darav pinched the bridge of his nose. "I'd like to say I forgot it was even happening but that'd be such a blatant lie I couldn't let myself get away with it," he said, "I hope Valos hasn't given you any trouble."

"A messenger or two. He's asked me to be his advisor like last time, as if he doesn't remember how that ended."

"A messenger *or two*, wow, he's really trying his hardest," Darav said sarcastically. Arran raised an eyebrow.

"My guess is you've gotten a few more than that."

"Oh, loads. A dozen for myself and another dozen for Ashfallow."

"I don't mean to speak ill of your brother. He is the King after all," said Arran, "but he does remember that the big lizard *can't read*, right?"

"I doubt he'd care to remember," Darav replied. "Regardless, Ashfallow wants nothing to do with it, and I'm inclined to agree with him for once."

"I figured both he and you said no."

"Of course we did, Ashfallow especially. He's not going to fight my brother's wars for him anymore," said Darav, "you'll remember that last time he nearly turned Delvor's lands into an ash-choked desert."

He exaggerated of course, but Arran knew what he meant. He looked around. For a split second he thought about what the dragon might say if he presented Eleyna's suggestion to him. "I know you've said no, and you'll keep saying no," he said. "But could I ask the big lizard for his opinion?"

"Ashfallow?" Darav asked. His face contorted into an expression of confusion and perturbed curiosity. "You think he'll agree with you?"

Arran shrugged. "I have no idea. I don't even like him, really, but that sword—" he pointed at Tyranny, "— he's responsible for it existing in the first place, it's his responsibility as much as it is yours."

Darav blinked and put his fingers to his temples, "I suppose ... you're not completely wrong." He got up from his seat and walked towards the table. "We'll visit him in the cavern, easier than trying to get him up here."

Back down the hill they went, right to the entrance to the cave, down the staircase and through the shadowy, narrow corridor, illuminated only by the faint red glow of Tyranny's bloodstone. The light reflected off the crystalline walls. Eventually they came to the main chamber. There was still water on the cavern floor. Ashfallow's breaths echoed quietly. He sniffed the air, then a loud rumble came from deep within his chest.

"**Speak,**" he said, now aware of his visitors.

"Good afternoon to you too, Ashfallow," Darav said. Arran couldn't see it but he was sure that the Lord's face was locked in the same irritated expression as he always had when speaking with the wyvern.

"**It appears you have been stirred into action,**" Ashfallow said, "**bringing the blade here is evidence of that.**"

"I wouldn't go that far yet," Darav said, "Arran here has some idea of what can get rid of our little titan problem."

The wyvern shifted his head. Arran could barely see through the darkness, but he could tell Ashfallow looked at him.

"**I would have you present your solution. Speak, Stormcleaver.**"

"It appears that the one thing that can kill Nimhailc is Tyranny, and we're here to ask you for your opinion."

"**No,**" the Wyvern said decisively. "**There can be no discussion about this.**"

Arran looked to his left, where he knew Darav to have stood moments before. He could tell that he wore a wide grin on his face, despite it being obscured.

"You're not even willing to entertain the idea?"

"**Not unless you provide evidence of this link between the Cruel Monarch and Tyranny.**"

Arran had to resist the urge to make a snarky comment. Instead he forced himself to answer the dragon's request. "I spoke with someone with more knowledge of titans than myself, and she informed me of a perceived weakness," he had to try his hardest to dance around Eleyna's identity, in case it would worsen his position.

"**I should like to speak to this more knowledgeable person.**"

"That's kind of difficult right now," Darav said, "she's within enemy territory. I don't think the Nederans are all too excited to host the King's brother and a dragon."

"I'm inclined to agree," said Arran. He could feel Darav staring daggers at him.

"**What reason would this person have to believe that this titan is any like she's known before?**" Ashfallow asked. He crawled forward, his snout now illuminated by the faint red light Tyranny emitted.

"She ... " Arran hesitated, but Darav stepped in before he could finish his sentence.

"She's the one who got us into this mess," he said. Now it was Arran's turn to stare daggers at Darav, "if it weren't for her we wouldn't be having this discussion."

"In more ways than just one, it would seem," Ashfallow said. The neutral response surprised both the men. **"This witch created him. She has a unique bond with the Cruel Monarch."**

"Which means what, exactly?" Darav asked.

"That her experiences are more valuable than your speculation, Ebonblade." If the dragon could sound snide, this was the closest he could come to it. **"She feels any pain he feels, every wound he suffers, at least while she still draws breath. If she believes the blade can kill him then we have every reason to believe her words to be the truth."**

"Even if she's the reason we're in this mess in the first place?"

"As I said, Ebonblade, that is exactly the reason why we should believe her."

"Then I don't think there's anything left to discuss, is there?" Darav asked, his tone laced with irritation. Arran agreed and turned to leave with him when Ashfallow drew his attention.

"You still possess the stone I gave you?"

"Yes, though I don't think I need you to protect me."

"**I would rather the weapon remain safe. Man is prone to lose their tools.**"

Darav called him from the other side of the tunnel.

"**We will see each other again during your travels, Stormcleaver. I will be following your progress,**" Ashfallow said before he let Arran go. Outside the cavern Darav stood waiting for him. Tyranny was wrapped up in the dragon skin which usually lay draped over the stone table in the mountaintop hall.

"Don't you dare touch this, not a finger on that hilt until you absolutely need to. No sooner. Once you're done you head back here immediately and return Tyranny to m— the fortress," he said sternly, "do I make myself clear?"

"Clear as glass, my Lord," Arran said. He couldn't hide his snarky tone.

"Good," Darav appeared to ignore Arran's intent as he handed him the wrapped-up weapon, "now get out of here and kill that titan before either I or the dragon change our minds."

Arran held out his hands as Tyranny was placed on them. The weapon was heavy — heavier than it looked, even heavier than he'd imagined it being. It felt like it bore with it the weight of every single thing it had been used to kill. Even though he'd seen it so many times before now, this was the first ever moment he was allowed to hold Tyranny in his own two hands.

"Lose it, and you'll regret it," Darav grabbed Arran's arm with an iron grip.

"I'll try not to."

***

As Arran started packing his things Darav approached him again. There'd been a change in his mood. As opposed to any other time Arran had seen him since the first time they'd retrieved Tyranny fifteen years ago he looked happy, elated even.

"Where are we going then?" he asked.

"Excuse me?" Arran said, an eyebrow raised in confusion. "What do you mean 'we'?"

"Well, I figured since you were going on your own you might like it if I joined you."

"This is strange. Really strange Darav," Arran replied, "you haven't left this place in years." His eyes narrowed. "Why change that now?"

"You said it yourself, I haven't left this place in years. I felt it was time to change that."

Arran scratched his beard, still confused, but now also slightly suspicious. "Fine ... " he said, "Pick a horse. I don't think Reed can lift us both."

Darav shrugged and looked around the stables, eventually coming back with a stallion. A proper war mount, some might've said. It looked like it could trample anything.

"Now, like I asked before: Where are we going?" Darav asked. "That letter did tell you where to go ... right?"

***

Arran's eyes shot open. He'd spent the entire night tossing and turning from nightmares. Every so often the night terrors were interrupted by imagery of Tyranny's crossguard. The pulsing red glow of the bloodstone sent shocks of fear through him. Immediately after Arran opened his eyes, he looked to his hand, which was clenched in a fist around Tyranny's covered blade. The sight scared him fully awake and he instantly pulled back his arm. It was only when he sat up that he could see what Darav had been doing. The prince was sitting cross-legged across from him. His shoulders were slouched forwards, and his eyes were focused on Tyranny in an enamoured stare. Arran called his name to draw his attention, but Darav didn't respond. He simply sat there, quietly staring. It took a good while before he reacted to the fact that Arran had woken up.

"Someone's awake," he said. His facial expression changed completely from how it looked before. He looked calm, relaxed even.

"It took you long enough to notice." Arran's voice was groggy. He thought to mention the strange behaviour Darav had been taking part in earlier, but instead he figured that the lord would simply shrug it off. Arran wiped the sleep out of his eyes. "We should probably keep going."

He got onto his feet before he picked up Tyranny. The greatsword got heavier the higher he lifted it.

"If it's not too much trouble, I was wondering if ... " Darav's expression had started to ease into the stare again.

"Go on ... ?" Arran was apprehensive. He already knew where this was going.

"If I could carry Tyranny instead."

Arran sighed and tilted his head to one side, "no, the answer is a resounding no." He felt like a father sternly telling off his child. Darav appeared to shrug it off, but as Arran turned around he could almost feel the lord's gaze burn into his back. He climbed back into his saddle and looked at Darav again.

"Get on your horse," he said, "we've got a long way to go."

***

Arran and Darav sat at the side of a small creek, and Arran could tell that the prince's almost malignant stare was focused on him again.

"How much further to Terridge?" Darav asked as he changed the focus of his stare from Arran to Tyranny. It was subtle, and yet it was noticeable.

"I'm not entirely sure, I thought you were the one who knew a thing or two about maps," Arran said. He'd never gotten the hang of map reading, but he assumed Darav must've, considering that he'd been in a leading position in the military.

"What town did we just pass through?"

"Aeverton, I think, I can't remember what the sign said," Arran stood up straight to stretch.

"Which Aeverton?"

"The southern one."

"And how far is that from Laketon?"

"Two days?"

"So that leaves about ... what? one day? two?" Darav scratched his chin. "At least we're not going to Southgate, we'd be on the road for another five." He stood up and looked at Arran with a disinterested expression. "I'm going to take a leak."

"You do that," Arran replied absent-mindedly. He didn't look back at Darav. As Arran started to pack up his things he heard a loud thud and the cracking of branches as a carcass hit the ground.

It went accompanied by the sound of leathery wings slamming against the air. The flaps increased in speed as the creature the wings belonged to landed on the ground. Arran looked up from what he was doing. Ashfallow now sat opposite to him. The dragon lowered his head to the surface of the creek, dipped in his lower jaw, and began to lap up the water, almost like a big, reptilian dog.

Arran carefully watched Ashfallow, as if any sudden move would immediately make the dragon rush for him. They might have been on the same side, but he'd be damned if he'd trust that wyvern.

"It's easy to forget sometimes," he said as he kept his eyes trained on Ashfallow.

"What is?"

"That you're just animals. Dragons I mean."

The wyvern raised his head. He couldn't sneer like a human would, but Arran would bet his life that the dragon would like to do nothing more than that.

"I trust you have a point to make?" He was correct. Ashfallow sounded exactly like how Arran had imagined he would.

"I mean, you're animals, but not." He looked away. "To a human you are."

"Animals that predate on your kind, animals which treat you as cattle, superior to mankind

in every way." Ashfallow bared his long, knife-like teeth.

"Forget I said anything," Arran said as he got back to what he was doing before, but it couldn't hold his attention for long as he got back to watching the dragon immediately after.

Ashfallow seemed satisfied enough with that as the ending of the conversation. He chose to turn his attention to his prey. In life it had been a mighty Fiaighan bull elk, one with the most magnificent set of antlers Arran had ever seen. Well, calling it a set may have been an exaggeration. One half of it was missing. Ashfallow had likely ripped it off before. The dragon pinned the corpse down and bit down on the remaining antler. With a jerk of his head he ripped it out of its socket and nearly tore the elk in half. It was a catch that could've fed a family, if not a small village, for a week or more, and now Arran had to watch as this dragon, this massive reptile, gorged himself on his prize. Ashfallow's jaws seemed to unhinge like a snake's as he wolfed down the carcass in one go. Head first, just down the dragon's throat. He wouldn't try saying it out loud again, but all Arran could think was what he'd said before. *They're just animals.*

"**You seem uneasy, Stormcleaver,**" Ashfallow said as he finished swallowing his prey. Perhaps it was that eternal "cultural" difference between dragons and humans, but it didn't occur to the wyvern that it may have been because of what he was just doing. **"If I were to make an attempt at guessing, it is due to our mutual ally,"** he said. Arran had to shake his head to stop thinking about the elk for a second. Darav did concern him, but he wasn't sure whether or not he should tell the dragon. He watched as the wyvern's throat contracted once, then again. The elk was gone now. For a second he feared that might happen to him if he spoke his mind. The wyvern turned to face him.

"Not entirely," Arran said apprehensively.

"Speak freely. He is relieving himself is he not? I doubt he will be able to hear you, and I have no reason to report your thoughts to him."

Arran sat down on the ground. It was cold and slightly damp from the brook splashing water onto the surrounding dirt.

"There's something wrong with him, it's like he's—"

"Obsessed, perhaps even drawn to the sword?"

"That would be putting it mildly."

The wyvern shook his head before scratching his neck with the thumb claw on one of his wings. **"This was already known to me,"** Ashfallow said, **"he would hardly be the first, and he will** not be the last." He seemed to wave off Arran's worries. "**It is no real concern of yours.**"

"I hope you're right," Arran said quietly. His curiosity had yet to be sated however. "What will happen to me?" He looked at the wyvern.

"**I do not understand,**" Ashfallow lowered his head, but tilted it to one side, "**perhaps make yourself more clear.**"

"If I wield it, the sword I mean."

"**You will be fine if you only do so once,**" Ashfallow said. Arran seemed to relax for a moment until the dragon finished his deliberation and said: "**or you might begin to hunger for it too.**" He spoke with a deadpan tone as he turned away. "**Either way, you will live, and the Cruel Monarch will not, and that is all I require of you.**"

Chapter XV:
The Black Flame

The calming sound of hooves trampling the dirt underneath increased in speed as Yara and Laras left the smouldering ruins of a city behind. They'd intended to stop in Southgate, only to find it burnt to the ground. Looking at it now it was obvious that the stone had been melted by the heat of the fire. There wasn't much they could do to help now, and so Yara and Laras had decided to keep going.

Not much later they got to a smaller village, just beyond sight of the city. The main road was loaded with caravans and carts. A crowd of people bustled around them — refugees, likely from Southgate, who'd only wanted to find a safe haven after their homes were destroyed. Most people there ignored Yara and Laras, and those who didn't threw them snide looks or occasionally mumbled phrases like "fat lot of good you were". Yara looked at them, feeling sorry for the fact that they hadn't gotten there earlier. It was their job to protect these people, after all.

She stopped when Laras did. Almost as quickly as they'd gotten to a halt did he start asking the crowd questions. "Assuming you're all from

Southgate, we'd like information on the creature that attacked your city."

"Why would you care?" an indignant man from the crowd asked sceptically.

"Because it's our responsibility to—"

"To what? Show up *after* a dragon burns down our homes?" a woman from the crowd interrupted Yara. Laras immediately took back the conversation.

"It's our responsibility to prevent it from happening again, or to other people," he said, "we were too late to protect you. Don't let that negatively affect someone else's life."

Murmuring came from the crowd. Some gestured in an agreeing manner, others shrugged, while those who were the most opposed to assisting the two Knights of Ash who'd just ridden into town simply walked away.

"You say you'll be able to stop this from happening again?" asked a younger man. Yara nodded, and Laras confirmed verbally.

"You didn't deserve what happened to you," he said, "if there's anything you remember seeing, anything that could help us figure out what burnt down Southgate and where it went, it would be more than helpful."

Again the crowd devolved into murmurs. This time they went accompanied by confused questions as the people asked each other if they did remember anything.

"Well it was a dragon!" One of them piped up. Of course it was a dragon, that's what they'd already figured out themselves. What they needed was more than that.

"Anything more specific about this dragon?" asked Yara. The crowd then erupted into a flurry of answers.

"It was big!"

"As black as night!"

"My chimney melted when it burnt down my house!"

"I remember it speaking."

"So do I! It was angry."

"I still don't understand why."

"Its throat was gold and red like the fires in a hearth."

"I think it ate my uncle!"

Yara started to get a little overwhelmed and Laras raised his hand when he noticed. His face was locked in a stern expression when he started to speak. "That's enough, thank you," he said. "I think that will do for a description. Did anyone see it go anywhere after attacking the city?"

A man who'd previously been sceptical of the two dragon hunters stood on the outskirts of the group. His expression changed when he heard that. "You mean to tell me you're going after it?"

"Well, obviously," said Yara. She wasn't quite sure why that was so strange to him. "How else would we prevent it from burning down another city?"

"If that *is* your actual plan, then I might know where it went," he said. "It fled to the south east after it melted our homes and ruined our lives."

"To the mountains?"

The man nodded. "Likely hiding in the foothills."

Laras looked at the man, then at Yara. "So that's where we'll be heading."

Yara nodded. They thanked the crowd for their help — something they were unwilling to reciprocate — and went on their way.

***

"You think it's him?" Yara asked. She didn't think so herself, but sussing out Laras' thoughts was a good way to pass the time. Not only that, but being on the same page would be helpful moving forward. The information that the refugees had given them didn't describe Nimhailc even a little. Sure, he was huge, but he wasn't black, and judging by her previous encounter with the titan she knew that his flames couldn't melt stone.

"No, I doubt it is," Laras replied quietly, "The molten stone, it being black as night ... it wouldn't make sense if that was him."

Yara kept her eyes focused on the road. "The molten stone in Southgate — that scared me when I saw it. I'm not sure I want to look the thing that did that in the eyes."

Laras looked at her and shook his head. "Neither would I, honestly. Sounds terrifying."

"I didn't even think a dragon could do that, almost like they shouldn't be able to."

"I'm almost inclined to agree," Laras said, "but that's just the thing with dragons, every time you think there's a limit to what they can do, they go beyond that."

***

"Foothills sounds about right," Laras said as he stared into the distance. The place they'd been pointed to was close to the Yilgran border, a series of foothills on the northern half of the mountain range bordering both nations. The landscape ahead was inundated by pine forest, an increasingly common sight the further south-east they went. The tall mountain peaks in the distance gave the appearance of spikes along a dragon's back.

"What do you think? A cave?" Yara asked.

"A cave for what?"

"For the dragon to hide in."

Laras scratched his head. "Finding a cave where this thing could be hiding is bound to be difficult," he said. His horse, Havor, stepped back a little at his command. "There's trees farther than I can see, and not a lot of exposed rock."

"I think it'll be a cave, the bigger question is whether anyone is even home," Yara peered into the forest to try and find an opening in the trees or any sign that a dragon had been there. "I guess we could just set an ambush for when it comes back, then wait. Though that might mess up our meeting with Arran."

"It's an alright strategy, and I'm sure he'll understand."

"Or he'll go sick with worry."

"Or he does that, that's true," Laras admitted. "You think our shields will be useful at all?" he asked as they both studied their surroundings.

"If it can melt stone I don't think they'll do us much good. I imagine the barrier we've got has its limits," Yara answered him quietly before she used the reins to command her horse. Despite the fact that this little detour was just a distraction they both felt it was a necessary one. Why not track down and slay the dragon that'd recently burnt down a large city?

Laras had started to flip through his encyclopaedia to try and find a dragon that fit the description they'd been given. His copy of the book was thicker than Yara's, but the pages were also smaller. She kept glancing over to see what page he was on. Every now and then she saw a drawing of a dragon she didn't recognize, one that wasn't in her edition. Some were small but covered in spikes, others long and almost like eels. Laras' hand stopped in the middle of turning a page and his eyes widened. Yara noticed that the sound of pages turning had stopped and looked over again.

"You found something?"

Laras nodded, but didn't say a word.

"Well? Are you going to tell me?" She raised an eyebrow playfully. Instead of saying anything he handed her the book. Yara's eyes were drawn to the rendition of the creature at the centre of the page. It was a six-limbed dragon. A knuckle walker. The front half of its torso was large and muscular, while the back half was more lean. Two impressive wings sprouted from its back. The four horns at the base of its head spiralled and twisted as they pointed backwards. A yellow and red dewlap hung from the bottom of its jaw. Its claws were as long as a man's forearm, and much like how the refugees had described it was black as night.

"A Drahali Black Dragon," Yara said out loud as she scanned the paper. As she read the description on the page she came upon one key detail: It was the only known kind of dragon with the ability to melt stone.

"They're from the south, the far south," Laras said with a surprised tone to his voice.

"You mean Meál south?" Yara asked, alluding to the southernmost point of Angalir.

"I mean Deserts of Asatir south," he said. They weren't just far, these deserts were two oceans away. "None of these have been seen on Angalir since ... "

"Since when?" Yara thought she might know the answer, but would prefer some confirmation.

"Since Yursin the Black was killed ninety years ago," he answered, "considering that it's been less than a century since she was killed I doubt any others would've made this trek north. That means we might be facing Yursin instead."

"And not as a dragon, but as a titan," Yara said. It wasn't like they couldn't kill any old titan. It didn't seem very likely for her to be an Ancient Titan either. No, the problem was that if they even had so much as a minor misstep they could end up immolated, or worse, a puddle of molten person and armour.

"We've taken too much of a detour already, we can't—" Laras stopped himself. When he took a breath he caught a certain smell. "Do you smell that?"

Yara caught the scent as well — the unmistakable stench of burning wood. She nodded. In the distance a plume of ash and smoke had kicked up and begun to rise from the treeline. Both of them urged their horses to gallop and leaned forward on their saddles. The air around them began to feel warmer as they approached the raging flames. They got down from their mounts to investigate further.

Before stepping any closer they both took their helmets and put them on. Each closed their visor so they wouldn't breathe in too much of the ash or smoke. Laras nodded at Yara to follow him.

"What about the horses?" she asked. Her voice sounded tinny on account of her helmet.

"They'll be fine!" Laras was being slightly disingenuous and she could tell. "If we leave them untied they can run when the fire gets too close. I'd rather have that than an overdone horse steak." He had a point, it was probably safer to not tie them down. The pair walked further through the forest. As they got closer to the source of the flames the woods seemed to become more claustrophobic, like the smoke was a set of walls that kept closing in on the two of them.

Above them was a rush of wind, followed by heavy flapping of leathery wings. After it came a deafening roar that frightened both of the dragon hunters simply with its sudden thundering. They looked overhead as a dragon flew past. Judging by its small size there was no chance it was the one which'd roared so loudly.

"What was that!?" Laras asked, the noise leaving him completely bewildered.

"I'm assuming it's who we're looking for," Yara said, as she recovered from the scare. They continued their climb. Fallen leaves dried by the heat crunched under their feet with every step. Eventually they'd gotten close enough to see the creature that could've taken their hearing completely had they been any closer.

It looked exactly like the depiction in Laras' copy of the encyclopaedia. Muscular upper torso, lean lower body. Scales black as night, and a colourful dewlap underneath the head. It was different in one major way, however. This creature wasn't graceful. It oozed death, both literally and metaphorically. Its physical form had started to decay slowly but surely. The titan was busy knocking over trees, attempting to dampen the fire before it could spread too far. If this creature had been the one to breathe fire it's likely nothing would've been left of the forest. The alternative was that the wood would've melted at the flame's lightest touch. After stamping out most of the inferno the creature retreated back to a cavern just behind it.

"Told you," Yara said as she glanced at Laras.

"What?" he asked.

"About the cave."

He sighed audibly. "Fine, you were right."

"That does mean we have to go in there, don't we?" asked Yara, perhaps somewhat apprehensive. Even though dragon hunting was her job it remained dead-terrifying to actually face one of these things in person, let alone one which could melt stone.

"Not sure what we're going to do if we do," Laras deliberated, "I think trying to fight her would probably just make things worse."

Yara thought for a second. "Talk to her, maybe? If she's a titan she must know something about Nimhailc." It was the only thing she could come up with. Whether it was Yursin or not didn't really matter, they wouldn't stand a chance if they tried to fight it.

"Talking it is then," Laras agreed, "if we can convince her that we're just here to talk, that is."

They carefully walked through the freshly-scorched woodland as they approached the cavern. Laras took the first step inside, before kicking a small stone at the entrance deeper into its bowels. Not much later he heard it bounce off the cavern floor. Both Yara and Laras then continued their descent. The light from the outside grew more dim with every step deeper into darkness.

At some point they reached a large grotto. At the centre of the open space lay the undead dragon, curled up and making her best attempt at sleeping after being awakened so rudely. Her large, reptilian head faced the entrance and as she heard them approach she slowly opened her eyes. The eye staring back at them was a fiery red, with a dark slit in the exact centre, and it darted around quickly like any stressed animal's eye would. Yara instinctively reached for her weapon but Laras stopped her. He undid the belt his sheath was fastened to and dropped Drakeblight on the ground. His weapon clattered as it fell on the hard stone floor. That sound made the dragon lift her head. She turned to the humans that'd started to approach her. In the centre of her head was a deep broad cut, almost as if it had been impaled once. Both Yara and Laras recognised it as the wound that had killed her.

"We're not here to kill you," Laras said as the dragon got up slowly. He nodded at Yara, who followed his lead and dropped her sword.

"I would hope not, for your sake," the titan replied apathetically as she blew smoke out of her nostrils. She spoke with a snakier voice than any other dragon they'd ever talked to. "Do you know what happened to the last group of humans that tried?"

"You burnt their city to the ground?"

"After I stripped their 'brave' soldiers of their extremities."

"Then we are lucky indeed." Laras minded his words carefully, like he was taking steps on a frozen lake.

"We came here to ask you for information," Yara said quietly. The echo of the grotto made sure the dragon heard her. "About another titan."

"How are you sure I hold the knowledge that you are searching for?" the titan cocked her head. "It seems quite a stretch to assume that I would know."

"It concerns a dragon commonly known as 'The Cruel Monarch'?" Laras asked. The dragon swiftly turned her gaze from Yara to him.

"That title I recognize," she replied and tilted her head slightly, "though that should be no surprise to you. That name lies on the tongue of every dragon, living or dead."

"We need to know where he is," Yara spoke as she stepped forwards. "If you know anything, of course."

"I do not recall seeing him since the day he raised me from the dead. When he did so I fled near instantly. I wanted nothing to do with him." Yursin focused briefly on Yara before looking back to Laras again. "I still don't. If you intend to destroy or bind him I will gladly share with you anything I know."

Yara raised an eyebrow, waiting for her to continue.

"Since my return to freedom I have only ever seen his purple flames burn west of here."

"We know, that's where we came from."

"We never set our own territories alight, or we would prefer not to at the very least." Yursin turned away from them. She laid down before the pair of hunters and rested her large scaly head on her arms. "He cannot range south, as there are mountains there, east as well. There's hardly ever prey in those areas."

"So he hunts to the north, or the west from where his lair is?" Laras asked calmly.

"If he went north, he would come into contact with dragon hunters. Since you even know of his existence in the first place that has undoubtedly already happened. Whether or not you can hurt him does not matter, he would rather avoid any altercation." Yursin spoke quietly. "This western country is at war with your own, correct?"

Both Yara and Laras nodded.

"A battlefield is the perfect place to attack, with enough easy prey there. Enough chaos to mask his presence and still wreak havoc."

"We ought to go east then, further east than we are now anyhow," said Laras. The undead dragon before them looked away, using one of her wings to hide her face. She made it clear she wanted them to leave, and Yara certainly wasn't keen on overstaying their welcome.

"I suggest you hurry, the sooner he's dead, the sooner his little underlings can begin to leave me alone," she said to them, likely referencing the dragon she'd scared away before. "I refuse to fight his battles for him, no matter how much mankind wronged me."

Yara and Laras thanked the titan and carefully left the cavern after retrieving their swords.

"So are we going east right away? or to Terridge first?" Laras looked at Yara. She deliberated for a second.

"We should group up with Arran first, he'll want to hear what we learned."

"Then Terridge it is."

Chapter XVI: Reunion

Arran and Darav looked at the imposing city of Terridge. Its impressive walls and gates were only a short distance away from them now. Ashfallow flew low overhead, his powerful wings creating a gust of wind which nearly blew the two men off their horses. Regardless of the large wyvern's allegiance it instilled a small level of fright in the both of them.

"I'll never get used to that," Arran said as he shook his head and laughed off the little fright he felt. "not back then, and definitely not now."

"Can't imagine what it must be like for him up there," said Darav. He looked up at Ashfallow. "I'm almost a little envious."

The wyvern roared loudly and farmers that were toiling in the fields looked up to the thundering sound above them. Some ran for their houses, while others simply went back to work the moment they saw Darav and Arran come closer. Arran turned his attention to the city walls. They were old, yet still well fortified. A palisade had been built around the stone barrier to protect from any attackers. He saw some guards look up in shock as Ashfallow flew close by. The dragon shook the banners on the walls and the men atop them with the blasts of wind created by his wings. Eventually he perched himself atop one of the towers. Arran could see the dragon lower his head, no doubt to get on eye level with the terrified men. It was hard to believe any of them counted themselves lucky to be face to face with even a "friendly" dragon.

Arran and Darav had approached the gateway into the large city. A guard nodded at the knight and hastily saluted Darav, as he had only just noticed that the King's brother had ridden past him. He looked away and winced. Arran snickered when he saw Darav mouth "please don't do that".

The crowded city behind its walls was a change of pace from the calm countryside.

"How do you propose we find either of your apprentices in this mess?" Darav asked. He had to increase the volume at which he spoke mid sentence to make sure Arran could hear him.

"I have no idea, we've never really split up before."

Darav sighed, "but you still thought splitting up was a smart thing to do?"

"Well I thought this way we could hit two birds— or rather two dragons with one stone," Arran replied absently as he surveyed the crowd. "If we're in any luck they'll at least have a general idea of where he might possibly be."

Darav was quiet as he stared ahead blankly, before quickly turning to look at Arran with a questioning expression on his face.

"I think that's about the biggest 'maybe' I've ever heard in my life."

"Figured I should stay optimistic," Arran laughed, "we agreed to meet on the main square, though if I know Yara even a little bit, she won't want to be where the crowds are."

***

"Saints, there's so many people here I can barely move!" lamented Laras as he and Yara made their way through the crowds. Going on foot and leaving their horses at the stables had been her idea. The rabble was making so much noise they almost hadn't heard the thundering of a dragon's roar overhead. Judging by the lack of panicked screams nobody was particularly concerned with the concept of a fire-breathing creature destroying the city. Either that or they, too, had simply failed to notice.

As Yara and Laras approached the broader main street that led to the square they finally got some room to breathe. Yara didn't say a word out loud the entire time. She had just been muttering to herself while resisting the urge to cover her ears. Laras lightly tapped her shoulder, something which startled her slightly. She turned to smack his hand away but stopped.

"You're okay right? Don't have to say it out loud if that's too difficult right now."

She nodded once.

"Good ... good," he replied. His voice sounded about as confident as Yara felt comfortable with the crowd around them. "Well, we should keep going, otherwise we're never going to find him."

Yara nodded again and followed Laras over the crowded streets. They had to dodge people bumping into each other. Yara looked all over the open space. She made an effort to spot any sign of Arran being there, and even then it took her a little while before she finally found him. Arran was sitting on the back of his horse still, and next to him was another person — someone she hadn't expected to see: Prince Darav. His attention was drawn to someone who had addressed him, and Arran was in the process of climbing down and out of his saddle. The second Yara was sure it was him she bolted over the square in a straight line. As she ran she knocked several people over while pushing them aside. Arran saw her coming just a tiny bit too late and she very nearly tackled him to the ground. She hugged him tightly as he held up his arms with his elbows at shoulder height. Arran slowly lowered them to pat her head.

"I missed you too," he said with a little smile. Laras had approached more calmly and got a pat on the back from Arran. "So you've found something I assume?"

"After a bit of a goose chase we—"

"We think we might know where he's made his home," Yara interrupted. She threw Laras a quick glance as a means of apology for interjecting like that. Arran had a knowing smirk on his face and was about to tell Darav that he told him so when he noticed the prince's face had contorted into a dead-serious frown, more so than usual. He still sat there, high atop his horse, with his stare focused on the letter he'd been handed.

"I ... I'm going to have to check up on something at the military garrison here ... " he spoke apprehensively, "to get some ... clarification on what it says in this thing." Darav waved the letter about. He rode away and left the three hunters on their own.

"So, how about we find a place to sit down and catch up?"

***

They did exactly that. After finding a quiet pub on the square's edge Arran told his side of the story to them. Most of what he conveyed to them consisted of trying to convince Darav of allowing him to use Tyranny. Yara and Laras then told him about what they experienced. That they rode past Southgate — or rather, what was left of it — and their meeting with Yursin. Arran grinned when he heard the Black Flame's name.

"That'd explain where the skull went," he said, recalling how during their last visit to Hillguard it had been missing from its plaque. "So she gave you a general idea of where he might be?"

"Yes, east of the country, he's only hunted to the west of where his lair is," Laras answered. Yara was too focused on stuffing her face with bread to say anything.

"East is a lot of land to cover," Arran replied, "that still leaves Estin, Meál, even the mainland."

"Crossing the sea would take too long for just a hunt" said Yara through her stuffed mouth, "I don't think he leaves the island."

"So that leaves the other two options."

"I don't think it does, he's only flown west according to Yursin. Dragons usually use mountains as natural borders for their territory," Laras interjected. "Hyghwing county is the only hold I think he could be hiding in."

Yara looked up from her food. "That's where you picked me up," she said, looking up at Laras. He nodded. "What'd be the point of hiding in that region? There's really not much there," she snickered as she kept her eyes on the table, "anymore, anyhow."

"Well there's virtually no competition I imagine. When we visited castle Hyghwing last autumn we didn't really encounter anything big," said Laras as he leaned back in his chair. "If there's anything an old dragon like him wants it'd be peace and quiet." He looked at Arran, who scoffed at that idea.

"Dragons aren't dogs," he said, "as they get older they get more prideful and more angry. They start looking for more fights."

"Maybe he drove them all away?"

"Maybe ... " Arran sunk into thought. "I suppose the only way to really find out would be riding east."

Yara's ears perked up at the mention of heading out. She looked at both Laras and Arran. Her eyes shot back and forth between them before she turned them downwards again.

"Someone's eager to get out of here," said Arran with a grin when he noticed her. She just nodded quietly and glanced at him again, as if to tell him that she was done being around all these people. "Best we get some supplies then before we leave." The knight got up from his seat. "Oh, and we should find Darav."

***

Arran found the prince sitting on the steps outside the garrison. He sighed as he hit his hand with the envelope a few times. Arran found him then and approached with Yara in tow.

"Bad news?" asked Arran as he sat down next to him.

"And how," said Darav with a sigh, "I don't think I can continue travelling with you."

Arran raised an eyebrow.

"Are you going to tell us or will you just keep us in the dark?"

"It turns out that we've been losing the war as of late, and hard," Darav explained, "my brother finally managed to get me a message informing me that Nedervar is using the dead as reinforcements." He put his fingers to the bridge of his nose. Arran's eyes widened as he looked at him. Had it not been for the few people also walking the street you would've been able to hear a pin drop.

Arran knew what — or rather who — could've been behind that sudden turn in the war. His stomach dropped when her name crossed his mind and anger followed soon after. The knight balled his fists and was about to punch a wall, however he caught himself just before he could.

"Is this the wrong moment to tell you 'I told you so'?" Arran cocked his head and crossed his arms. "I mean, I do distinctly remember telling you in no uncertain terms that putting her in that prison was a bad idea."

"No, it's not the wrong moment. You'd just be telling the wrong person, exactly like you did about sixteen years ago. It was Valos' idea, not mine," said Darav before he put his hands to his face. "Right now he's looking for someone to blame that isn't himself."

"That's very like him."

"I'm just wrestling with how I'm going to break it to Ashfallow.

"You already know he won't join you." Arran looked at the tower on the city wall with the wyvern perched atop it.

"I'll have to take—"

"You're not taking the sword with you." Arran cut him off. "We need it to kill Nimhailc, something a little more important than you running off to fight your brother's war."

Darav looked at him, appearing dumbfounded. He was about to say something in response, but he stopped himself. "Fine," he mumbled, "you're right." His voice carried a malcontent tone with it. He almost sounded like an angry child after a scolding

"Send Valos my regards, will you?" Arran spoke sternly and with a hint of sarcasm in his voice.

"And mine," Yara had a more genuine tone to what she said. Most likely due to the fact that she didn't pick up on the subtleties of Arran's words. The knight snorted and had to stop himself from laughing. Darav stood up.

"I will, if I get to see him at all."

***

Once again Arran was nearly blown off his horse by the wind Ashfallow made as he swooped down from the sky above. Now he was joined by Yara and Laras too, as opposed to just Darav and the wyvern. Ashfallow landed a short distance away from them, and once the trio reached him they stopped.

"**Ebonblade is not with you,**" he stated, "**you forced him to leave?**"

"It wasn't exactly me who forced him," Arran said. He avoided looking at the dragon.

"**I know you still carry the sword, you did well to deny him.**"

"If he took it with him we would've had nothing to use against our mutual friend," Laras interjected with an attempt at a clever comment.

"We're going east," Arran said to the dragon, who shook his head.

"**Then I shall scout ahead, to see if I can find him before you do,**" Ashfallow said. He took to the skies again before either Arran, Yara, or Laras could respond to what he said. The wyvern flew off into the distance and far out of their view.

***

The flatter landscape of Surriver and the city of Terridge was now a little while behind them. Arran, Yara, and Laras had entered Hyghwing county. The plains gave way to deep, dark green forests and rolling hills that merged into the distant mountains. The morning fog that surrounded the imposing ridge had begun to fade out. Distant winds from the north carried a howl or a roar, however it had faded too much to tell what made the sound.

Not an hour earlier the hunters stumbled upon a small village to ask for directions, where they'd discovered it had been completely abandoned. This had been the same for several farmsteads and another village they encountered before it as well. There were no people for miles around other than themselves.

Normally Yara would've preferred the lack of people, however this time around it was nearly unsettling. They arrived at a crossroads with a signpost that pointed them where to go. The largest sign of the three had a crude imitation of the Hyghwing crest — a Peryton flying upward —

hastily painted on it. Next to the image was the castle's name.

"Think we'll find anyone there?" Laras asked with an uncertain tone. He pointed at the sign.

"It doesn't sound too far out," Arran said, "the places we passed were probably abandoned out of fear, and castles make people feel secure."

"Who wouldn't be afraid with Nimhailc hanging around here," Yara said.

"Well, us, I suppose," Arran replied calmly. He commanded his horse to keep moving past the crossroads.

A mile or so away from the crossroads they came across a singular man walking alongside a cart. Arran and Laras didn't slow their pace. However, Yara nearly stopped Helena in her tracks to talk to him. His cart looked to be in poor condition, like it was falling apart, and the ox which pulled it looked too old to be doing any sort of work. The man looked up from the path. His head was tilted slightly and he moved his hand to tip his hat, only to remember at the last minute that he was in fact not wearing one.

"Afternoon."

"Afternoon to you as well," Yara threw him an awkward stare. She glanced over the side of his cart. There she saw a collection of metal tools, two small cages with a chicken in each, and a small chest no doubt containing what little valuables the poor man had. "Sorry to bother you," she said, "but did you ... leave your home recently?"

"Oh, only a day or two ago, I've been walkin' ever since."

"Could you tell us why?"

The man looked at her barding and saw the Knight of Ash crest on it. He must've felt reassured by the symbol.

"Well to tell you the truth," he began to stammer, "I'm deathly afraid of the beast that's been lurking the hold."

"Beast?" Yara pretended to sound surprised. A little ahead of her Arran and Laras slowed their pace.

"Aye, and it's up your alley too milady." The farmer took a moment to stop walking and catch his breath. "a great winged monster, with a crown of horns adorning its head."

"Has it attacked anyone?"

"Not me personally, though I can't speak for others. It patrols the skies, keeps us normal folk up at night."

"Anything particular about it?" Arran turned back and rode up to them, looking the man in the eyes. "Size, colour, et cetera?"

"I can only remember how big it was when it flew over. That's when I took to the road."

Arran thanked him. The farmer nodded in return and focused on keeping his cart on the road.

***

Castle Hyghwing's gates were lifted and let the three dragon hunters in. The safety of its walls had not been ignored by the larger population of Hyghwing county. People from all around the hold had sought it out to save their lives and it had led to the courtyard being overcrowded. Lord Hyghwing stood on his balcony overlooking the wide open space in the castle. He had seen the three hunters enter the courtyard. The guards on the walls had alerted him to them prior to their arrival and so he'd allowed them to enter. Lord Hyghwing had quickly taken notice of the fact that Yara was one of the three he'd allowed in and so he ran down the stairs to greet his latest guests.

"Hail!" he shouted excitedly. Arran saw him first and responded by waving, while Yara was too focused on what was going on around her. "Have you come to bring her back?" Hyghwing asked. He sounded like he meant it as a joke, though it wasn't unlikely that he'd have liked that as well.

"I'm afraid it's a little late for that now." Arran laughed. "Besides, I doubt you'll have room for her. You're housing more people than usual," he said, eager to change the subject. Lord Hyghwing looked around and chuckled.

"Truthfully, it's become somewhat of an issue," he answered. "all the commoners suddenly decided that their homes weren't safe anymore."

Arran was already aware of why that was, and he assumed Lord Hyghwing would be too. Still he decided it'd be best to ask him if he knew at all. Before he could, however, Lord Hyghwing slapped him on the back.

"Come, we should go to the hall," he said, "it's incredibly noisy out here and dreadful to speak over."

***

"It's terribly convenient you've arrived at this time," Lord Hyghwing said. He was looking at his hands while two of his servants brought his visitors something to drink and eat. Arran thanked them when they left. "We were about to send a carrier pigeon to the hold to ask for assistance, but it seems that's unnecessary now."

"I would ask you why, but we came across a farmer who might've already told us what's happening," said Arran, "we came here to ask if you knew more."

"That depends on what you want to know," Lord Hyghwing answered his guest. He looked at

Yara and noticed the scar on her face. "Oh dear. What happened?" he wanted to reach out to her but she leaned back to avoid his hand. Touch was off-limits for everyone, especially with how her cheek was now.

"I made a mistake," Yara said quietly. "I'm fine."

"To get back to the glaring issue at hand," Arran attempted to steer the conversation, "we need to know about whatever is forcing all these people to relocate here."

"Right," Lord Hyghwing agreed, "ehm, I myself am not quite certain — the peasants below I've spoken with all told me it's a dragon."

"We got that far ourselves," Laras interjected before Arran threw him a glare. He then quickly apologised and shut his mouth.

"Well it's technically not a dragon," said Arran as he scratched his chin, "technicalities aside, what have you learned from them?"

"uhm ... It's a particularly large dragon, green as well apparently."

"Sounds like who we're looking for." Yara looked at her mentor as she spoke.

"I need more specifics," Arran said to Lord Hyghwing, "did any of them mention a location?"

"Not that I can remember," he sunk into thought, "the only specific thing I can think of is that the first civilians to flee here primarily came from the east?"

"The east?"

Lord Hyghwing nodded.

"I don't think there's anything other than mountains east from here," Laras said quickly before shutting up again.

"Not true," Yara interjected, "there's Castle Delvor," She quickly glanced at Lord Hyghwing and Arran's face, both of which looked at her. "Its ruins I mean," she turned her eyes towards the table. Arran rested his elbows on it and put his hands together. He closed his eyes and sighed.

"Figures ... " he muttered, "you're dead certain that's where they came from?" he made eye-contact with Lord Hyghwing, who simply nodded.

Arran stood up abruptly. His chair scraped over the wooden floorboards and he turned around to face one of the hall's many windows. The knight gazed down at the courtyard.

"We should leave," said Arran; his words were almost contrary to how hesitant he felt about where they had to go. He refused to turn away his gaze from the glass pane before him, "the sooner we get this over with the better."

Arran turned to leave, feeling both Yara and Laras' eyes on him as he walked out of the room. They followed Arran out, and Lord Hyghwing didn't seem to mind what just happened.

Arran was already in his saddle when Yara and Laras had just left the hall. They both rushed to their own mounts but before they could reach them Arran had quickly left the castle behind him.

"Arran WAIT!" Yara shouted after him. They both hastily gave chase to catch up.

Chapter XVII:
Knight of Ash

An hour is all that it took for Yara and Laras to catch up to Arran. He'd slowed down after noticing that they had fallen behind. Arran hadn't left to get rid of them, he just wanted to get out of Hyghwing castle. He told himself that he simply wanted to get their hunt done and over with, but in reality his reason was far more personal. He hated castle Delvor. Arran had only ever been there once before, but he didn't need much experience with the place to despise it.

"Arran, are you okay?" Laras was the first to ask him. He'd approached him the fastest out of the two of them and he'd been riding next to him ever since.

"You were just ... gone," said Yara, "we looked outside and you were out of there. Scared me a little too."

"I'm fine, really," Arran gave them a tight-lipped smile, "I couldn't really tell you why I ran like I did," if that was meant to reassure her it did its job very poorly. Yara raised an eyebrow, clearly sceptical of him, while Laras seemed content enough to simply accept what he was given.

"Your face went white when I mentioned where we'd have to go," Yara said, prompting her mentor to talk more.

"It was a name I'd hoped I wouldn't have to hear for another long while," Arran said as he turned to look at Yara. His eyes made contact with hers for just a second. "Castle Delvor isn't exactly a fun place to visit. In fact I'd say it's downright depressing to get anywhere within a mile of that place," he explained, "having been before, it's not an experience I was hoping to relive."

"Add its history to that pile of depression ... " Laras added, "and you get a less than pleasant cas— ruin." He had to correct himself mid-sentence. All three of them stopped talking, right until Yara broke their silence with a change of topic.

"Do we have a plan?" she asked.

"Same plan as we usually follow," Arran answered confidently, "the main difference being the weapon I use," he jerked his head to Tyranny. The greatsword hung from the side of his saddle, still wrapped up in that same dragon skin as before.

"I feel bad that I didn't read up on Titans a bit more," Yara said, "I don't know if they get tired, if they have to land to rest. How will we make sure we get him on the ground?"

"If we've really got no other options he can always throw it like a javelin." Laras said, stifling a chuckle. He imitated a throwing motion. "You know, to close the distance."

"It looked too heavy to throw the last time I saw it," Yara said. She looked at Arran, who stayed quiet for the most part. He'd sunk into thought to try and find answers to Yara's very fair questions. How would they get Nimhailc to ground anyway? He probably wouldn't get tired, or need to eat. He could stay in the sky indefinitely and never land. They'd be sitting ducks at that point. Arran had one solution, of course, but he didn't want to tell them. Frankly, he'd like to avoid using it too.

The one time Arran had killed a titan, back at Rivertop now nearly half a year ago, the creature had been so waterlogged that there was no way it could've taken off. It didn't seem to need to breathe, judging by the fact that it'd been submerged for what was probably several days. That thing was only driven by a need to destroy, it didn't think about survival, it just wanted to kill. It was nothing like Nimhailc. The Cruel Monarch would probably toy with them — treat them like his playthings before killing them. The thought of that definitely made Arran rethink his decision to go directly into the dragon's den.

"Arran?" Yara had tapped Arran on the shoulder.

"Yes?" he said when he turned to look at her.

"It's getting a bit late, should we rest here?" she asked. "We could also keep going, if that's what you think is better."

"No, no you have a point," said Arran, "thinking about it now it's probably better that we're all wide awake while fighting."

All three of them stopped their horses and walked them to the side of the road. Looking for anything other than a comfortable ditch would be a waste of time and effort. There were no inns in the area, manned or otherwise, for them to stay in, so a roadside camp would be enough. They made an agreement to switch guard every now and then, and soon after two of the three of them were asleep.

***

The next morning Arran awoke to Yara sitting opposite to him with her legs crossed. The sun had only just risen so she couldn't have been awake for too long. She was deeply immersed in her copy of the encyclopaedia. Yara glanced at Arran's face quickly before looking back at the book. She quietly mouthed the names of the dragons she passed the pages of.

"I've been looking through the book," Yara whispered to avoid waking up Laras, "I can't find Nimhailc."

"He won't be in there by name," Arran replied, equally quietly.

"What should I look for then?"

"Last I recall," Arran grunted as he made an attempt at sitting up, "he should be under ... Royal Green Dragons, I think? It's been a while."

Yara flipped through the pages until she got to the index at the back of the book. It listed exactly what dragon was found on what page. She dragged her finger over the alphabetical list until she found it.

"Royal Green Dragons, page ... one-hundred-and-eighty," she muttered as she closed the book, then opened it at the halfway point and flipped a few pages until she got to the right number.

"The colour of his fire is weird," Yara said, "it says here it's supposed to be deep red but his is purple."

"Titans are an entirely separate beast, who knows what being undead does to anything." Well, he had some idea of someone who would, but he refused to mention her. Yara nodded.

"I guess that's true," she said, "I'm looking for weak spots he might have."

"Here." Arran pointed at a part of the page she hadn't looked at yet.

"Oh, thanks," Yara murmured as she read the words to herself. "Naturally the wing shoulders are where you'll want to hit him first," she said, pointing to that part of the image on the page.

"Of course," Arran said as he watched her get absorbed by the book. By now Laras had opened his eyes and sat up on his bedroll.

"I couldn't help but hear the two of you whispering," his voice was groggy from having just woken up, "you weren't talking about me were you?"

"Not unless you're a dragon," Yara smiled a little. Arran looked to the road they'd rested beside.

"We should get moving again," he said as he slowly got up on his feet, "we're almost there anyway."

***

If Ashfallow's Hold was an imposing citadel and symbol of might and protection, then the dilapidated ruins of Castle Delvor was one of failure and regret. In its day the fortress had been one of the most impressive buildings to ever have been built on perhaps all of Angalir. Delvor Hall had been at its centre. Built to house a captive dragon, it was once a long, tall building. After that dragon had escaped she'd reduced the tall spires and walls of the castle down to ashes and molten stone. Now the ruins felt like nothing other than a grim reminder for those who dared to let their hubris get the better of them.

Arran, Yara, and Laras passed by a partially collapsed tower. It was built along the road, meant to guard the way to the now destroyed citadel above. From its crumbling side hung a ripped banner. In the past the fabric depicted a chained white dragon on a black background, however now it was torn and slightly burnt. The symbol was still recognizable, but damaged. Arran looked away as he passed it and focused on the ground instead

"They really wanted to up-sell their achievement, didn't they?" Laras, as opposed to Arran, had his gaze fixed on the banner. It was difficult to look away from something like that.

"Wouldn't you?" Yara asked, "killing a dragon is one thing—"

"Capturing one and keeping it locked away is another," Arran interrupted with a beleaguered sigh. He really did not want to be there. Castle Delvor meant something else to him than what it meant to others. He was tangentially related to the people that built this place, this monument to their power and wealth. He was the illegitimate child of a Draehal, just like the founder of this house, the cause of so much misery. The last time he'd been there was something he'd rather forget, too.

"I really, really never wanted to see this place again," said Arran. Being privy to the execution of a count and his children was not a thing he was keen on reliving.

He stopped Reed in his tracks when they got to the gate. Both Yara and Laras followed suit.

"Bringing the horses with us would be a deathtrap," Arran said as he got out of his saddle and started to lead his horse by the reins.

"Should we hitch them to a tree?" asked Yara, Arran shook his head and looked around before he pointed at a nearly collapsed stable. It looked safe enough for their mounts.

"Leave them over there," Arran answered as he tied Reed's reins to one of the rotted wooden fence posts. He took Tyranny from his saddle, "I'll be going in first."

Yara and Laras didn't say anything to try and stop him. They simply followed his lead. It didn't get any less grim as they passed through the gates. The streets of the lower town surrounding the actual castle were littered with burnt homes and debris. Broken supports of treated oak were thick with the rain water they had collected over the years. Burnt wood and melted stones like

Yara and Laras had seen at Southgate inundated the debris, homes and lives abandoned nearly a century ago now. Even after all that time the rain had failed to wash away the soot stains on the streets. They outlined the shape of people who'd once walked there— now they were just a ghost made of smoke.

If there was any place a dragon could call home it would be at the ruins of Delvor. Nobody of sound mind would ever dream of looking here, which, Arran supposed, is exactly why he and his two companions were there. He walked further through the ruinous streets, further up the hill and to the castle.

What used to be the citadel's courtyard had been cleared of debris ninety years ago to create space for a monument at the centre. An upturned mound of dirt, with a tall, menhir-like grave marker knocked onto its side, found itself as the only "intact" structure in the area. Everything else was crumbling around them. Just in front of it was a smaller stone, still upright. Both the stones had inscriptions. Arran took a closer look at the smaller obelisk once he, Yara, and Laras reached the middle of the courtyard. Its plaque had faded since his last visit, and become nearly illegible.

He'd read this one before, yet could only scarcely remember what it said. The obelisk' plaque had also faded, but from what he could recall it was Yursin's gravestone. She was very obviously no longer there. Outside from the fact that Yara had told him about their meeting it was obvious enough from the upturned mound alone. There was the scalp of a human skull poking half out of the sand — likely Evan Delvor's. He'd been buried there, in the same grave as his greatest folly.

Arran remembered being here when Valos had essentially already won the war. Silvergrass Plain had been nearly a month before at that point. They'd captured the remaining three members of house Delvor and executed them right there — execution by dragon for the crime of their grandfather's treason. Watching three teenagers meet their end like that had turned his stomach, a feeling he felt now just like he had then.

Arran kept looking around him for any sign that Nimhailc had been there. Tyranny's wrapped-up blade felt heavier in his hands when he walked away from Yursin's empty burial mound. The closer he came to the palace gates the stronger the stench of rotting flesh became. That was really all the confirmation he needed. He entered into the main hallway, or what was left of it. Eventually Arran walked into the throneroom, and what he saw made him want to turn around.

It had become a macabre mausoleum for dragons. The skeletal remains of at least three different creatures had been used as some sort of decoration for Delvor's old throne. Around it and placed against the walls were piles made out of a dragon or two each. The stench inside was worse than it was outside. Whoever these dragons may have been when they were alive, Nimhailc must've felt it was important to kill them. As to why he had put up such a display made of their corpses, only the titan would know. Arran turned around to leave and as he walked back through the corridor he saw Yara and Laras had reached the gate of the great hall.

"You said you've been here before?" asked Yara.

"I have," answered Arran. He pointed back at the knocked-over obelisk, "back when that thing was pushed over onto its side, when Valos murdered the last owners of this place," he looked at Laras, who held something in his hands.

"I went back because I thought I forgot something, and I found this in your bags," he said. Arran looked down and put a hand on his hip.

"You didn't have to bring—"

"What's it for?" Laras asked as he handed the small object to Arran.

"It's for luck," he answered, lying through his teeth. He took the shard in his hand and looked at it. It was the piece of volcanic glass Ashfallow had given him. For a second he thought that it might prove useful after all. "Saw anything on your run over here?"

"No."

"Heard or smelled anything?"

"Definitely not," Yara said, "since the castle is so close to the mountains I don't think we'll be able to smell him coming. Very little wind in this direction and all. Besides, it already smells like death here."

"I've got an idea," Arran looked at the small piece of black volcanic glass in his hand. He walked back out of the hallway and into the courtyard, followed by both Yara and Laras. Arran carefully laid Tyranny down on the ground before he unsheathed Skycleave.

"What are you doing?" Laras asked, one of his eyebrows raised.

"Calling on my luck," Arran answered, playing on what he'd said before. He put the tip of his weapon on the cold, hard ground, kneeling next to it. He then slowly dragged the obsidian along the weapon's blade until he very nearly touched the ground. It produced a sound so very shrill it could've shattered a nearby window, had there been any left in their frames.

"What was that for!?" Laras shouted as he checked his ears.

"I wasn't being entirely honest, it's for something else, not luck." Arran said. "It should make what we're doing just a little easier."

"Are you calling Nimhailc or something?" Yara asked, her head cocked to one side.

"Just wait," Arran replied. And so they waited. It felt like hours crawled by. No change in the sky above, not a roar, nor the flap of a wing to be heard. The only change being that the clouds had started to gather, coating the normally blue sky in a tapestry of dark grey and even black. The stench that permeated the air from inside the great hall had become stronger somehow. When Arran noticed that change in potency he tested the direction that the wind was blowing. Just like how he'd done at Dragoncrown he stuck a wet finger in the air, and his gut feeling was proven correct. It had changed. The strong gales that'd blown down from the mountains had calmed down and had been replaced by even colder ocean winds.

"He's getting closer," Arran said as he stared out into the distance.

"How can you tell?" Laras asked as he got up. He'd sat down for the time they were waiting.

"He can smell it," Yara said, "I can too, but with all the stench from around here I wasn't sure if it was Nimhailc," she covered the lower half of her face.

"Eugh that's awful," Laras said as he caught a whiff of it too. Immediately they started looking for places to hide. Catching the titan by surprise would make this much easier for them. All three of them donned their helmets. The shrinking distance between Nimhailc and the ruins became more clear with the sound of his wings increasing in volume, his rotten leathery wings slammed down on the air to move forward. The flapping sound became deafening the closer he came.

Nimhailc appeared through the mist, still that same poison green with yellow underside as before. In his monstrous claws he carried the corpse of a smaller dragon. The titan approached the hall and entered it through its broken open roof, where he dropped his victim on the hard floor before landing next to it. Arran stepped out from where he was hiding. His face was still covered by the visor of his helmet. In the knight's left hand he held the wrapped-up greatsword Tyranny. Nimhailc turned his head to look at who was approaching him.

"The Knight of Ash returns," the beast spoke with a grin, "it would appear the blood of Dorum continues to accompany fools."

Arran didn't say a word. He simply removed the dragon hide covering Tyranny. The rotting grin on Nimhailc's face shifted to a look of fright for just a split second as the greatsword's black blade was revealed to him. Regardless of the titan's efforts to hide it as quickly as he could, Arran had noticed. That one tiny moment was all he needed as confirmation that what he was doing was the right thing. He put one hand around the hilt of the weapon, followed by the other as he continued to walk forward. Now the titan turned his full figure to face Arran. He spread his forelimbs wide as he leaned on them in an attempt to make himself look larger.

"You dare bring that thing here?" Nimhailc's eyes shot back and forth between Arran and the weapon he carried in his two hands, the blade resting on his shoulder. The undead dragon spread his wings as much as he could. "It will kill you if you use it." A little waver haunted his voice with every word he spoke. "You know this."

"A small price to pay," Arran's voice echoed from inside of his helmet. He marched further towards the monster, who quickly took to the air. Still his wing showed difficulty moving from their previous encounter. He flew in place as he continued to speak.

"You will pay it without reward," He grinned before looking toward the sky. Arran looked up as well, and for just a second he thought that he'd failed, that he'd have to track the dragon down again. Then he remembered what he'd done earlier, who he'd called for. Nimhailc flew out of the hall in an attempt to flee.

Arran couldn't see what happened from the ground, but not long after the titan had disappeared into the clouds did he re-emerge. He was falling, and fast, barely able to catch himself before crashing into the central town square, where Yara and Laras had been hiding. Arran ran over as quickly as he could.

***

Nimhailc seemed to struggle to his feet following a fall he'd barely been able to slow with his torn up wing. He looked around. Yara and Laras watched as the green dragon sniffed the air, likely to try and find them. As he searched for the two hunters he would occasionally knock over rocks and shove aside debris, one building fully collapsing when his tail crashed into it. Yara's breaths quickened as the dragon approached. Laras had trouble staying calm himself, but tried his hardest to settle down when he saw how Yara was doing.

"We're going to have to run, okay?" he asked, trying to make eye-contact. "Yara?"

"Huh?" she looked at his shoulder, "run ... got it," she'd heard him, but Laras still wanted to make sure. He put his hand on the hilt of his sword. It wouldn't do much against an ancient titan but the feeling of his sword in his hands made him less afraid in the face of danger.

He got up and sprinted away from where they'd been hiding. Once Laras had gotten to a place he could catch his breath he looked back and saw something that pushed his heart into his mouth. Yara was standing still directly in front of the monster they both intended to hide from. She had picked up her shield after dropping it before and stood ready to face Nimhailc on her own. The undead dragon laughed.

"I'd almost call it bravery," he said. Yara didn't respond. Flames grew in the back of the dragon's throat and they bellowed forward, directly at Yara.

Laras watched as the young huntress braced herself and mere moments passed before the sheer force of the blast began to push her back. It must've taken all the strength in her tiny body to stay up. The longer it went on, the more her barrier visibly weakened. Nimhailc continued to spew his purple inferno every step he took, his throat shaking as he belched the fire forwards. Finally, when he reached his young adversary, he stopped.

"Not wavering once? I'm almost impressed," the titan said in a mocking tone as he struck at her. She jumped aside, and in a moment of either pure bravery or stupidity she thrust her shield arm forward in a punch, puncturing Nimhailc's rotting skin with its sharpened front edge.

The titan smirked and let out a hollow chortle, then clawed at her again, this time hitting his target. She cried out in surprise and pain as she hit the ground with a clatter. The titan sniffed the air again.

"I wonder ... you have a similar foolhardiness to—" He was interrupted as a tiny sharp rock hit him in one of his azure eyes. The small stone was followed by a bladed weapon piercing his throat from the side. Laras had charged forward and stabbed Nimhailc. It had no real effect other than as a distraction. Naturally, the titan felt nothing of what just happened. Nimhailc responded to Laras' attempt at an attack by swiping at him with his tail, which sent him to the ground, much like what he'd done with Yara.

Nimhailc flew off with visible difficulty when he realised that Arran had nearly reached them, still with Tyranny in both hands and its blade resting on his shoulder as he advanced.

Laras watched as the monster flew up with his sword still embedded in its throat. After being carried with Nimhailc for no great amount of time it came loose and fell to the ground with a loud clatter. Laras immediately ran to retrieve his weapon before Arran could reach them, and came back just in time to greet Arran. Once the knight got to where the two young hunters had confronted the titan he instantly turned his attention to Yara. Laras watched as Arran carefully helped her up and then grabbed her by the shoulder. She flinched and went wide-eyed. As far as Laras knew Arran had never been this stern while addressing her.

"*Never* do that again," Arran said. "I know what you were trying to do, but don't ever do something like it again. I can't have you getting hurt."

Yara moved to shake his hand off at first but clearly decided against it once their eyes met. He was frowning. Yara nodded and Arran then let go of her shoulder before he continued to track the undead dragon in the sky above.

***

Nimhailc was in the air again, that much Arran could see. This time around the titan had decided to fly near the mountain range. A thick, black cloud appeared from above just as it had before. There was a cacophony of roaring. Nimhailc shouted something, but Arran was too far away to make out what it was.

Then, as quickly as it had appeared, the cloud of smog and ash dissipated, and a bolt of gold and black shot through the sky from the clouds above. It collided with Nimhailc and he fell to earth again, even more quickly. He plummeted downwards and hit the ground not too far away, at the highest part of the fortress: a lonesome watchtower overlooking the ruinous remainders of the city. A thundering roar, quelled by a squeal, filled the air as the Titan and his attacker made landfall.

"TRAITOR!" Arran could hear Nimhailc shout. He continued up the path, past the debris and the overgrown streets, increasing in speed as he went further uphill. It was now or never. As he made his approach he could tell what had happened. Ashfallow had darted down from the sky above and tackled Nimhailc, forcing him to the ground. One of Nimhailc's wings had been ripped clean off, and now lay twitching on the mossy stone of the ruin.

"I should have taken more than just your eyes," Nimhailc hissed as he retreated away from Ashfallow. Arran watched as Ashfallow lunged forward.

"You should have," the wyvern said, almost snarling, **"and now I will outlive you once more, Venomous Tempest."**

The Cruel Monarch glanced at Arran. "The fool approaches," he said, refusing to let up in his arrogance. Nimhailc moved to attack and swipe at Arran, but as he tried Ashfallow pounced on him, locking his jaws around the titan's remaining wing.

The two creatures fought like wounded beasts — no holds barred, simply an animalistic need to destroy each other.

Nimhailc made another attempt, and instead felt Tyranny's blade slice through his claws, severing each digit with ease. The pieces fell to the ground with a dull thud. His eyes darted between the sword and what remained of his claw. Again he snapped at Arran, which only resulted in the sword cutting deep into the top of the titan's beaked maw. Nimhailc pulled back his head, moved it to the side, and then Ashfallow's jaws locked around his neck as the Ash Wyvern climbed on top of him. The dragon's weight pinned him down in place. Nimhailc's chest heaved with every straining breath.

Arran raised the sword to above the titan's neck. Just cut off the head, that's all he needed to do to get this over-and-done-with. As he was about to bring it down he heard the dragon speak.

"I have ... a request," Nimhailc pleaded pathetically, all pretence of arrogance, pride, and power gone from his voice.

"A request? Arran asked, his head tilted in curiosity. He relaxed his arms, letting Tyranny's razor sharp edge rest on Nimhailc's tender, rotting neck.

"Something simple ... only a few last words."

Ashfallow released his toothy grip on his victim, **"you are not owed a single thing, Cruel Monarch,"** he said, **"yet again you fail. Your efforts proved futile."**

"Still you fear my name, still you prefer my titles, even now that I lay dying a second time," Nimhailc said. He looked at Arran, the milky film over top making it difficult to discern what exact emotion they were meant to communicate. "Ah yes ... and like the last time ... to the blood of Dorum as well, yet another dragon slayer." Nimhailc let out a hollow chuckle, or at least a sound similar to one. "Until just now I failed to notice that the scent has lost its potency."

"Probably because of your stockpile in the ruins."

"No, it is something else. A dragon can always smell the blood of those significant to it," The undead dragon said absently as he looked off into the distance. A foul, rotten grin then found its way onto his face.

"What then?" Arran was being led in by his curiosity, exactly what the downed monster wanted.

"The girl," Nimhailc said, "I noticed it from her as well."

Arran's stomach dropped. "What do you mean?" he asked, his tone infused with anger. "SPEAK!"

"She is not with you now. Alone, below in the ruins instead is where she finds herself." The undead dragon's voice returned to its former arrogant tone. "She made the scent stronger. She has the blood."

"You're lying."

"Were you unaware or did the thought simply never cross your mind? Did you not once look at her and think what I know to be true? That hair, those eyes, perhaps they were yours after all."

Arran raised Tyranny and drove it downwards and into Nimhailc's neck. He discovered the weapon had blunted itself mid-cut. The sword was allowing the undead dragon to speak, if it could even process such a thing.

"Your blood runs through her veins just as Sander Dorum's does through yours, knight of ash," The monster spat his words in disgust, each one taking more energy to speak than the last.

He didn't want to hear anything more from the titan. Arran raised the weapon and brought it down again. Each and every time that it failed he repeated what he'd done until finally the part was severed from the whole. Splatters of blood and rotten flesh had gotten almost everywhere. The wound oozed decaying clumps and blood. Arran then raised Tyranny one last time, now pointing its tip directly at Ashfallow. The wyvern recoiled.

"Did you know?" he asked, and when Ashfallow didn't reply he repeated himself. "DID YOU KNOW!?"

Again the dragon said nothing.

"I'm asking you a very simple question," Arran hissed. "Did. You. Know?"

***

"Is everything alright?" Laras asked when he and Yara finally reached Arran. Yara's eyes were immediately drawn to Nimhailc's headless, fingerless, and wingless corpse. She threw the severed head a single glance. It was likely that that was all she needed.

"I'm fine," Arran lied. He was fortunate that neither of them noticed.

"So you did it," Yara said as she stepped closer to the rapidly decaying body. She quickly directed her gaze to Arran's hands, which were still very much holding onto Tyranny's hilt. They were clenched tightly — every muscle in his arms was tensed up.

"Arran, I think you should let go of that ... " she said. He looked at his hands as well and quickly lost his grip. The weapon hit the ground with a loud, echoing thud. It didn't bounce or clatter, just that single thump when it landed. Arran then took off his helmet and tossed it to the ground.

Ashfallow looked down at Tyranny without saying a word. He couldn't see, but knew exactly where the weapon was.

Arran stepped towards Yara and Laras, and embraced both of them. His hand rested on Yara's head as he kept her close. She wasn't just his student, she was his *daughter*. The girl he'd trained to fight for the past few months was his child. Deep inside he'd hoped she was, but he was afraid of it too. He'd put her in danger so many times already.

Arran had to hold back tears. He couldn't stop thinking about that revelation. He'd hurt *his own daughter*, left a scar, for life. He let go of both Yara and Laras, and quickly turned around to look at the wyvern behind him, mostly to hide any tears.

Ashfallow was still perched atop Nimhailc's corpse. He didn't speak, either because he refused to or because of what he'd told Arran before Yara and Laras had met up with them. Laras started to inspect Nimhailc's unmoving, headless corpse.

"That's that then? He's gone, no more titans?" he asked. Yara nodded.

"Hopefully for good," she said as she squatted down next to the severed head.

"I want to get out of here," Arran said. He picked up his helmet and slowly walked away from the corpse, down the path he'd walked up only shortly before.

"Shouldn't we burn it?" Laras yelled after Arran, he was afraid that he'd gotten out of earshot, "and what about Tyranny?"

"I don't care."

***

Yara and Laras watched as Arran walked away.

"Well, what do we do now?" Yara asked. Laras shrugged in response. "Should we ask Ashfallow?" She glanced at the dragon. Again, he refused to speak.

"You don't have anything sagely to say?" asked Laras. "Normally you're the one with the apathetic wisdom here."

Still, no response. He lowered his head to the corpse and sniffed it. He clambered over it, to Nimhailc's head. His nostrils flared, followed by his teeth being bared in a snarl. "**Victory, at long last,**" he said, satisfied, raking the claw on his wing thumb through Nimhailc's dead, dull eyes. Ashfallow pulled one of his legs forward, his long talons ready to tear through the dead titan's skull. Then, he struck. He did what that very dragon had done to him long ago: he took his sight from him. Yara figured it must've been cathartic for him.

"**Leave Tyranny,**" he said, turning his head to Yara and Laras, "**Ebonblade can recover it when he is done cleaning up the mistakes of his sibling. You may go, Stormcleaver has more need of you than I.**"

Ashfallow raised his head and stretched his wings before he started to lift himself into the air. Tightly locked in his claws was Nimhailc's severed head, his rotting tongue drooping out of his now open mouth. The tongue had decayed so much already that moments later it was separated from the rest of the head and hit the ground with a wet slap. Yara and Laras turned around and left, running after Arran.

***

"Are you really okay?" asked Yara when she and Laras finally caught up to their mentor

"I'm fine." Simply looking at his apprentice — he corrected his thoughts — his daughter made his heart ache. "I'm only a little tired," he lied through his teeth, like he'd done for years any time his emotions had come up.

"If you say so," Yara replied. "So what are we going to do now?" she asked, "is there anyone we should inform? Anywhere we should go?"

"Not anywhere other than home," Arran answered, forcing himself to look ahead, "and I thought that maybe ... "

"Maybe what?"

"You already have your sword, and you've proven with this titan business that you can handle this kind of work just fine," Arran said. He wanted to feel pride, but something ate away at him too much to do so. "So I could try and see if Darav could let you graduate."

Epilogue

Arran found himself in the hall at the top of the hold. The stone table at the centre of the room had been moved aside. Instead he stood there, next to Yara. She was nervous. Her usually neat crown braid had been discarded, and her hair was now done up in a slightly messy bun. She didn't wear her scabbard, nor did she have her sword with her, mainly because she couldn't find it that morning. Both her and Arran faced the large opening at the back of the hall. It was raining outside. Darav stood in front of them. In his open hands he carried a folded-up amber cloak. He stepped forward and handed it to Arran.

"Kneel, please," Darav said. He made an attempt at sounding more official than he normally did. Yara got down on one knee, and rested her elbow on the other.

"For your exceptional service," Darav repeated the words he'd said to countless other members of the order, "and for future servitude." He handed the cloak to Arran. "I place with you the responsibility of our work, and the expectation that you will fulfil your duty."

Arran then draped the cloak over his student's — his daughter's — shoulders, and fastened the band around her neck.

"Yara, ward of Arran Stormcleaver," said Darav, "rise, please, and meet me as an equal."

Yara got up as requested. The weight of the cloak pulled back her shoulders and made her stand upright. Another member of the order then walked up to Darav, carrying in his two hands Yara's sword. He gave it to the Lord, who then extended it to the newest official member of their order.

"This is now truly yours," he said, refusing to budge from his rather official-sounding tone. "Wield it with pride."

Yara took hold of the sword, and its scabbard, accepting both quietly.

"Welcome, Knight of Ash," Darav said. The group around them, made up of a small number of people at Yara's request, erupted into cheers and applause. The sound was amplified by the echoing of the room. Arran smiled as he patted her on the back. Yara looked at him, her face locked in a grin as well. Just in that moment Arran felt pride, real pride. He didn't feel regret, or shame for teaching his own daughter to fight like he'd expected. For the first time what felt like forever, he was just happy, and in that moment that was all he needed to feel.

Afterword

It took years for me to get even a first draft finished, and then even more to get this book to a point where I was happy with it. I couldn't have done it without the help of some very special people who had to put up with me and my lore dumping. It's because of this that I ought to thank them here.

Nina Cruz
It means the world to me that you were willing to read this all the way to the end and give me criticism throughout. I know I wasn't always easy to work with, and so I'd like to thank you for being so patient with me.

My parents
I might not have talked about what I write all that often or dumped my lore at you like I did to people online, but you still had to live with me, and that deserves a dedication in and of itself.

Hero & Aly

You're some of the best friends someone could ask for. You stuck with me and hyped me up through so much of this process. I can't thank you enough for just being my friends, let alone for all that support you've given me.

Noah Dietz

Thank you for being in the background of Nina's microphone and occasionally offering valuable criticism.

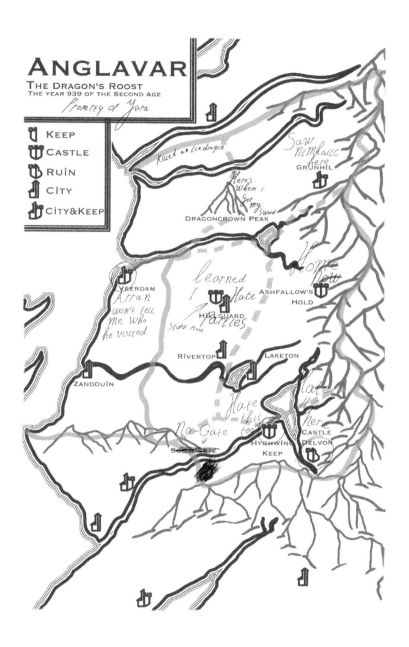

About the Author

Sebastiaan C. van Doorn is an independent author, artist, and amateur palaeontologist from North-Holland in the Netherlands.

Sebastiaan grew up with creative interests and began pursuing writing as a hobby at the age of thirteen. He began working on what would one day become Knight of Ash: The Venomous Tempest sometime in 2016. It would eventually take just over half a decade to complete and self-publish the first book.

Art of the characters featured in Knight of Ash, palaeontology, and discussions of works written by Sebastiaan C. van Doorn can be found on the twitter page @Basilisk_art.